W9-AVG-831

RALPH COMPTON:
RIDE THE HARD TRAIL

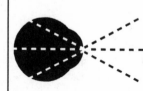 This Large Print Book carries the
Seal of Approval of N.A.V.H.

A RALPH COMPTON NOVEL

RALPH COMPTON:
RIDE THE HARD TRAIL

DAVID ROBBINS

THORNDIKE PRESS

A part of Gale, Cengage Learning

GALE
CENGAGE Learning·

Detroit • New York • San Francisco • New Haven, Conn • Waterville, Maine • London

Copyright © The Estate of Ralph Compton, 2008.
Thorndike Press, a part of Gale, Cengage Learning.

ALL RIGHTS RESERVED
This is a work of fiction. Names, characters, places, and incidents either are the product of the author's imagination or are used fictitiously, and any resemblance to actual persons, living or dead, business establishments, events, or locales is entirely coincidental.
Thorndike Press® Large Print Western.
The text of this Large Print edition is unabridged.
Other aspects of the book may vary from the original edition.
Set in 16 pt. Plantin.
Printed on permanent paper.

LIBRARY OF CONGRESS CATALOGING-IN-PUBLICATION DATA

Robbins, David, 1950–
    Ralph Compton : ride the hard trail : a Ralph Compton novel / by David Robbins.
        p. cm. — (Thorndike Press large print Western)
    ISBN-13: 978-1-4104-1124-2 (alk. paper)
    ISBN-10: 1-4104-1124-9 (alk. paper)
    1. Large type books. I. Title.
PS3568.O22288R36 2008
813'.54—dc22   2008035361

Published in 2008 by arrangement with NAL Signet, a member of Penguin Group (USA) Inc.

Printed in the United States of America
1 2 3 4 5 6 7 12 11 10 09 08

Western
Robbins, David, 1950-
Ralph Compton. Ride the hard
trail [large print] : a Ralpl

THE IMMORTAL COWBOY

This is respectfully dedicated to the "American Cowboy." His was the saga sparked by the turmoil that followed the Civil War, and the passing of more than a century has by no means diminished the flame.

True, the old days and the old ways are but treasured memories, and the old trails have grown dim with the ravages of time, but the spirit of the cowboy lives on.

In my travels — to Texas, Oklahoma, Kansas, Nebraska, Colorado, Wyoming, New Mexico, and Arizona — I always find something that reminds me of the Old West. While I am walking these plains and mountains for the first time, there is this feeling that a part of me is eternal, that I have known these old trails before. I believe it is the undying spirit of the frontier calling, allowing me, through the mind's eye, to step back into time. What is the appeal of the Old West of the American frontier?

5

It has been epitomized by some as the dark and bloody period in American history. Its heroes — Crockett, Bowie, Hickok, Earp — have been reviled and criticized. Yet the Old West lives on, larger than life.

It has become a symbol of freedom, when there was always another mountain to climb and another river to cross; when a dispute between two men was settled not with expensive lawyers, but with fists, knives, or guns. Barbaric? Maybe. But some things never change. When the cowboy rode into the pages of American history, he left behind a legacy that lives within the hearts of us all.

— Ralph Compton

CHAPTER 1

They were night and day.

The older brother had neatly combed hair the color of straw. He was wide of shoulder and narrow of waist, and rode with his back straight and his blue eyes alert. His clothes were those of a cowman: a high-crowned hat and cowhide vest, both brown, a green homespun shirt and denims.

The younger brother had a shock of hair as black as a raven. He was thin and sinewy and rode slouched in the saddle, half dozing. His hat was black with a deep crease and a wide brim. His shirt was blue. He also wore denims.

The dust that caked their clothes and mounts testified to the many miles they had ridden. The blond brother rode a palomino, or buttermilk, as they were sometimes called. The black-haired brother rode a zebra dun.

The trail they were following across the

prairie was marked with hoofprints and wheel ruts. Presently it brought them to the top of a hogback sprinkled with sage.

Drawing rein, the older brother pushed his hat back on his head and bobbed his square jaw at a cluster of buildings a quarter of a mile off, nestled at the foot of the Big Horn Mountains. "Yonder is a settlement. We will stop there for a spell, Chancy."

The younger brother looked up and frowned. "A gob of spit in the middle of nothing. We came all this way, and for what, Lin?"

Lin Bryce sighed. The crow's-feet around his eyes crinkled as he tiredly rubbed them. "You know as well as I do why. And you would do well not to remind me."

Chancy's frown deepened. "I hate it when you take that tone. You are not Pa."

"If he were still alive, we would not be here," Lin said wistfully. "We would still be on the ranch. Ma would be her old self, and it would all be as it was when we were young."

"You live too much in the past, Big Brother," Chancy said. "It is now that counts."

"You never think of him? Of how things used to be?"

Chancy yawned. "Why live yesterday all

over again? What is done is done. He died and Ma died and we lost everything and are drifting God knows where."

"We need not have drifted," Lin said harshly.

"Don't start. I am not in the mood. I will be damned if I will listen to another of your lectures." Chancy gigged the zebra dun.

Lin clucked to his buttermilk and followed. He studied the buildings as they drew near. Most were so shabby, they looked fit to blow away with the next Chinook. The exceptions were a general store and a saloon. Horse and pig droppings littered the short street.

Lin brought the buttermilk to a stop at the hitch rail in front of the general store. Chancy had already dismounted and gone in. As Lin alighted, an elderly man in an apron appeared holding a yellow dog by the scruff of its neck.

"When will you listen, you ornery mongrel?" Setting the dog down, he gave it a hard shake. "Stay out of my store! I won't have you underfoot, and I don't want your fleas." With that, he kicked the dog in the backside. Yelping, the animal ran off. Chuckling to himself, the man smoothed his apron.

"Are you as friendly to strangers?" Lin asked.

The man started. "I didn't see you there, mister. And no, as a general rule I don't kick people."

"Where might I be?" Lin asked.

"Wyoming."

Lin waited, and when no more information was forthcoming, he remarked, "You are downright comical."

"Be specific. I can educate you, but I can't make you think, and you don't want to go through life with a puny thinker."

Chuckling, Lin strode around the hitch rail. "I take it back. You are not comical. You are a philosopher."

The man smiled and offered his bony hand. "Abe Tucker. What might your handle be?"

Lin hesitated. He noticed the color of the man's suspenders. "Gray," he lied. "My name is Lin Gray."

"Well, Mr. Gray," Abe said, encompassing the hamlet with a sweep of his bony arm, "this here is Mason. It is named after an old trapper who lived in these parts nigh on forty years. We have a population of fifteen if you count that dog."

Lin gazed to the southeast, out over the rolling grassland he and his brother had crossed, and then to the west at the emerald foothills and the timbered slopes of the towering mountains beyond. Nowhere else was there sign of human habitation. "You must not aim to die rich."

Abe Tucker laughed. "If money was all I cared about, I'd have opened my store in Sheridan. Last I heard, they have pretty near two hundred souls. That is too many for me. I can only abide people in small doses."

"We passed through Sheridan on our way here," Lin mentioned. "I counted three saloons and two churches."

"If parsons served liquor at their services, Sheridan would have five churches and no saloons." Abe arched an eyebrow at the doorway. "You said 'we.' Is that young gent who walked in a minute ago with you?"

"My brother."

"He is not very polite. He bumped into me and did not have the courtesy to say he was sorry." Abe paused. "I almost gave him a piece of my mind, but something in his eyes stopped me."

"He is peaceful enough." Lin told his second lie of the day. "But he is not much on manners."

"The young usually aren't. They reckon they know better than their betters, and strut around like roosters." Abe smiled. "I

11

did the same when I was his age. But we all grow up eventually."

"Some of us," Lin said. He went in.

The store was dark and cool, a welcome relief from the sun. For a small settlement the store was well stocked, the merchandise neatly arranged. Salt, sugar, molasses, eggs, butter — all could be had. Canned goods lined a shelf on one wall. Tools, knives and firearms were on display.

Chancy was at the counter next to a pair of kegs. One was marked APPLE CIDER. He was filling a glass from a spigot. "This gob of spit is not entirely hopeless."

Lin stepped to the cracker barrel. "You would do better to eat. We did not have breakfast."

Abe Tucker moved behind the counter. "Anything that you boys want that you don't see, just ask."

"How about a filly in a tight red dress?" Chancy responded.

"I am not in the painted-cat business, son. The nearest women to be had for money are in Sheridan."

"I figured as much," Chancy said. "And I am not your son, nor will I ever be," he coldly added.

"No offense meant."

Lin held a cracker to his lips but did not

take a bite. "Don't start," he told his brother. "You would think you had learned your lesson by now."

"I am just saying, is all," Chancy said. "People should not call you their son when you are not."

Abe glanced at Lin. "A mite touchy, this brother of yours."

"You have no idea," Lin said. But he did, and he worried that Chancy's touchiness would cause them to continue their flight. He changed the subject. "Tell me, Mr. Tucker: Are there many ranches hereabouts?"

"If four are a lot, then yes," the storekeeper said. "Looking to hire on, are you?"

"I am a tolerable hand," Lin said.

"When you leave Mason, head southwest. In about a mile you will come on Laurel Creek. Follow it west six or seven miles and you will be on the Bar M. That is the biggest outfit in these parts. But the owner, Seth Montfort, is particular about who he hires. It is not enough to know cows these days."

"No?"

"Of late he has been hiring gents who are fond of tie-downs," Abe Tucker revealed.

Chancy's interest perked. "You don't say? What does this Montfort need with leather

13

slappers?"

Abe stared at the pearl-handled Colt high on Chancy's right hip, then at Lin, who did not wear a six-gun. "You would have to ask him. I took you for one, what with that fancy smoke wagon of yours."

Grinning, Chancy patted his Colt. "Cost me a hundred dollars, but it was worth every cent."

"Throwing lead always leads to trouble, young man. You would do well to imitate your brother."

"Don't tell me what to do." Chancy bristled. "I will live as I damn well please."

Lin moved between them, saying, "Simmer down. He was only suggesting, and he is right."

"Here you go again."

"No," Lin said. "I have talked until I am hoarse, and you refuse to listen. So wear it if you want, and I pray to God it doesn't get you killed." He faced the owner. "You mentioned four ranches."

Abe nodded. "The other three are small outfits. To the northwest is Aven Magill. He lives alone and likes it that way, so there is no sense asking him for work. Besides, he is a grump, and you would not want to work for him if he did hire you." Abe paused. "To the west are two ranches. The farthest out is

Cody Dixon and his family. A bit closer is Etta June Cather's spread."

"A woman?"

"Her husband got kicked in the head breaking a raw one about a year ago. Etta June has a boy and a girl, but they are only ten and eight. Too young to be of much help. She runs the ranch herself and does a fine job, but she works herself to death."

A rustling sound caused them to glance down the aisle. A woman was standing there. She was tall and full bodied. Her plain dress and Zouave jacket, which had seen a lot of wear, hinted at frugal means. Sandy hair spilled from under a floppy hat. "I thank you for the compliment, Mr. Tucker," she said, her hazel eyes twinkling.

"Dang it, Etta June," Abe said. "You ought not to sneak up on people like that."

She smiled and came to the counter, paying no attention whatsoever to Lin and Chancy. "I need a few things on account, if that is all right."

"Your credit is always good with me," Abe said kindly.

Chancy held out his half-full glass. "Care for some cider, pretty thing? I do not mind sharing."

"Since when is it proper to address a lady so familiarly? I am not a tart." Etta June

15

Cather reached into a pocket and pulled out a folded sheet of paper. "Here is my list, Mr. Tucker." She went to hand it to him, but Chancy snatched it from her.

"See here," Abe said. "What do you think you are doing?"

Chancy wagged the paper. "I will not be treated as a no-account. She will say she is sorry, or she does not get it back."

"Why, you upstart," Abe said.

Lin held out his hand, palm up. "Give it to me."

"You heard her," Chancy snapped. "I was only being sociable. Where was the harm?"

"Give it," Lin repeated.

"Sometimes you go too far. If you weren't my brother, I would have bedded you down — permanent — a long time ago."

Lin wiggled his fingers.

Scowling, Chancy slapped the paper into Lin's hand. "Here. Take it. But I will not put up with much more of this. I can manage on my own if I have to."

Wheeling, he stalked toward the door, his spurs jingling. As he went out, he slammed the door after him.

"Temperamental, that youngster," Abe Tucker commented.

Lin leaned back against the counter and folded his arms across his broad chest. "He is seventeen. There are ten years between us, and sometimes it seems like fifty."

Etta June said, "I am sorry if I upset him, but he had no call to do that."

"I don't blame you, ma'am," Lin told her, giving back her list. "In fact —" He stopped. Spurs had jangled near the front of the store. "Listen, Chancy," he began, turning.

It was not his brother.

The man who had entered favored black: a black wide-brimmed hat, a black jacket, a black vest and belt and boots. The garb of a gambler. A nickel-plated Smith & Wesson in a studded black holster was slanted across his left hip, butt forward. His face seemed perpetually pinched, as if he were sucking on a lemon. A thread of a mustache adorned his upper lip. He ignored Lin and Abe Tucker and walked up to Etta June Cather, his mouth curling in a grin that was more of a leer. "Well, look here. My favorite female in all the world. I am right pleased to see you, Etta."

"I cannot say the same, Mr. Pike," the ranchwoman responded. "Not if you are going to carry on again as you have been."

"I do not take no for an answer," Pike said. He placed a hand on her wrist. "How about if you and me take a stroll and talk?"

"We have nothing to talk about."

"Don't be contrary," Pike said, pulling on her arm. "You have been without male company for a long time now."

"Release me, if you please," Etta June said. She tried to twist free, but his grip was too strong.

"I will not," Pike said. His leer widened. "Not unless you are nice."

Lin Bryce straightened and squared his shoulders. Balling his big fists, he said quietly, "Let the lady go."

CHAPTER 2

Lin was as surprised as the others by what he had done. He'd vowed to tread lightly after what had happened in Cheyenne. He did not want to draw attention to himself — or to his brother. But here he was, butting in to a matter that did not concern him. Inwardly, he wanted to kick himself. He was a fine one to criticize Chancy.

"What did you say?" the man called Pike demanded.

"You heard me," Lin said. "I will not see a woman abused by you or anyone else."

Pike looked Lin up and down. "Big talk for someone who does not go around heeled."

Lin stepped up to him, looming large. "Don't let that stop you."

Abe Tucker quickly said, "I don't want trouble in here."

"Stay out of this," Pike snapped.

"I will shut up after I say one more thing,"

Abe said. "And that is that Seth Montfort won't be none too happy to hear about how you are treating Etta June. Or don't you care if you rile him?"

"You are a nuisance, old man," Pike said. But he released his hold and lowered his arm. To Lin he said, "I won't forget this." He touched his hat brim to Etta June, hooked his thumbs in his gun belt and departed with a swagger.

Abe waited until the door closed to say, "You can always tell a blockhead. They go around with chips on their shoulders."

"Someone will knock his off one day," Lin commented.

Etta June smiled up at him. "I thank you for stepping in. It was awfully kind."

A warm sensation crept from Lin's collar to his hairline, and he knew he was blushing. "A man should not mistreat a woman."

"I wish I had some way of repaying your gallant gesture." Etta June held out her hand and properly introduced herself.

Lin did likewise, growing hotter. He did not use his real name.

"He mentioned being in need of work," Abe Tucker brought up.

"You don't say?" Etta June Cather's brow knit. "I have been thinking of hiring someone. But I can't pay much. Board and meals, and a few dollars when I have a few to spare."

"Are you offering me a job, ma'am?" Lin asked, breaking into a broad grin. He could not believe his luck. It was just what they needed. The thought sobered him. "Because if you are, I am afraid there is a complication."

"Oh?"

"That scalawag who took your shopping list. Where I go, he has to go. As you saw, he needs looking after."

"So if I hire you, I have to hire him?" Etta June stared at the floor. She bit her lower lip, then said, "I suppose I could feed the both of you. But I am not so sure he is right for the job. How hard will he work?"

"As hard as I make him. And you need not fret in any other respect. He will behave himself. I give you my word."

"You have that much influence over him, Mr. Gray?"

"I like to think I do, yes, ma'am. And you can call me Lin."

"We will keep our relationship formal, if you do not mind," Etta June told him. "And before you agree, there is something else you should know. I do not have a bunkhouse. You and your brother would have to sleep in the stable or out under the stars."

"That is nothing new to us, ma'am."

"I have hundreds of head scattered over a thousand acres. They need to be rounded up and branded, and then we can drive some to market. There is fence to put up. I might even have you build a bunkhouse so you will have a roof over your head."

"I am not afraid of hard work."

"Neither was my husband," Etta June said.

"Abe here told me about him," Lin replied. "I am sorry for you. Losing someone you love is always hard."

"I warned Tom not to try to break that mustang alone. But he was prideful and had to prove to me that he could do it. So in a way I am to blame for his death."

"That is plumb ridiculous," Lin said.

Etta June gave him a sharp look. "Everything Tom did, he did for me. He came to Wyoming from Missouri because I wanted to live in the West. He bought our land because I wanted to have a ranch. He built our house to suit me. And he was breaking that mustang because I wanted more horses and we could not afford to buy them."

"It was the mustang that busted his skull, not you."

"I would rather not talk about it, if you don't mind."

"Certainly, ma'am." Lin backed down the

aisle. "I will go give the good news to my brother. How soon would you want us at your ranch?"

"I intend to head back in an hour. You may accompany me if you still want the job."

"I will not change my mind," Lin assured her. Pivoting on a boot heel, he ambled outside. He was so happy at the turn of events that he momentarily forgot about his clash with Pike. The sight of the gambler talking to his brother across the street reminded him. He headed straight for them, surprised to see they were smiling and laughing.

Pike turned, his hand rising toward his revolver. "Well, look who it is. Mr. High-and-Mighty, as big as life."

"My brother?" Chancy said.

"Your what?" Pike grinned as if it were humorous.

Lin halted.

"Him and me had words over in the store," Pike explained to Chancy. "I can't say as I like him much."

"I will not lose sleep over it," Lin said.

Chancy stepped between them. "Sheath your horns, Big Brother. I happen to like this hombre. His handle is Efram Pike, and we have a lot in common."

"You just met him."

"I can make friends, can't I?" Chancy said. "He has invited me to play cards to-night."

"And have him win what little money you have?" Lin shook his head. "Besides, we won't be here. We will be settling in at our new job."

"You found us work already?"

Lin noticed that his brother did not sound particularly pleased. "On a ranch. The pay is not great, but we will eat regular, and it gives us time to hash over what we want to do."

"I know I do not want to ranch."

Pike said, "I don't blame you. It is hard, brutal work. I did it for a while years ago and never had more blisters in my life."

"It is decent," Lin said.

"You make too much out of right and wrong," Chancy responded. "And there are easier ways to make money than by break-ing our backs."

"You don't mean that," Lin said.

Efram Pike started walking off. "I have better things to do than listen to you two squabble. If you care to join me tonight, kid, my invite holds. But don't bring your brother. He puts on too many airs." Pike glanced over his shoulder at Chancy. "And to prove I am not out to fleece you, leave your money with him. I will stake you in the game, and you will not need to pay me back." He sauntered on into the saloon.

Chancy glared at Lin. "You made a jackass of yourself just now. And a fool of me."

"You are the one who was rude to a lady."

"What the blazes does that have to do with how you talked to Pike?" Chancy swore. "You worry me sometimes, Big Brother. You can be worse than Ma used to be."

"Ma was as fine a woman as ever drew breath, and she would still be alive if —" Lin caught himself.

"If not for Pa?" Chancy prompted. "Is that what you were fixing to say?"

"We have about an hour before we head out to the ranch where we will work," Lin said. "We should check that there is nothing we need."

"You didn't answer me," Chancy said.

"Let's not go into that again." Lin crossed to the buttermilk. He opened first one and then the other of his saddlebags and rummaged inside, verifying he had enough coffee and jerky and whatnot. When his brother did not join him, he looked around. "What are you waiting for?"

"I am not fond of your company at the moment."

"You are too prickly," Lin said.

Motioning in disgust, Chancy made off down the street. "I want to be by myself a while."

Lin opened his mouth to say something, but just then the door to the general store opened and out came Etta June Cather. She came to the hitch rail, raised a hand over her eyes to shield them from the sun and studied him.

"So."

"Ma'am?"

"Mr. Tucker will be a good twenty minutes filling my order. How would you like to take a walk?"

"Me, ma'am?"

"I am not addressing your horse," Etta June said. "Why do you sound so surprised? Or is it that you do not like to walk with women?"

"I guess I would be flattered to walk with you, ma'am," Lin said.

"You guess? For a man your size, you are not a mountain of certainty." Etta June took a few steps and glanced back at him. "You can follow behind if you want, but it is easier to talk when we are side by side."

"Yes, ma'am." Lin scooted over and matched his normally long stride to her shorter one.

"First things first," Etta June began. "I

want to thank you for agreeing to work for me. I need a good man — a man I can depend on; a man who will not try to take advantage — and the way you stood up for me shows you are a gentleman at heart."

"Take advantage, ma'am?"

"Oh, please. We are adults. I am a widow, and in the minds of some men, that is the same as wearing a sign on my back that reads 'I miss it and I want it.' "

"Dear God," Lin said. "Do you always talk like this?"

Etta June took off her floppy hat and swiped at a stray bang that fell over her left eye. "You are a grown man. I would not have suspected your sensibilities to be so fragile."

"Ma'am?"

"I am frank in my speech but never coarse. If that offends you I am sorry but I cannot be anyone but me."

"Our ma never talked like you do, ma'am," Lin said. Nor, now that he thought about it, had any woman he'd met. But then, he had not had words with all that many. He was always shy around females.

Etta June halted and faced him. "That is another thing. Call me ma'am one more time and I am liable to scream. You may call me Mrs. Cather or you may call me Etta June."

"Yes, ma—" Lin caught himself. "Sorry. I was taught to always respect my elders and females."

"A commendable trait if not carried to excess." Etta June resumed walking, her hands clasped behind her. "Now, suppose you tell me a little about yourself. I am taking a risk hiring on two strangers. My instincts tell me you are a good man, but I would like to know more about you."

Icy fingers clutched at Lin's chest. "There is not much to tell. My brother and me were raised on a ranch. Our pa died about five years ago. Our ma died last year. We have been footloose ever since."

"You didn't stay and run the ranch yourselves?"

Lin realized he must be careful around her. She did not miss a thing. "We had to sell it. My pa left us in debt when he died, and we were barely ever able to make ends meet."

"I see."

Lin felt bad lying to her, but he had done so much of it since Cheyenne, the lying did not bother him as much as it used to.

"It is not easy making a living these days," Etta June sympathized. "I was lucky. My

Tom believed in paying for everything with cash. No credit for him. When he died I had few debts. But I did not have much money, either, since we always spent what little we made."

"A thousand acres is a good-sized spread," Lin mentioned.

Etta June snorted. "In these parts it is nothing. Cody Dixon has two thousand. The Bar M has ten times as many, and even that is small compared to some of the ranches to the south. Why, I heard of one with close to a million acres. It is run by a syndicate. They sell more cows in one year than I will in my entire lifetime. Can you imagine?"

"No," Lin said.

"But a thousand is enough for a family to get by if they manage their cattle smart," Etta June went on. "My Tom was as smart as they come except when it came to taking advice about breaking mustangs." She paused. "I refused to sell after he died although Seth Montfort pestered me to. Some men have the silly notion that women can't run a ranch alone."

They came to the end of the street and walked past the last of the ramshackle buildings. Before them rose the foothills. Beyond were the imposing peaks that formed the backbone of the Big Horn range.

"I love this country, Mr. Gray."

"Who?" Lin absently asked. He was entranced by the miles-high peaks, several with mantles of snow.

"Didn't you say that is your last name?"

"Yes, sorry," Lin quickly answered. But he was upset with himself. He had to be more careful or the truth might come out, in which case Etta June Cather would regret ever hiring them.

CHAPTER 3

The Big Horn Mountains were spectacular. Few ranges in all of Wyoming boasted higher peaks. More than a dozen were over nine thousand feet, with the highest over thirteen. Timber was plentiful, with firs and a sprinkling of aspens at the upper elevations, and spruce and pines everywhere else. Cottonwoods lined the streams. The valleys were lush with grass.

For a rancher, the Big Horns were paradise. All the graze and water that cattle needed.

But the Big Horns were so far from civilization, there were few settlements like Mason, and few ranches. The newspapers predicted that one day the whole region would have more spreads than stars in the sky, but for now the number was barely enough for a constellation.

Lin Bryce drank it all in with a sense of wonder. He had seen mountains before, notably on a visit with his father to the Tetons when he was a boy. But that had been long ago, and his memory was fuzzy. In his estimation, the Big Horns were as grand as nature got.

Lin tried to put what he was feeling into words as he rode alongside Etta June Cather's buckboard, but all he could come up with was, "They sure are something, aren't they?"

"God's footstools," Etta June said serenely. "I fell in love with them the first time I set eyes on them. They reach to heaven, and their heartbeat is the beat of life in all of us."

"You sure have a way with words."

"Thank you. If I do, I have my mother to thank. She insisted her children learn to read and write. She taught us mostly herself since there wasn't a school within fifty miles."

Chancy, on the other side of the buckboard, stifled a yawn. "Mountains are mountains."

"You don't see the splendor?" Etta June asked.

"I see rock and snow and trees, lady. Hardly anything to get all excited about."

"It is true I am a lady, but you will not address me as such. I have a name. You make my gender sound like a disease."

"There are days when I think it is."

"Chancy, stop," Lin intervened. "After she has been kind enough to hire us, you will treat her with respect."

"That is all right. I would like to hear him out." Etta June smiled. "What is it you have against women, exactly, young Mr. Gray?"

"They are strange."

"Strange how, pray tell?"

Chancy appeared to be bothered by her questions. "Strange in every way. Women do not think like men, they do not act like men."

"Isn't it good that we don't? Would you want men and women to be the same?"

"Women nag. Women carp. They pick and pick at a man until they have chipped out his insides. They tell him what he can and can't do. They keep him on a leash and get mad if he dares take the leash off. They throw fits when they don't get their way, and are forever shedding tears over one thing or another. They are a mess, and it is best for a man to have nothing to do with them."

"My word," Etta June said. "Where did you ever get such a low opinion of womanhood? Surely not from your mother."

Lin quickly said, "Our ma was as sweet

33

and kind a woman as could be. He did not get it from her."

"Ma was all right," Chancy conceded. "But her sisters are harpies, and her own ma was worse. Bossy does not begin to describe her. The married men I have talked to say that is pretty much normal."

"I would say you have a jaundiced view," Etta June said. "Women have a lot to recommend them."

"Not as far as I am concerned," Chancy said. "I want nothing to do with any of you."

"Nothing at all? What about long walks on warm summer nights? Church socials and county fairs? Picking a flower for your girl, and her thinking you are the handsomest man alive?"

"That is for fools drunk on perfume," Chancy said. "I would rather be drunk on the real thing."

"I had no idea," Etta June said.

Again Lin spoke up. "I am sorry. I should have warned you. He holds some peculiar notions. I don't know where he got them from because he sure did not get them from anything our folks did or said."

"I get my notions from me," Chancy declared.

The trail they were winding along had brought them out of the foothills and into the mountains proper. Off a ways an eagle soared high on outstretched pinions. Songbirds warbled in the woods.

Lin breathed deep and said, "I could learn to love it here."

"That is good to hear," Etta June said. "How about you, Chancy?"

"Need you ask? Trees and squirrels do not mean much. Give me a saloon and a bottle of whiskey and a card game and I am in heaven."

"You are young yet."

"So? Are you saying I do not know my own mind? That when I am older I will think a mountain is God's gift to creation?"

"That was harsh," Lin said.

"I don't know why some people seem to think I should think like they do," Chancy said to Etta June.

"I would never presume in that regard."

"Then maybe we will get along. For my brother's sake I am willing to try."

"May I ask you a personal question?" Etta June said.

"What do you call what you have been doing?" Chancy laughed. "I suppose one more won't hurt."

"What do you want out of life?"

"See what I mean? Only a woman would ask a thing like that." Chancy shrugged. "I don't reckon I want anything."

"Everyone wants something."

"There you go. Telling me what I should think. But I honest to God don't want a thing. Except maybe to be left alone to do what I want and not have people saying as how I should do this, that, or the other."

"He means me," Lin said.

They climbed until they came to a broad shelf. The afternoon was waning, and Etta June brought the buckboard to a stop near a ring of blackened rocks that showed the spot was regularly used as a campsite.

"We are stopping?" Lin asked in some surprise.

"We are," Etta June confirmed. "The mountains at night are dangerous. A horse can easily break a leg. And there are bears and mountain lions and Indians."

Chancy pressed a hand to the small of his back and arched his spine. "How far is this ranch of yours, anyhow?"

"We will reach it tomorrow afternoon."

Lin was more interested in another of her comments. "Abe said something about Indians too. Has there been an outbreak?"

"A small band has been spotted a few times," Etta June revealed. "Some say they are Crows; others say they are Blackfeet. Everyone suspects they are out to make trouble, but so far they have not gone on the warpath."

"Let them give us trouble," Chancy said, patting his pearl-handled Colt. "I will kill redskins as soon as anyone."

About to climb down, Etta June paused. "You make it sound as if you have killed before."

Again Chancy patted his Colt. "I do not wear this for bluff or ballast."

Lin had dismounted and offered his arm to Etta June, saying, "That is his age talking."

"I will be glad when I am thirty," Chancy said. "I am sick to death of being thought a shaver."

Smoothing her dress, Etta June regarded his Colt. "I trust you will not wear your artillery when you are working."

"You might as well ask me to shed my nose or my ears," Chancy said.

"What if I insist?"

"Then we might as well part company now," Chancy replied. "You just got through saying redskins are on the prowl, yet you want me to ride the range unarmed? If that is female logic, it proves what I have been saying."

"Very well. But you are not to let my son or my daughter handle it or shoot it without my consent."

"It will be a cold day in" — Chancy stopped and grinned — "Hades . . . before anyone but me touches my hardware."

Lin had listened to enough. "Why don't you fetch some firewood while I help Mrs. Cather unhitch the team?"

Later, seated near the crackling flames, with the aroma of brewing Arbuckle's in his nostrils, Lin watched as Etta June opened a can of Van Camp's beans. Stretching out his legs, he leaned back against his saddle and gave a contented sigh.

"You seem quite happy at the moment," Etta June remarked.

"I am." Lin gazed at the stars sparkling in the firmament. "I want to thank you again for taking us on."

"Thank me after you have been at it a month," Etta June said. "Ranching is hard work."

Chancy, his arms wrapped around his chest, his hat pulled low, grunted. "Don't we know it. Our pa worked from dawn until dusk to make ends meet."

"Did you admire him for that?"

"What is admirable about working your-self to death?" Chancy rejoined. "I do not rate calluses all that high."

Etta June removed the lid and upended

the can over a pan. "You prefer the easy life, I take it?"

"Who doesn't? If given their druthers between breaking their backs ten to twelve hours a day or playing cards all night long, most men would choose the cards."

"That simply is not true," Etta June said. "My Tom was devoted to his family. He would never jeopardize our future by squandering our hard-earned money at poker."

"He would if he was any good at it," Chancy said.

About to stir the beans with a large wooden spoon, Etta June glanced across the fire. "My Tom was good at a lot of things, but that is neither here nor there. A man who cares for his family does not indulge in immature habits."

"So cards are immature, are they?"

"When you have mouths to feed besides your own and a roof to keep over their heads, gambling is as irresponsible as you can be." Etta June looked at Lin. "You are conspicuous by your silence."

"I agree with you. A husband and father should put his wife and family before everything else."

Etta June smiled. "I like your answer."

"That is not for me," Chancy said. "There is too much of the world I have not seen, too many things I have not done. I will not let myself be tied to apron strings or bibs."

"Some folks would call that selfish," Etta June said.

"It is his age speaking again," Lin interjected. It seemed to him that the two of them could not open their mouths without clawing at each other's throats.

"Folks may call it whatever they like," Chancy said. "If there is one thing I do not care about, it is what others think."

"I wish I had that luxury."

Chancy poked at the unlit end of a burning brand with a toe, pushing it into the fire. "Are you saying you don't?"

"I am a widow with two children," Etta June said. "People expect me to behave a certain way. Were I to take up with men and keep all hours, I would be branded a harlot."

"There are worse things to be branded," Chancy said.

"Not if you are a mother. Loose morals are frowned on. I would lose my credit at the store. The few dollars I have saved would not last long. When the money ran out I would lose my ranch. I would need a job or we would starve. And when you are female and have a reputation, there is only one sort of work you can get."

"We are back to the harlot."

"Some women might not have qualms about lying in bed with total strangers, but I do."

Lin gestured at his brother, who was about to say something more. "This is hardly fit talk."

"She started it."

"Be that as it may," Lin said, "I would like to hear about her cows and anything else she considers important."

The next moment one of the horses raised its head, stamped a front hoof and nickered.

Chancy was on his feet in a twinkling, his hand on his Colt. "Something is out there."

"He caught a whiff of a cat or a wolf or a bear," Etta June said. "Whatever it is, it will leave us be."

"But what if it's a grizzly?" Lin brought up. He had heard stories about grizzlies — formidable monsters that could not be stopped once their dander was up. Or if they were hungry enough.

"Most of those that are left are higher up," Etta June said.

"Most?"

"Oh, we get one down here from time to time. But they pretty much leave people alone."

"Pretty much?"

Etta laughed. "You two should move back

east where the most you have to worry about are rabid raccoons. Relax. Nothing will bother us."

As if to prove her wrong, the night was suddenly shattered by an inhuman shriek.

CHAPTER 4

The cry was enough to freeze a man's blood. Rising to a piercing wail, it wavered on the wind, then gradually faded.

Lin Bryce felt the short hairs at the nape of his neck prickle. "God in heaven."

"What the hell? Where did that come from?" Chancy asked, anxiously turning every which way.

Etta June was unfazed. Chuckling, she said, "Haven't you ever heard a mountain lion before?"

"Are you sure that is what it was?" Chancy peered into the dark as if expecting something to rush out at them.

"I am sure," Etta June said. "Unless I miss my guess, it was a female letting the males know she is feeling romantic."

"A hell of a note," Chancy said, straightening. "If people did that, the nights would be bedlam."

Etta June laughed. "That they would." She

cocked her head at him. "But that makes twice you have used language I do not want you to use in front of my children. I will thank you to limit your cussing from here on out to inside your head."

"You ask too much," Chancy said, sitting back down. "The words just pop out. There is nothing a man can do."

"Not all men swear. Your brother, here, hasn't cursed once since I met him."

"I never got into the habit," Lin said.

Chancy sighed. "I will try not to do it around your sprouts, but don't blame me if I slip up now and then."

"Try your best is all I ask," Etta June told him.

Lin faced into the wind and breathed deep of the crisp mountain air. It had a vaguely piney scent. "This sure is wild country," he said to change the subject.

"None wilder," Etta June agreed. "It is not like down Colorado way, where the mountains have been overrun by gold and silver seekers, and most of the big game has been killed off. Here it is like it has always been. Savage beasts, savage men and a savage land — and none show mercy to the weak and the helpless."

Lin looked at Etta June. "If it is as bad as you say, why do you stay? Why put yourself

44

and your children in danger?"

"Because I love it here. I love the mountains; I love the freedom."

"But the dangers," Lin persisted.

"Safe is overrated. Safe is living in a town or city where you can't turn around without bumping into someone. Safe is living by others' rules and always having someone looking over your shoulder."

"I hate that," Chancy said.

"A lot of folks would rather stick their heads in the ground like one of those ostriches than face the fact that life was never meant to be safe," Etta June said. "We come into this world with no guarantee of how long we have before we are called to the other side. Whether it is an arrow or a bear or old age, it is all the same."

"You have it all thought out," Lin said.

"I like being able to live as I please. If the only place I can do that is a place like the Big Horns, then that is where I will live, dangers or no."

Chancy gave her a strange look. "It could be I was wrong about you. You have grit, ma'am."

"Thank you," Etta June said.

She filled their tin cups with steaming coffee, and for a while the three of them sat in silence, listening to the sounds of the night

45

and drifting with the tides of their own thoughts.

Lin was troubled. He had known Etta June Cather less than a day, but he was growing powerful fond of her. In a way she reminded him of his ma before the awful event that changed their lives forever.

Soon the beans were simmering. Etta June heaped spoonfuls on tin plates for each of them. She added a thick slice of bread smeared with butter.

Lin was ravenous. He dipped the bread in the tomato sauce, bit off the end, and chewed with relish. If there was anything better than eating food, he had yet to come across it. He caught Etta June staring at him. "What?"

"You look just like my Tom used to look when he was eating. From his face you would think he was in heaven."

Lin's ears grew hot. "I like to eat," he admitted.

Chancy snickered. "All my big brother asks out of life is a full belly and a roof over his head and he is content."

"What about you?" Etta June said. "What will make you content?"

"My share," Chancy said.

Etta June took a sip of coffee. "Your share of what?"

46

"Of all there is. I want to bite into life and chew it like my brother is chewing that bread. I want to taste all it has to offer, to never settle for being one of the common herd."

"That is a tall order."

Lin lost some of his appetite. He hated to hear his brother talk like that. Not after all they had been through. "There is a lot to be said for a roof over your head and three meals a day."

Chancy's laugh was harsh. "For sheep in a pen that will do, but not for those of us who think life is for living."

Later, lying on his back with his head and shoulders propped on his saddle, Lin gave silent thanks that Etta June had offered them work. It bought him time. Time to convince his brother that sheep had one advantage over curly wolves; they lived longer.

Sunrise found them on their way. The clatter of the buckboard was nearly drowned out by the creak of a rear wheel.

Lin reined close to the seat to say, "That wheel needs greasing. When we get to your ranch that is the first thing I will do."

"You think ahead. I like that."

Lin wished his ears would stop burning.

"I knew it had to be done, but I had too

47

much to do and didn't get to it before I left," Etta June said, and lowered her voice. "I will only say this to you and deny it if you ever tell anyone, but running a ranch, even a small one like mine, is too much for one person."

"From what Abe Tucker said, you do as good as any man could," Lin brought up by way of praise.

"I try my best," Etta June said, "but there are days when I miss my Tom severely. A day of toting bales of hay and winching them to the loft leaves me so sore and tired, I can barely stand. It is all I can do to work the plow. I have the will but I lack the muscle."

Lin's tongue moved of its own accord. "I have plenty. Enough muscle for both of us."

"I will put them to hard use, on that you can count," Etta June said with a smile. "To tell you the truth, I would have hired someone sooner, but there aren't any men hereabouts I trust."

"None at all?"

"None I could count on to do an honest day's work. Take Efram Pike. He would rather loaf his life away drinking and playing cards."

"So you take a gamble on a complete stranger like me," Lin said.

Etta June looked him in the eyes. "It is no gamble."

Midmorning came and brought with it, to the west, tendrils of dust that grew into a cloud filled with riders. Etta June brought the buckboard to a stop, reached under the seat and pulled out a Winchester.

Lin hid his surprise. He glanced at his saddlebag and started to reach back but closed his hand into a fist and placed the fist on his thigh. "No," he said softly to himself.

Chancy drew rein on the other side of the buckboard. "Know those folks?" he asked.

"The man in front is Seth Montfort, owner of the Bar M," Etta June said. "He does not often come this far north." The brothers barely heard her next comment; "Unless he is paying me a visit."

The rumble of hooves swelled. Seth Montfort held up an arm, as if he were an army officer, and his men slowed their mounts to a walk. He held it up again and they stopped. Montfort sat his saddle much as a dumpling would sit a griddle, which was fitting given that he was short and plump and had two chins. His attire was Eastern, from his bowler to his suit to his boots. The gold chain to a pocket watch gleamed brightly on his vest. His double chin quivered when he spoke. "Etta, my dear. It is a distinct pleasure to run into you."

"How are you, Seth?"

"Fine, fine." Montfort's dark eyes shifted from her to Lin to Chancy. "You have new friends, I see."

"New hands," Etta June said.

"You don't say." Montfort frowned. "Why hire them when I have offered time and again to have my men help you whenever you need it?"

"I could not impose."

"Nonsense, my dear." Montfort reined closer. "I would do anything for you. Anything at all. Surely I have made my feelings plain?"

"Yes, you have," Etta June said. "And I have made mine plain, as well. It is much too soon for me to even consider anything like that."

"He died over a year ago."

Lin had divined what they were talking about, and he did not like it. Not one bit. Anger welled, but he smothered it. He had no right. She was his employer, nothing more.

"Please, Seth," Etta June said. "Don't start."

"Very well." Again Montfort looked at Lin and Chancy. "I do not know who you

50

gentlemen are or where you came from, but I trust you are dependable. Mrs. Cather is a close personal friend of mine, and I would not take it kindly were you to slight her in any way. I would not take it kindly at all."

Chancy snorted. "Why, you little butterball."

Montfort stiffened. "What did you just call me?"

"You heard me," Chancy said. "Who do you think you are, threatening us? I have half a mind to pistol-whip you to teach you some manners."

Seth Montfort's chins twitched. "How dare you talk to me like that," he snapped.

A rider on a piebald straightened and lowered his right hand close to his holster. Of middling height, he wore a high-crowned hat and a vest fringed with silver studs. His clothes were typical work clothes, but there was nothing typical about his nickel-plated Hopkins & Allen revolver with ivory grips. "Want me to deal with this kid, Mr. Montfort?"

Before Montfort could answer, Chancy laughed and said, "Oh, my. A gun shark. Should I tremble in fear?"

Lin jumped in with, "Don't provoke them, Chancy."

"Chancy?" the rider said, his eyebrows

meeting over his nose. "I have heard that name somewhere."

Seth Montfort swiveled at the hips. "When I want your assistance, Mr. Stone, I will ask for it. Until I do, kindly refrain from interfering."

Etta June motioned at Montfort's men. "What is this, Seth? You have a lot of new faces with you, as well."

"I have been hiring hands too," Montfort said.

"So I hear. Word is, they know more about guns than they do about cows. What would you need with men like this?"

"They are for my own protection, my dear."

"From whom?" Etta June asked skeptically. "Indians? You already had enough punchers to deal with them. You did not need to bring in a tie-down crowd."

Montfort sniffed and smoothed a sleeve on his jacket. "Red savages do not worry me any. I am concerned about the rustlers."

Etta June sat up. "What on earth are you talking about?"

"Some of my cattle have gone missing. Granted, it is only a few head so far. But if I do not nip it in the bud, there is no telling how many I will lose. I will not stand for that."

"Where did these rustlers come from?" Etta June asked.

"I never said they were outsiders. In fact, I have reason to believe one of your neighbors is involved. We followed tracks in the direction of his ranch but lost them. I just paid him and his family a visit. He denies it, of course, but he does not fool me."

"Family?" Etta June said. "Dear Lord. You must mean the Dixons."

"I do."

"Are you loco? Cody is one of the most honest souls I know. The same with Patricia. To even suggest they would stoop to stealing your cattle when they have more than enough of their own is preposterous."

Seth Montfort lifted his reins. "Think what you will, but the facts speak for themselves. I have warned Dixon that if any more of my cattle disappear, I will hold him to account."

"Can we talk about this?" Etta June requested. "How about if I have you over to my place for supper tomorrow? About seven?"

"I would be honored," Montfort said. "Now, if you will excuse me, I must arrange to have a letter mailed." He smiled, then clucked to his roan and rode off toward the settlement. Some of his men gave Lin and

Chancy looks of outright contempt.

"I don't like that hombre," Chancy declared.

Neither did Lin. But he owed it to his employer to be civil. "Are you all right?" he asked, noticing worry lines that etched her face.

"No, I am not," Etta June said, twisting in the seat to stare after the knot of horsemen. "I have an awful premonition."

"About what?"

"Comments Seth Montfort has dropped over the past six months or so. Little things I did not think much of at the time. But now I see they were not so little, after all."

"You are making no kind of sense," Chancy said.

"I pray I am wrong," Etta June said. "For if I'm not, before long these mountains will run red with blood."

CHAPTER 5

Tom Cather had done things right. In addition to the ranch house, he had built a stable with an attached corral, a blacksmith shop, a chicken coop and a number of sheds. Modest in comparison to some spreads, the log structures were as solid as rock. The ranch was not situated near a stream as Lin had expected, but near a small lake.

"The Big Horns are home to a lot of lakes," Etta June said when he brought it up. "Unlike some of the streams, they do not dry up in the summer."

The buildings were situated at the east end of a valley that meandered along the base of steep wooded slopes. At the west end a high peak glistened white with snow.

Cattle were scattered throughout the valley. Some had even strayed up into the timber.

"You will have your work cut out for you," Etta June informed them.

As the buckboard rattled past the corral, the front door to the house flew open, and out ran a pair of sandy-haired youngsters. Squealing with delight, shouting, "Ma! Ma!" they raced to meet her. The boy was lanky, his limbs more bone than muscle. The girl had an uncommon amount of freckles and wore her hair in a braid.

Etta June brought the buckboard to a stop and jumped down. Sinking to a knee, she spread her arms wide. Her children practically hurled themselves at her and clasped her to them as if afraid she would get back up and leave again.

"We missed you, Ma!" the little girl squealed in delight. "We missed you so much!"

"It has only been a few days," Etta June said, and kissed her daughter on the cheek. "What will you do if I ever have to go away for a week or more?"

"Don't ever do that, Ma," the boy said. His chin on her shoulder, he closed his eyes. "We heard a wolf near the house last night and sissy got scared."

"I did not," the girl said.

Etta June rose. Holding them to her, she smiled. "These two are my reasons for living. Tom Jr. is my oldest, Elizabeth my youngest. We have taken to calling her Beth for short." She introduced Lin and Chancy and explained why she had brought them.

"I am pleased to make your acquaintance," Lin said formally.

"I will be pleased so long as you leave me be," Chancy said, dismounting. "I do not like kids."

"Why?" Beth asked.

"I would like to know too," Tom said.

"Because all your kind do is pester people with questions," Chancy said. "If you have a question to ask me, ask it a year from now."

"You might not even be here," Tom said.

"Then you can ask whoever is."

Beth giggled and whispered in her mother's ear.

"She says she likes you," Etta June relayed.

Chancy muttered under his breath, then announced, "I will tend to my animal." He led his zebra dun away.

Beth immediately ran after him.

"Go with her," Etta June said to Tom. "Don't let her make a nuisance of herself."

Lin swung his leg over his saddle horn and slid down. "You have fine young ones."

"That I do," Etta June proudly agreed. "I was not joking when I said they are my reason for living. I only pray I can do half as well by them as my husband and I planned."

"They are lucky to have someone who cares for them so much." Lin was thinking of his own mother, and how she had been toward the end.

"What a kind thing to say."

Lin coughed. "So where do you want us to start? I saw a broke corral rail. We could put in a new one."

"That can wait," Etta June said. "Take the rest of the day off."

"But you brought us here to work." Lin was eager to show her he was the dependable sort she wanted.

"The rail will still be there in the morning. Strip your horse, then relax. Take a stroll. Get acquainted with what is where. I will expect you and your brother for supper."

"Us tonight, and Seth Montfort tomorrow night? Do you always have so many folks over?" Lin meant for it to make her grin, but instead she grew sad.

"If I never set eyes on him again, it would be too soon by half. But I need to find out what he is up to." Etta June shook herself, blinked and smiled. "Listen to me. Prattling away. There is a washbasin out back of the house. I will fill it with water and leave lye soap so you and your brother can clean up before supper."

"We will," Lin said. He watched her hurry off, then turned and headed for the stable. The buttermilk came first.

Conflicting emotions tugged at him. On the one hand, he was happy to be there. He liked Etta June. He liked the notion of working for her. He liked that they were in the middle of nowhere. But on the other hand, trouble appeared to be brewing, and the last thing he needed was to become involved in another shooting affray.

Why isn't life ever easy? Lin asked the thin air. When he was a boy it had been easy enough. Back then his parents were as kind and loving as could be, and everything was right with the world. Lin sighed. Lately he was thinking too much. It took too much effort, and half the time he could not work out the problems he was trying to solve.

Lin would be the first to admit he was not all that smart. He accepted that. A man should always be aware of his limitations, and one of his was that his brain did not work as well or as fast as most others. But that was all right. As his pa liked to say, the important thing was that a man stayed true to himself. And that was one thing Lin would always do, no matter what.

Lin grinned wryly. Who was he kidding?

He was being — what was that word? Oh, yes. He was being a hypocrite. He had lied about his last name. And anyone who lied was hardly being true.

The sound of laughter brought Lin out of himself. He reached the open double doors of the stable and saw Chancy about to place the zebra dun in a stall. The children were grinning and chortling, and looked around as Lin entered leading the palomino.

"Your brother is funny," Tom said.

"He called us bugs," Beth piped up, and giggled. "He says we are a couple of spiders."

Lin smiled. His brother hated spiders and stomped every one he saw. "Pay him no mind. He says a lot of strange things."

"I do not," Chancy said.

"You sure have a pretty gun," Tom remarked. "Can I hold it?"

Chancy glanced at the boy, and for a few seconds Lin worried he would let him. "You may not. Guns are for adults, not spiders."

"I only want to hold it," Tom begged. "I won't shoot it or anything."

"Do I ask to hold your cows?" Chancy said.

Beth cackled.

The stall next to the zebra dun was empty. Lin brought the buttermilk over, saying,

"Keep it up and you will be more popular than hard candy."

"It is not my fault," Chancy said. "No matter what I say, they take it the wrong way."

"Be nice," Lin said.

Chancy went to a bin, opened it and scooped oats into a bucket. "I do not know how long I can do this."

"We just got here."

"This is your kind of life, not mine," Chancy said. "I like cards and whiskey and a dove to warm my knee."

"Give it a try," Lin said. "For me."

"You ask too much," Chancy replied. "But for you, and only for you, I will hold out as long as I can." He came back to the stalls. "When I cannot take it anymore, though, I am saddling up and heading for Mason. After that, who knows?"

"You would go off on your own?"

"I am a grown man, Lin. We are family, but we will have to go our separate ways eventually."

"I just thought —" Lin said, and fell silent. It was foolish of him, he supposed, to imagine they would be as close now as they had been when they were the same ages as Tom Jr. and Elizabeth.

The children followed them on their tour.

61

Beth mentioned that one of the chickens always pecked when they tried to take her eggs, and both kids laughed when Chancy suggested they eat her. Tom talked about a dog they once had, which they always tied up at night so it could not run off. One morning the family came out and the dog was gone.

"Pa said a cougar or a wolf must have got him," Tom said. "We looked, but all we found were Indian tracks."

That made Lin wonder. Some tribes were partial to dog meat.

The smith shop had not been used much since their father died. The forge was cold. Tongs and other tools hung neatly on pegs on the wall.

Tom Jr. placed a hand on the anvil. "I liked to watch my pa work in here. The metal would get so hot, it glowed."

"I miss him so much," Beth said, her eyes misting.

"Let's keep going," Chancy said.

Their circuit presently brought them back to the stable and the corral. Tom pointed at a spot near the gate. "That is where we found him. His head was crushed."

"Ma shot the horse that killed him," Beth said. "Shot it over and over with the rifle until there were no bullets left."

"You must be careful around horses," Lin advised.

"I don't like them much anymore," Beth said. "Ma wanted to get me a pony, but I don't want one."

"You could always throw a saddle on a cow," Chancy said.

Beth brightened. "You say the silliest things."

The clang of a triangle on the front porch let them know supper was ready. Etta June had changed into a clean dress, and wore an apron. "I hope you are hungry."

Lin sniffed a few times. Something sure smelled good. He doffed his hat, then nudged Chancy so he would so the same. They were about to step onto the porch when young Tom turned and pointed.

"We have company coming, Ma."

Two riders were galloping down the valley. Even at that distance, the fact that they were not men was apparent.

"Who can it be, Ma?" Beth asked.

"Only one person we know rides an albino," Etta June said. "I will put another plate on for her." She hurried in.

"It has to be Mrs. Dixon and her daughter, Sue," Tom Jr. said. "But I never saw them ride like that."

The woman on the albino was quirting it

as if she could not get to the ranch fast enough.

"How old is the daughter?" Chancy asked.

"No one ever told me," Tom answered, "but she is about your age, I would reckon."

"She sure is a fine-looking filly."

"She is a girl," Tom Jr. said in disgust.

Lin leaned toward his brother. "You better behave."

"I will be so polite, you will gag."

The women did not slow until they were almost to the house. Then Lin saw the older of the pair notice him and Chancy, and she hauled on the reins and said something to the younger woman. The last twenty yards, they came on at a walk.

"Pat! Sue!" Beth squealed in delight and ran to greet them.

The mother was a square block of a woman. Gray at the temples, she had thick arms and thicker legs, and when she dismounted, she planted them as if she were a tree. She also yanked a rifle from her saddle scabbard. "You are growing like a weed, little one," she said to Beth, and bending, hugged her.

The daughter had the same black hair, only without the gray. She was nicely formed, a flower in bud that would soon bloom in the full beauty of womanhood.

She nodded at Lin, then intently regarded Chancy. "How do you do?"

When his brother did not reply, Lin looked over and saw that Chancy was standing as rigid as a statue.

"I am Patricia Dixon," the older woman said. "Who might you two be?" she asked suspiciously.

Lin was spared having to explain by the timely return of Etta June, who greeted her visitors warmly and invited them in.

"So you have finally taken my advice and hired a couple of hands to help out?" Pat said. "I wish Cody would hire a few. We might need them, if things go as I fear."

"I ran into Seth Montfort on my way home," Etta June revealed. "I couldn't believe my ears when he claimed that Cody was rustling his cattle."

"I couldn't believe it, either," Pat responded. "Montfort rode right up to our house and accused Cody to his face. I was never so glad we keep our rifles and revolvers in a case in the parlor. Cody might have tried to shoot him and been shot to ribbons by Montfort's men."

"Surely it will not come to that."

"You know as well as I do that Montfort has always acted as if he is better than everyone else. He looks down his nose at smaller spreads. I used to think he was just putting on airs, but now I am not so sure."

"What do you mean?"

"The look on Montfort's face. The things he said." Patricia Dixon put her hand on Etta June's shoulder. "I am scared, Etta June. Have you heard about all the shootists Montfort has hired? I think he aims to unleash them on me and mine."

She sucked in a deep breath. "He is going to wipe us out."

CHAPTER 6

The food was delicious. It reminded Lin of his mother's cooking.

Chicken stew was the main course; the broth was thick and creamy, heavy on the milk. Potatoes and coleslaw were the side dishes. The former had been fried, the latter fresh made, so that the bits of cabbage crunched when Lin chewed. Corn dodgers were an added treat. But the best came last; for dessert there was brown Betty, a favorite of his when he was growing up. They had a choice of beverages: coffee or lemonade.

Lin and the children seemed to be the only ones enjoying the meal. The guests barely touched theirs. Etta June also ate sparingly. Even Chancy did not display his usual healthy appetite, which surprised Lin considerably. Although his brother did not make the big fuss Lin did about eating regularly, when Chancy did eat, he consumed as much as a hungry bear just out of hibernation.

As they ate, Tom Jr. and Beth chatted about the things they had done while their mother was away. Tom had discovered an ant hill and dug down until he unearthed the queen. Beth reported that a pigeon had laid an egg in the stable rafters.

Etta June broke her silence. "How would you know that unless you climbed up to see?"

"I didn't do the climbing," Beth said. "Tom did."

Etta June focused on her oldest. "What have I told you about playing in the rafters?"

"I used the ladder."

"That shows common sense," Etta June said. "But you still could have fallen and broken a leg or an arm, and then where would you be? With me off at Mason?"

"I was real careful."

To Lin's amazement, Chancy, of all people, wagged a finger at the boy and said, "Listen to your ma. She knows what is best. If I had listened to mine, maybe I wouldn't have gotten into some of the trouble I did."

Sue Dixon uttered the first words she had spoken since she arrived. "I bet you handled it right fine, though."

Lin nearly choked on the coffee he was swallowing. His brother had blushed, and

Patricia Dixon gave her daughter a look that made Lin think of twin daggers.

"I am still breathing," Chancy said. Then he became interested in a corn dodger.

Only after the meal was over and the children had been whisked to bed did the adults get to the business at hand. Etta June started it off by saying, "You can't be serious, Pat, about Seth Montfort wanting to exterminate you and yours."

"Then why all the short-trigger men?"

"Seth says cows have been disappearing off his range," Etta June said. "That is cause enough. Remember, most punchers are not all that gun wise."

"I could see hiring one or two," Pat said. "But he has upwards of fifteen. He told us so. Bragged about them as if they were prized bulls."

"Seth does like to crow about himself," Etta June said.

"Talk to him for me," Patricia requested.

"What?"

"That is why I came over. Everyone knows he is sweet on you. The next time you see him, ask about the gun crowd. Find out why in heaven's name he has accused Cody of having a sticky rope. We are not brand blotters."

Etta June fingered her glass of lemonade.

"As a matter of fact, I am having him over tomorrow night."

Pat reached across the table and squeezed Etta June's hand. "I knew I could count on you. This needs to be settled before blood is spilled, or worse."

"What can be worse than spilling blood?" Lin interjected.

"A strangulation jig," Pat said, anxiously. "In these parts brand artists are turned into human fruit, and I do not want my husband or either of my sons dangling from the end of a rope."

"How old are your sons?" Lin asked.

"Tyler is twenty-two; Hank is eighteen. They are good boys." Pat stopped and swallowed, but she had nothing in her mouth. "When Montfort showed up and accused us, Tyler said he was willing to swear on a stack of Bibles that we never rustled a head in our lives. And do you know what Montfort did? He said my boys would not know the truth if it jumped up and bit them."

"He didn't!" Etta June exclaimed.

"I heard it with my own ears," Pat confirmed. "If you ask me, Seth Montfort was trying to provoke my menfolk. I honestly think he was hoping they would go for a gun so he would have an excuse to have his hired killers bed them down permanent."

"Surely not."

"Who is to stop him? We are awful short on law. Mason is not big enough to have a marshal. We don't have a county sheriff because the legislature has not gotten around to creating counties this far north. All that leaves is a federal marshal, and getting hold of one of them can take months." Pat wrung her hands. "No, we are on our own. Seth Montfort can do pretty much as he pleases, and there is not a thing we can do about it."

"If he dares to harm you I will go to the governor," Etta June vowed. "I will tell Seth that too when I see him tomorrow."

"I thank you, but it won't stop a man like him. He is used to having his own way."

The talk drifted to other matters, and at one point it was agreed that Pat and Sue should stay the night.

"These mountains are not safe after dark," Etta June said. "Especially not with rustlers and Indians on the loose. Get a good night's sleep and head home in the morning."

Lin and Chancy could sleep anywhere that struck their fancy — so long as it was not in the house.

"I figure one of us should stay near, just in case, while the other beds down in the stable," Lin proposed. Some Indians were

71

as fond of helping themselves to horses owned by whites as they were of counting coup on the whites who owned them.

"I will sleep near the house," Chancy promptly said.

Lin looked at him. It would be more comfortable in the stable. "Are you sure? I don't mind sleeping under the stars."

"Neither do I, Big Brother."

Etta June had a contribution. "Why not sleep on the porch, Chancy? I will give you extra blankets and you will be as cozy as can be."

"I am obliged," Chancy said.

The women indulged in more small talk. About the weather, about a new dress Pat was making for Sue, about how much manure to add to a rose garden and the prices Abe Tucker was charging these days for essentials like sugar and flour.

Typical female prattle, Lin thought to himself. He did not take part. Neither did his brother, who was being unusually quiet. Chancy did speak when Sue Dixon asked him to pass the bowl of sugar so she could add some to her lemonade.

"Of course."

It was probably Lin's imagination, but he had the impression their hands brushed as Chancy slid the bowl to her.

Then the meal was over, and Etta June escorted Lin and Chancy to the door. Lin thanked her for a fine time.

"The first of many," Etta June said with a smile. "You were perfect gentlemen, the both of you."

"The next time I will try to be more rowdy," Chancy said.

Laughing, she held the door open for them. As Lin went past, she snagged his sleeve. "Both of you be careful. What with the Indians and the wolves and now this business with Seth Montfort, there is no telling what might happen."

"Have you always had a wolf problem?" Lin asked, mainly so he could stay near her a bit longer.

"Not until the last year or so," Etta June revealed. "All the ranchers have lost a few calves and yearlings."

"Strange," Lin said. Where game was abundant — and the Big Horns had plenty — wolves normally let livestock be.

"Might be a lobo."

"I suppose," Lin said. It was rare, but every now and again a lone wolf took to killing stock and went on killing, often because the wolf was so old it could not run down wild game, or it had been crippled.

"Keep your rifle and revolver handy," Etta

June advised.

Chancy placed his hand on his pearl-handled Colt. "I never let this out of my reach."

"Ever since my husband died, I have taken to sleeping with a rifle by my bed," Etta June mentioned. "Give a holler and I will come on the run."

Lin idly wondered why she had stopped referring to her departed spouse as "my Tom." He put his hat on, touched the brim with a finger and went out. As the door closed he was filled with regret that the meal was over.

"I will go with you to the stable to get my bedroll and Winchester," Chancy said.

"Nice folks." Lin bobbed his head at the house.

"The sprouts can be a nuisance."

"They did not act up once during supper," Lin observed. "What did you think of the Dixons?"

"The mother is a she-bear. Get her riled and she shows her claws. Seth Montfort had better watch out."

"What about the daughter, Sue?"

"What about her?"

"She must be awful shy. She hardly said a word all night. She is pretty, though, don't you think?"

"I didn't notice," Chancy said stiffly.

"The young men in these parts are bound to. She probably has more suitors than you can shake a stick at."

"Don't you have better things to talk about than romance?"

Lin looked at him, hiding a smile. "Why are you so prickly?"

"Men should talk about manly things and not who is courting who," Chancy said.

"What do you want to talk about, then?"

"Not Sue Dixon."

The stable was quiet, the interior mired in shadow. Lin lit a lantern that hung on a peg near the door.

Soon Chancy, his bedroll under one arm, strolled back out. "Don't sleep too tight, Big Brother, or you might wake up without your hair."

Lin did not find that amusing. He once met a man who had been scalped and lived to tell the tale, but when his head healed, the man's hair had not grown back. These days the man hardly ever took his hat off.

Where to sleep was the question of the moment. Lin decided on the hayloft. He blew out the lantern, waited for his eyes to adjust to the dark and walked to the ladder. He climbed carefully. The hay smell re-minded him of his childhood. He stamped some of it down and spread out his bedroll.

Weariness nipped at Lin, but he shrugged it off. He had left the stable doors open in case Chancy or the women needed him in a hurry. Now he knelt at the hayloft door. It opened at his second tug, and cool air blew over him. He put his rifle down and leaned out.

The night was peaceful. A few windows were still lit in the house. He could not see Chancy thanks to the porch overhang.

Lin pushed his hat back on his head. He liked the ranch, he liked the kids, he liked Etta June more than ever. He hoped — no, he prayed — that it worked out so he and his brother could stay for as long as they wanted. If only he could keep a rein on Chancy. His brother's recklessness had already brought them enough trouble. They did not need more.

Lin yawned. On hands and knees he crossed to his blanket. Sinking down on his side, he place the Winchester next to him, removed his hat and closed his eyes.

The hay was as good as a bed. Lin drifted into dreamland, and in his dream he was stalked by a pack of starving wolves. He was on his horse, but they chased him, and one of the wolves brought the buttermilk down by ripping a rear leg with its fangs. He heard the horse whinny, felt the jolt of striking the hard ground.

Suddenly Lin was awake. He lay in a cold sweat, unsure whether the dream had woke him, or something else. He had about decided it was the dream and was closing his eyes to go back to sleep when a sound came through the hayloft door. It was faint, but he would swear it was the rasp of metal on metal.

Puzzled, Lin rose onto his elbows and cocked his head, waiting for the sound to be repeated. When it wasn't, he sank onto his back.

Another sound reached him, only from inside the stable, the suggestion of a stealthy tread.

Lin sat up and jammed his hat on. With infinite caution he crept toward the edge of the loft. He tried not to rustle the hay, but it was everywhere. Easing one leg forward and then the other, he reached the ladder. But he did not descend. Not yet. Not until he had some idea of who or what was down there.

The open space between the loft and the front of the stable was empty. At least, it appeared to be.

Lin craned his neck to scan the center aisle. Only a few stalls were visible, and they were plunged in darkness. None of the horses were acting up, which suggested it was a person, not a wild beast. The scent of a big cat or a bear would have them in a panic.

Lin leaned out — and froze.

A vague shape was almost directly below him.

Placing a hand on the ladder, Lin leaned farther out and strained his eyes to pierce the gloom.

Suddenly the shape bounded forward. Before Lin could guess its intent, the ladder was wrenched out from under him. He tried to catch himself, but it was too late.

Headfirst, Lin plummeted from the loft.

CHAPTER 7

For an instant Lin imagined crashing to the ground and hearing the snap of his neck. Then instinct took over. He twisted as he fell, contriving to land on his side. He succeeded, but the pain nearly blacked him out. He thought his chest burst, so hard did he hit.

Aware that whoever pulled the ladder away was still there, Lin struggled to sit up. He had dropped his rifle when he fell and desperately groped about to find it.

Movement registered.

Lin glimpsed a furtive form darting from the stable. He almost shouted for the prowler to stop, then realized how silly that would be. Besides, it was better this way. He was in no shape to defend himself.

Sinking back down, Lin pressed a hand to his side. Lord, he hurt. Gingerly probing, he established that as near as he could tell, none of his ribs were broken. When he could, he slowly sat up. His fingers brushed something, but it wasn't the Winchester; it was his hat. Placing it on, he got to his hands and knees.

Lin thought of his saddlebags, and what was in them, and how foolish he had been to have only the rifle. But he refused to use the other. It was a matter of principle. Maybe to his brother it did not matter, but it mattered to him.

A short search produced the Winchester. Propping it under him like a crutch, Lin stood. He shuffled to the open doors. The lights in the house were out and the ranch lay serene under the multitude of sparkling pinpoints above.

Lin moved toward the house. He needed to tell his brother so Chancy could be on his guard. Whoever had been in the stable might still be lurking nearby. He was forty feet from the porch when he spotted a darkling silhouette a stone's throw from it. Squatting, he jammed the Winchester to his shoulder. It had to be the skulker. Or so he assumed until the silhouette split down the middle and became two people. One of them, he was sure, was wearing a dress.

Lin heard whispering. It was Chancy — and Sue Dixon! Her skirt rustled as they strolled toward the rear of the house.

Lin was dumfounded. He debated whether to intrude and decided against it. Chancy would resent it, and the girl might be embarrassed.

As quietly as he could, Lin rose and turned and retraced his steps to the stable. The night was a bundle of surprises. He should be mad, he supposed, that his brother was sparking and not keeping watch. If Chancy had been doing what he was supposed to, he might have spotted whoever snuck into the stable. But what was done, was done, Lin reflected. Besides, for his brother to show an interest in a female was a miracle in itself.

Provided the interest was genuine.

The prospect troubled Lin. He would not put it past Chancy to trifle with her affections. A harsh thing to think about his own brother, but there it was.

Lin made a circuit of the stable. The horses in the corral were fine, the valley beyond peaceful.

Instead of going into the stable, he slipped between the left-hand door and the front wall. There was enough space for him to sit with his back to the wall and stretch his legs. No one could see him, and he would hear if anyone came near.

Lin massaged his shoulder. The pain was

almost gone. He would be badly bruised but that was all.

The time crawled by. Lin could not stop yawning. His chin dipped to his chest several times, but he snapped his head up.

Gradually, Lin's eyelids became more and more leaden until finally his chin fell and did not rise. He slept sitting up. He stirred only once, when a faint noise punctured his slumber. He listened, and far off a wolf howled. When nothing else happened, he went back to sleep.

A pink blush tinged the eastern horizon when Lin stirred and stiffly rose. He could use more sleep, but dawn was breaking.

Several chickens had come out of the coop, and soon the rooster would emerge.

Cradling the Winchester, Lin went into the stable. The ladder lay where it had fallen. He propped it against the loft, then checked on the buttermilk. As he emerged, the rooster was about to do what roosters always did; it flapped its wings, arched its neck and crowed.

On a ranch, that was the signal to start the new day. Lin figured Etta June would be up soon, if she wasn't already. He strode to the house.

Snores came from under a pile of blankets on the porch. Lin kicked them, lightly, and was rewarded with a grunt. "It is a new day, Little Brother."

"Go away."

"Our new boss expects us to rise and shine early," Lin said. "We can impress her by being up and raring to go."

The blankets shifted and Chancy poked his head out. He blinked, rubbed his tousled hair and scowled. "I never have liked getting up at the crack of dawn."

"Cows can't milk themselves," Lin said, then innocently asked, "Didn't you get enough sleep?"

"Not as much as I would have liked, no," Chancy answered, his scowl disappearing.

"Work hard enough today, and tonight you will sleep like a baby," Lin predicted.

Just then the front door opened. Etta June had an apron on over her dress and was holding a large wooden spoon. "You are both awake. Good. Breakfast will be in fifteen minutes. Then we will saddle up and ride up the valley."

"I am not all that hungry," Chancy said.

"Nonsense. I may not be able to pay you much, but you will not work on an empty stomach while you are working for me."

"Can I help?" Lin offered.

Etta June smiled. "You can fetch the eggs if you want. I keep a bucket out by the coop." The door closed behind her.

Lin stepped from the porch. "I expect you up when I get back. Roll up your blankets while you are at it."

"Should I shine my boots and iron my clothes too?"

"You can be a trial," Lin said.

"*Life* is a trial," Chancy glumly responded. "It beats on us from the day we are born until the day we die."

Lin stopped. "Is that what you think? Good Lord. There is more to life than that. What about all the good things?"

"I must have missed them. All I remember is that we lost Pa and then we lost Ma, the two people who cared for us the most."

"What about the fun we had growing up? Going fishing and hunting with Pa. Riding and playing and hiking. And how Ma always tucked us in at night and read to us. Have you forgotten all that?"

Chancy said in disgust, "You always look at the bright side, Big Brother."

"Where is the sense in always dredging up the worst? Yes, our folks are dead. But everyone dies sooner or later. We mourn, and we get on with our lives."

Rising onto his elbows, Chancy stared hard at Lin. "You are not being honest with me. You miss them as much as I do. You wish we were back living with them, and everything was as it used to be."

"Sure I do," Lin admitted. "But we can't let our heartaches sour us on life."

"I can," Chancy said.

Lin could think of nothing to say to that, so he went on to the chicken coop. He wished he was good with words. His brother used to be so happy and carefree. It hurt seeing him so bitter.

More than two dozen eggs were waiting to be gathered. An irate hen pecked at Lin's hand and he had to shoo her off.

Chancy was not on the porch when Lin came back with the bucket. He knocked, and little Beth answered. She took the eggs, thanked him and hurried down the hall toward the kitchen.

Lin went around to the back. His brother was at the washbasin, stripped to the waist, splashing water on his face.

The back door opened and Sue Dixon emerged, carrying folded towels. She held them out to Chancy and started to say something, then noticed Lin. Catching herself, she said, "Etta June told me to bring these out for you and your brother there."

"Lin?" Chancy half turned. "Oh." He accepted the towels. "Thank her for us, Miss Dixon, if you would be so kind."

Sue colored pink and hurried in.

"Nice girl," Lin commented.

"I hadn't noticed."

"Pretty girl too, don't you think?"

"I hadn't noticed that, either."

"It might be nice to get to know her better. She is about your age. The two of you could be friends." How Lin did not laugh, he would never know.

Chancy raised a comb to his hair. "I cannot be bothered with females at the moment."

"Is that a fact?" Lin said.

"Women are nothing but trouble. I would rather talk about cows and chickens and such."

"Any minute now the world will come to an end," Lin joked. When his turn came at the basin, he scrubbed vigorously with the lye soap. Once he was clean enough to suit him, he slicked his hair. His shirt could use washing too. He had a clean spare in his saddlebags, along with the object he had vowed he would not touch, no matter what, but the spare was for special occasions.

Lin settled for dipping a corner of the towel in the sudsy water and wiping at a few spots.

Breakfast was fit for a pasha. To go with the eggs, Etta June had fixed sausages and ash-pone. She also made buckwheat cakes and poured maple syrup over them. For those still hungry,' there were apple dumplings.

Lin was not shy about putting the food down. Even as a boy he'd had a healthy appetite, and while his mother was alive he ate enough for an ox. Since then, pickings had been lean, and when he did eat, he did not feel the same zest. It surprised him that he felt as hungry now as in the old days.

Little was said. The children were not talkative and Sue Dixon ate with her head bowed, only now and then raising it to glance sheepishly at Chancy.

The dumplings were being served when Patricia announced, "We are leaving as soon as I help wash the dishes."

"Must you go so soon?"

"I am worried about Cody and my boys. Whatever Seth Montfort is up to, I want to be there when he makes his move against us." She paused. "Don't forget to talk to him tonight. I am counting on your help."

"You will have it."

Lin had forgotten about Montfort coming for supper. The thought irritated him. Then Montfort was forgotten; Etta June had a question.

"How did you two sleep last night?"

"Fine," Chancy said.

Pat forked a piece of dumpling into her mouth. "I could have sworn I heard someone moving about in the middle of the night."

"It might have been our cat, Ma," Tom Jr. said.

The time was right to tell them about the incident at the stable, but Lin kept quiet. He was unsure why, and felt a twinge of guilt afterward.

A gorgeous morning was unfolding. The sky was a vivid blue except for a few puffy clouds. Here and there cattle were grazing. About a score were sprinkled along the shore of the lake.

Etta June clasped Patricia Dixon's hand in parting. "Don't worry. We will work this out. I will impress on Seth that he is being unreasonable."

"I hope you can," Pat said earnestly. "My family is everything to me."

Sue Dixon smiled at Chancy, who abruptly developed an interest in a cloud.

"That girl seems to like you," Lin commented as the Dixons rode off. But his brother did not rise to the bait.

It was down to work.

Etta June saddled a mare. Lin offered to do it for her, but she refused to let him do something she could do herself. "I am not helpless and will not be treated as if I am," was how she summed up her sentiments. She led them past the lake and on up the winding valley floor. Stretches of grass alternated with tracts of brush where the cattle liked to lie up.

"Some of them have become wild and will not take to being rounded up and branded," Etta June said.

"That is why rope was invented," Lin responded. But it would be a chore. He spotted a number of bulls as well as steers, cows and calves.

"Do you two have much experience at roping?" Etta June asked.

A reasonable question. Lin answered it by reining toward a cow and calf and shaking out his rope. He held the loop and the line at his waist, the honda lower down. As he neared them, the cow moved in front of her offspring, her horns lowered. He reined to the right. The cow instantly shifted, but the buttermilk was quicker. His horse had done this hundreds of times.

The calf started to run.

Lin's arm snaked out. He did not swing the rope around his head before he threw it but tossed it straight and true so that the loop settled over the calf's head and neck.

Lin promptly took a half hitch around the horn and the calf was nearly yanked off its feet. It bawled in alarm for its mother.

Etta June and Chancy rode over, Etta June nodding in approval. "That was mighty slick."

The cow had retreated a short way and was letting her displeasure be known.

Dismounting, Lin released the calf and gave it a smack on the rump. He began gathering up his rope and caught his new employer eyeing him speculatively. "What is on your mind?"

"When I met you I took you for a cow-man. Your rigging, how you ride — you were born to the range. So how is it you haven't signed up with any of the big outfits? The ones that can afford to pay you top dollar? Why come to work for a nobody like me?"

"I don't think of you as a nobody," Lin said, evading the issue.

"Besides, ma'am" — Chancy came to his rescue — "on a big outfit we would not get to have supper and breakfast with the boss."

"Don't get me wrong," Etta June said. "I am glad I hired you. You are the answer to my prayers."

"We will not let you down," Lin promised. Come what may.

CHAPTER 8

Lin had received some shocks in his life. His father's death was one. It had been so sudden. His mother drinking herself to death over it had been another, although not her actual dying. The bank foreclosing on their ranch had been a surprise, since the banker had pretended to be so friendly. To that list he could now add Etta June's invite.

He and his brother had spent most of the day looking the ranch over and searching out the bottomlands and ravines where the cattle liked to lie up.

Etta June spent the morning with them but rode home at midday. She had a lot to do to get ready for Montfort's visit, she explained.

Along about five, Lin and Chancy returned. They stripped their horses and were just coming out of the stable when Etta June appeared on the porch and beckoned. They went over.

"So, what do you think of the EJ Ranch now that you have seen some more of it?"

Lin had never thought to ask what it was called. "Your husband named it after you?" he guessed.

Etta June nodded.

Chancy said, "That was right sweet of him."

"Tom was romantic that way," Etta June said sadly.

"You picked good land," Lin commented. "There is a lot of good graze and plenty of water. Tomorrow we will begin rounding up the cattle."

"I filled the washbasin out back. You have plenty of time to wash up for supper."

"Should we wait at the back door for the food?" Lin inquired.

"Why on earth would you do that?"

"Seth Montfort is coming over," Lin reminded her. "You won't want us to eat with you."

"On the contrary. I do."

Lin's reaction must have shown.

"Is something the matter?"

"He is not liable to like that very much, ma'am."

"Seth Montfort's likes and dislikes are of little interest to me. And I have told you before to call me by my name."

"But he might get mad," Lin pointed out. "He is right fond of you."

"I am not fond of him. Any other objections?"

Her tone caused Lin to say, "I am just thinking of you. I figured you would want to stay on his good side, what with the situation with the Dixons and all."

"I want you there, and that is that." Etta June wheeled and went back in, her back as stiff as a board.

"Well," Chancy said.

"She sure is something," was all Lin could think of to say.

"I like her spunk."

Lin reckoned her guest would show up early, and they should get ready. "What do you say to putting on our clean clothes for the occasion?"

"The hell with that," Chancy said. "It is only Seth Montfort, not God Almighty." He glanced at Lin's right hip. "How long are you going to go around naked?"

"I wear clothes."

"Don't play dumb. You know very well what I mean." Chancy gestured. "I could not do it. I would feel undressed."

"If you had been undressed, as you call it, when that banker rode up to our ranch, we would not be where we are," Lin observed.

"How long are you going to hold that over my head? There is only so much a man can take and still call himself a man."

Lin did not take the bait. They had argued about it so many times that all they did was argue in circles. "Let's wash up." They walked around to the back of the house. In addition to filling the washbasin, Etta June had laid out two clean towels and wash-cloths, besides.

"That gal thinks of everything," Chancy said. He reached up to remove his hat while idly gazing to the north. Suddenly he stiffened. "Company is calling, and he is not alone."

Four riders were approaching the back of the house. They were too far off to distinguish details beyond the fact that the rider in front wore a suit and bowler.

Lin was puzzled. What was Montfort doing north of the ranch when the Bar M was to the south? "He had more men with him yesterday."

"Maybe he sent them to his spread," Chancy suggested. Pulling his hat brim low, he hooked his thumbs in his gun belt.

"You behave yourself," Lin cautioned.

"I wish you would stop telling me that. I am not Tom Jr. I do not need a nursemaid."

"Tell that to the banker you shot."

The four riders slowed from a trot to a walk. Seth Montfort was flanked by the gun shark called Stone and two others cut from the same cat-eyed cloth. When Montfort drew rein, his gunnies did the same.

"The Gray brothers, isn't it?"

"Pleased to see you again." Lin added to his list of lies.

"I can't say the same." Montfort dismounted and handed the reins to Stone. "You and the others will wait out here for me," he commanded. "I do not know how long I will be, but it will be late." He walked toward the washbasin.

Chancy stepped in front of him. "Hold on, there, hoss. We were here first. Wait your turn."

"I am a guest, if you will recall. That gives me certain privileges. Out of my way." Montfort went to push Chancy aside but froze when Chancy's fingers flicked to his Colt.

"Touch me and see what happens."

Lin was watching the hired guns. He saw Stone's hand slide toward his revolver, and taking a bound, he grabbed Stone's leg, wrenched his boot loose of the stirrup and heaved.

Stone swore as he tumbled. He landed on

his shoulders and rolled up into a crouch, drawing and thumbing back the hammer as he rose.

But Lin had sprung around the horse, and kicked. He caught Stone on the wrist and the revolver went flying. It went off when it struck the ground, the slug digging a furrow in the earth. The horse bolted. Lin thought that would be the end of it, but Stone's hand streaked to the top of a boot and came up holding a knife.

"You son of a bitch!"

Lin backpedaled. Stone came after him, the knife flashing. It would have gutted Lin like a fish had he been a shade slower. Stone stabbed at Lin's chest but Lin sidestepped. Furious, Stone slashed and thrust. Lin avoided meeting his maker by whiskers. Cursing, Stone speared the blade at Lin's throat. Lin dodged, and as he did he gripped Stone's wrist and wrenched — hard.

Stone roared with pain but did not let go of the knife.

Vaguely aware that someone was shouting, Lin swept his leg behind Stone's ankles and hooked Stone's legs out from under him. The next moment Stone was on his back.

Lin dropped straight down, his knee slamming into Stone's gut. The breath whooshed from Stone's lungs and he went momentarily limp, long enough for Lin to tear the knife from his grasp and toss it away. Lin cocked his fist to smash Stone in the face.

"Lin! That is enough!"

Etta June was framed in the doorway. She was pale, a hand to her throat.

Slowly straightening, Lin ignored Stone's glare. The other gun sharks had their hands out from their sides, with good reason. Chancy was covering them with his cocked Colt.

As for Seth Montfort, he was beet purple with rage and trembling from the violence of his barely contained emotions. *How dare you!*" he exploded.

Lin nudged Stone with his toe. "This mongrel of yours was fixing to shoot my brother."

"He what?" Etta June said, advancing. "Why on earth would he want to do that?"

Chancy answered. "Because your neighbor thinks he has the right to shove folks around."

"Your conduct was uncalled for," Seth Montfort snarled. "I demand an apology!"

"When cows lay eggs," Chancy said.

Etta June put a hand on Lin's arm. "Are you all right? Did he cut you anywhere?"

"You saw the whole thing?"

"Just part of it." Etta June looked him up and down. "You are not bleeding, as near as I can tell."

"I am fine," Lin said. Once again his ears grew warm. When she took her hand away he swore he could still feel the gentle pressure of her fingers.

Seth Montfort was still trembling with fury. "What about me, my dear? Or don't you care how your hired help treats visitors? If I were you, I would fire the both of them."

"I am not you," Etta June said.

Impossibly, Montfort darkened even more. "I must say, I expected better of you. I have made no secret of the high esteem in which I hold you."

Etta June turned to Chancy. "You can holster your hardware. There won't be any more trouble."

"Tell them that," Chancy said, waving his Colt at the men on horseback.

Stone sat up, a hand on his stomach.

"Seth?" Etta June said.

Montfort's chins worked. He let out a long breath and some of the color faded from his cheeks. "There will be no reprisals. Is that clear?" he addressed his men. "Anyone who acts up will answer to me."

Stone pushed to his knees. "No one does to me what he did and gets away with it."

"Did you hear what I just said, Mr. Stone?" Seth Montfort demanded. "You are in my employ. You will do as I require."

"You ask too much."

"There is a time and a place for everything," Montfort said. "Give me your word, Mr. Stone."

"I would rather eat thistles."

Montfort stepped close to him. "I am waiting, Mr. Stone. And keep in mind, I do not like to be crossed. Will you or will you not give your word that you won't lift a finger against either of Mrs. Cather's hired hands?"

"You are the boss," Stone said angrily. "If you want my word, you have it. But I will neither forget nor forgive."

Etta June turned to Montfort. "Might I suggest your men wait at the stable? I will have my son take food and drink to them."

Lin did not say a word until the three leather slappers were gone and Etta June and her visitor were inside. "We handled that badly. There will be hell to pay and it is our fault."

Chancy had stepped to the table and was removing his shirt. "You did what you had to."

"When I said 'we' I meant 'you,'" Lin said. "Would it have killed you to let Montfort wash first?"

"She set out the water for us, not for him," Chancy said. "He thinks because he owns the biggest ranch in the Big Horns he can put on airs."

"That, and the small army of quick-trigger artists he has riding for his brand," Lin said.

"They don't scare me."

"Listen to yourself. You have shot one person and you act like you are Wild Bill Hickok." Lin paused. "You worry me. There is reckless and there is stupid, and you are a little of both."

"Insult me all you want. I am your brother and I will stick by your side." Chancy bent over the basin and immersed a washcloth. "Someone has to keep you out of trouble."

"You are the hothead."

"I only wounded that banker. Someone else shot his three guards, or whatever they were, and killed two of them." Chancy gave Lin a pointed glance. "I wonder who that was."

"I could not let them shoot you in the back," Lin reminded him.

"For that I am grateful," Chancy said. "But don't go throwing stones at me when you deserve to have a few chucked at you."

They were ten minutes cleaning up. Lin swatted dust from his denims, then took off his blue bandana, soaked it in the water, and did the best he could with his boots. He wet the bandana again, wrung it out, and retied it. Checking his hair in the mirror, he ran a hand over his cowlick.

"You would think you were going to church," Chancy teased.

Hats in hands, they went in. Lin took the lead. A narrow hall brought them to the kitchen. Etta June was at the stove. Tom Jr. and Beth were seated on the far side of the table. Seth Montfort was at one end, and at sight of Lin and Chancy, he frowned.

"What are they doing here?"

"I pay them partly in food," Etta June said while upending cooked cut green beans into a bowl.

"So that is why they were in here so long last night."

"I beg your pardon?"

"Nothing. But doesn't it strike you as improper to feed them in your house? Were it to get out, your reputation would be tarnished."

"Oh, please. Not a soul who knows me would ever accuse me of being a loose woman. What would you have me do? Make them eat in the stable?"

"It is good enough for my men," Montfort pointed out.

"They brought that on themselves. I would have invited them in but I could not count on them to behave. Now, will you desist so we can get on with our supper?"

Seth Montfort fell silent. But the look he gave Lin was a look of pure hatred.

CHAPTER 9

Lin could hear each crunch, each sip. No one said anything. It was unnatural.

Seth Montfort was so mad, apparently he did not trust himself to speak. He attacked his food as if out to destroy it. He did not cut his meat so much as hack at it, and he speared each morsel with his fork as if intending to kill it all over again.

Etta June ate quietly, her gaze fixed in front of her.

The children sensed that something was amiss and did not joke and laugh as they normally would.

Chancy was silent too, lost in his own thoughts.

Lin refused to let Montfort spoil their meal. He took it as long as he could; then he coughed and said to Etta June, "How many of the cattle do you aim to sell once we have all of them branded?"

Etta June smiled as if grateful. "I don't

know yet. I must go over the books. We have built up the herd to where we can part with a goodly number, but I don't want to sell too many. We still have a lot of herd building to do."

"That sounds wise," Lin praised her. "Unless there is a die-off, in a few years you can buy yourself fancy clothes and whatever else you want."

"My needs are simple," Etta June said. "A roof over our heads and clothes on my children, and to eat regular. All the rest of it is frills."

Chancy broke his silence. "That is darned sensible for a woman."

"You are one of those, then?" Etta June said, but she grinned.

"One of what? You know I am right. Some women are not content with what they need. They have to have everything they want, as well. Clothes, carriages, servants — you name it." Chancy chuckled. "Why, I hear there is one rancher's wife who takes a trip to Europe each year."

"That will not be me," Etta June said. "I have simple tastes. My Tom used to complain they are too simple, that I should treat myself now and again."

Seth Montfort stopped stabbing his food. "Your husband was right. You deserve to reap the fruits of your labors. You are an exceptional woman, but you have your flaws."

Lin grew warm once more, but not the pleasant warm as when Etta June touched him. "How is it you do not have a wife of your own?"

About to lift his coffee cup, Montfort jerked his head as if he had been hit on the chin. "That is a personal question. But to be polite I will answer it." He took a sip. "I have simply been too busy building up the Bar M. The work never ends. From dawn until eight or nine at night, seven days a week, month in and month out. I simply have not had the time to spare for courting."

Chancy said without looking at him, "If you ever get down Cheyenne way, there are plenty of females to be had."

"I have my sights set closer to home," Montfort said, and bestowed a glance on Etta June.

Lin grew so mad he had to look down at his food so it would not be obvious.

Again the table became quiet.

Etta June picked at her carrots, then set her fork down and stared at Montfort. "We might as well settle this once and for all. I respect you, Seth, but you would be better off looking elsewhere. I am not ready to remarry. I am not sure I even want to."

"Perhaps another time would be more appropriate for us to discuss it, my dear."

"I am not your dear, and now is as good a time as any. I should have told you months ago and not let you get your hopes up."

"When I want something I generally acquire it."

"I am not a bull or a cow or land," Etta June said. "I am a grown woman with a mind of my own and the right to choose who I will be with." She paused. "Even if I were thinking of remarrying, it would not be to a man who threatens my best friends."

"So that is why you are so testy," Montfort said. "I suspected that Mrs. Dixon's visit would not bode well."

"Who told you she came to see me?"

Montfort hesitated. "No one. I suspected she would, is all."

"She is afraid for her family, Seth."

"She has reason to be."

"They are as honest as I am," Etta June declared. "Cody Dixon would never steal your cattle. He would never rustle, period."

Montfort smiled smugly. "Tracks don't lie. I have given him fair warning, as I have Aven Magill. If they are smart, they will pack up and leave before I must take steps to protect my interests."

"Wait. You have been to see Aven?"

"He is a stubborn old coot. I demanded to inspect his herd cattle, but he refused to let me."

"You accused him of rustling too?" Etta June's eyes narrowed. "What are you up to, Seth?"

Montfort forked a piece of beef into his mouth. "I am doing something I should have done long ago. I was here before the Dixons. My mistake was in letting them settle."

"You were not here before Aven Magill," Etta June said. "By your way of thinking, he should not have let you build your ranch."

"That is neither here nor there," Montfort said with a dismissive wave of his hand. "The important thing now — the only thing that matters — is that my cattle are being stolen and I intend to put a stop to it by whatever means necessary."

"Oh, Seth."

"Don't look at me like that. I am not the first big rancher who has had to take steps to protect himself from those who would build up their herds the easy way at his expense rather than by the sweat of their brows."

"Cody Dixon is the hardest-working man

I know."

"You make it seem as if everything I say is wrong or a lie," Montfort said peevishly.

"The Big Horns are not big enough for any ranch but yours? Is that how it is?" Etta June asked. "Where do me and mine fit in? Surely you are not going to accuse *me* of rustling."

"Never, my dear." Montfort placed his elbows on the table. "Since you insist on bringing this up in front of your hired help, I will be frank. I hope to join the Bar M and the EJ together. Not by driving you off and taking it over, but by the two becoming one, if you will." His face split in a grin.

"And if I oppose your land grab? If I side with the Dixons and Aven Magill against you?"

Montfort straightened. "Have you listened to a word I have said? You make me out to be the villain when I am the victim."

"I see what you are up to. Your groundless accusations. The quick-draw artists. Your infatuation with me."

Lin stopped eating. It had occurred to him that he and his brother had blundered onto the outset of a range war.

"Etta, Etta, Etta," Montfort said, his tone patronizing. "You have it all wrong. In all that I do, I will be legal and aboveboard."

"Only so you do not end up in prison."

Montfort sighed and took his napkin from his lap and placed it by his plate. "You are ruining my appetite."

"Don't do it, Seth," Etta June said. "There is enough range for everyone. Don't turn the Big Horns red with blood."

Lin could tell she was wasting her breath. Montfort had made up his mind, and no amount of pleading on her part could change it.

Chancy pushed his chair back. "Say the word, ma'am, and there will be no blood spilled but his."

Seth Montfort came partway out of his seat. "Murder me and my men will appoint you the guest of honor at a string party!"

"Enough of such talk!" Etta June said sternly. "My children are present, in case you have forgotten."

"My apologies, ma'am," Chancy said. "But my offer holds, whether here and now or elsewhere and later."

Montfort had sat back down, but he was a study in suppressed fury. "Is this how I am to be treated, Etta June? You invite me to your house and force me to share your table with these drifters. You make all sorts of wild accusations. And now you don't object when this young simpleton threatens me?"

"Who are you calling simple?" Chancy snapped.

Etta June held out her hands. "Please. Both of you. I want us to get along, not be enemies."

"I know who my friends are, and it is not these two," Seth Montfort declared. He stood. "I am sorry. I will only abide so much. If you want me over again, I look forward to coming. But don't bother if you include your new hands. I will have nothing more to do with them."

Lin had listened to enough. He stood too, towering over the table, and over Montfort, who took a step back. "You would be wise to listen to her. Start a range war and you will suffer the same as everyone else."

"Another threat," Montfort said. Wheeling, he stalked toward the hall, but stopped and looked back at Etta June. "I will give you a month to decide whose side you are on. Get rid of your new hands while you are at it."

"I will feel the same in a month as I do now. And I hire who I like, thank you very much."

Montfort took his bowler off a peg. "I can't tell you how disappointed I am, my dear. For a year now I have bided my time, but I will not bide it forever. A change is coming, and it is my fondest desire that you are a part of it, and not against it." With that, he wheeled and stomped out.

"Well," Etta June said.

"Good riddance." From Chancy.

Little Beth leaned toward Etta June and whispered loud enough that all of them heard. "Why was Mr. Montfort so mad, Ma?"

"He is not nice," Tom Jr. said.

Etta June folded her arms. "Never speak ill of others behind their backs, Thomas." She indicated their plates. "Finish eating, both of you, and then go into the parlor."

"Will you read to us tonight before you tuck us in?" Beth asked.

"Don't I always? But be sure all your clothes are put away, and remember to wash behind your ears."

Presently the children scampered off. Chancy finished eating and excused himself. That left Lin. He had been done for some time, but he did not want to leave, so he nursed a cup of coffee.

Etta June's face was drawn. "I tried but I am afraid I did not do any good. Pat will be disappointed."

"There is no talking to a block of wood," Lin said.

"So much is at stake. Do you really think

he will do it? Unleash his curly wolves, and the consequences be hanged?"

"I gave up predicting what people will do long ago," Lin said. His mother was the reason. He had always thought of her as strong willed and levelheaded. But after their father's untimely death, after his wagon overturned and crushed him, she proceeded to drink herself to death. It took her five years.

Lin had begged his mother to stop. Tears in his eyes, he had pleaded with her to give up the bottle. But she never got over her loss. She did not want to live without the man she loved, and since she regarded suicide as a sin, she killed herself the slow way rather than putting a bullet in her brain.

Lin suddenly became aware that Etta June was addressing him.

"— if he goes through with it. The Dixons and Aven Magill do not stand a prayer against him. Neither do we, if it comes to that."

"I will stand by you no matter what," Lin pledged.

Etta June reached across and placed her hand on his. "I appreciate that. But I cannot ask you to endanger your life at my expense. We hardly know each other."

Lin gazed into her eyes — into those

incredibly lovely hazel eyes — and felt an urge to kiss her. He smothered the impulse.

"If a range war does break out, I will not hold it against you and your brother if you pack up and head for more peaceable pastures," Etta June informed him.

"I could never look at myself in the mirror again if I did." Lin was surprised she had not removed her hand. He liked it there — liked it there a lot.

"You might think differently once lead starts to fly. And don't you worry about me. Whatever else Seth might do, he will not harm women. It is just not done."

"He might not pull the trigger, but he could give the order," Lin said. "Paid assassins are not particular about who they are paid to kill."

Etta June rose and came around the table. Averting her eyes, she said softly, "May I tell you something?"

"Sure." Lin assumed it had to do with Montfort.

"I like you."

"Ma'am?"

"I am sorry to be so forward, but I find it easy to talk to you and be around you. I have not felt this way since my husband died."

"Oh." Lin broke out in a sweat.

"Please feel free to come to me at any time with any concerns you have," Etta June told him. "I will go out with you tomorrow when you start the roundup, but I can't stay the whole day."

Lin was about to suggest that she did not need to go along but held his tongue. He enjoyed her company as much as, if not more than, she liked his. "Would six be too early?"

"Make it seven. That way you and your brother can have breakfast with us." Etta June smiled. "I must say, your coming to work for me is the best thing that has happened in a long time. You are a godsend."

Lin was glad she felt that way. But as she walked him to the door, unease gnawed at him like termites gnawing at wood. She did not know the truth about him. It might well be that instead of being a godsend, he would bring the wrath of hell down on her head.

CHAPTER 10

Abe Tucker was doing inventory when three strangers came into his store. He glanced up from the tins of salted meat and fish he was counting.

All three wore dusty slickers and broad-brimmed hats. They came toward the counter. The man in the lead was big and broad and notable for twin Remingtons in black leather holsters adorned with silver eagles, high on his hips. His slicker was pushed back so he could draw them quickly if need be.

The second man was almost as tall but as thin as a broomstick. He carried a Sharps buffalo rifle in the crook of his left elbow.

The third man stayed near the door. His salt-and-pepper beard marked him as the oldest. A bulge in his cheek hinted that he was fond of chewing tobacco.

"How do you do, gentlemen," Abe said. "Welcome to Mason."

"Is that what they call this pimple?" the big man rumbled in his barrel chest.

"Let me guess," Abe said. "You three have hired on with the Bar M. I can give you directions on how to get there."

"Never heard of it." The big man placed his hands on the counter, close to his revolvers.

"Ah. Just passing through, then, and you need to buy some supplies," Abe surmised.

"I am Lute Bass," the man said, as if that should mean something.

"Abe Tucker, at your service."

"We are hunting the Bryce brothers."

"I can't say as the name is familiar," Abe said, "and I know most everyone in these parts."

Lute Bass' eyes were almost black. "They might be using a different handle. The oldest is almost as big as me. He has corn-silk hair and rides a palomino. The younger has hair as black as ink. He owns a zebra dun."

"I never pay much attention to horses," Abe said. "What would their first names be?"

"Lin and Chancy."

Abe looked down at his shoes, then at the shelf of salted meats and fish and finally back at Lute Bass. "You say you are hunting them. Are you the law?"

"Do you see tin stars on us?" Lute Bass responded. "We hire out to those who can afford us to do what the law can't."

Abe regarded the broomstick with the buffalo gun and then the older man chewing the wad. "Hired killers, I take it?"

"You say that as if it were a disease," Lute Bass said.

"I do not approve of killing people for money. Do not take it personal. I happen to believe in that book at the end of the counter, and it has something in it about 'thou shalt not kill.' "

Lute Bass glanced at the Bible. "It also has something in it about an eye for an eye and a tooth for tooth."

"You are choosy about your scripture," Abe said.

"And you aren't?" Lute Bass lowered his big hands. "We are staying the night. If you should recollect the pair I mentioned, look us up. If your information leads us to them, it is worth money to you."

"Mind if I ask what they did that you intend to buck them out in gore?"

"They shot a man," Lute Bass said. "It was him who hired us."

"He must hold grudges."

"You would too if you were crippled for life," Lute Bass replied. "His name is Pettigrew. He is a banker in Cheyenne. His bank had to foreclose on the Bryce ranch."

"Know any more of the particulars?" Abe asked.

"It seems their pa died some years back and left them in debt," Lute Bass related. "They got behind on their bank payments. Pettigrew rode out to tell them they had thirty days to pack up and clear out. He expected trouble so he took three men with him."

"Why expected?"

"The younger brother is a hothead. Pettigrew tried to reason with them. He explained he was only doing his job. But one thing led to another and the younger one shot him in the arm. Broke his elbow and tore the nerves so he can never use it again."

"Oh, my," Abe said.

"That is not all. The men Pettigrew brought to protect him went for their hardware, but the older brother drew and shot all three before they could clear leather. Two of them died."

Abe Tucker whistled. "He must be mighty fast."

"He is no slouch," Lute Bass said. "I look forward to finding out exactly how good he is when I catch up with him."

"No interest in old age?"

Lute Bass smiled. "Ever climbed on a bronc that was a man killer to test your mettle?"

"I can't say as I have, no."

"I have. It is what I do. I test myself all the time. This Lin Bryce will be another test. They say he is good with an iron. I think I am better. And there is only one way to find out."

"Better you than me," Abe said. "Your profession is too dangerous for my temperament."

"I also get three thousand dollars when the job is done."

Abe whistled again. "Now *that* I can understand. But my conscience and my maker would still hold the killings against me."

"Did you ever hear about that mother and baby down in Denver? The mother got sickly and died. The baby cried for days in its crib. Neighbors heard, and did nothing, and the baby starved to death."

"I did not hear of it, no, and I can't say as I would want to. What was your point?"

"You mentioned our maker," Lute Bass said. "That mother and her baby prove that God does not give a good damn about what goes on down here."

"You blaspheme, sir. And I will not have

anyone speak ill of the Lord in my presence."

The broomstick carrying the Sharps snickered. "We've got us a regular Bible-thumper here, Lute."

Lute Bass shrugged. "He can believe what he wants. We will leave him with his Bible and go ask around about the Bryces. They were heading this way. Someone had to have seen them."

"They could be in Montana by now," Abe said.

"I doubt it. We are not that far behind them. But Montana or Canada — it makes no difference. I will trail them to the ends of the earth if I have to. They will not escape me this side of the grave."

"To take pride in your work is commendable."

About to turn, Lute Bass stopped. "Spare me your scorn, storekeeper. When I take a job, I see it through. You can call that pride if you want. I call it earning my pay."

"I meant no disrespect."

The three manhunters filed out.

Abe went around the counter and over to the front window. He watched them confer, then separate and amble off in different directions.

Just then someone came out of the saloon.

It was Efram Pike.

Lute Bass made right for him.

Abe returned to the counter. Reaching underneath, he brought out a silver flask. He opened it and tilted it to his mouth, and his Adam's apple bobbed. After a few chugs, he capped the flask and put it back under the shelf.

"Hell in a basket," Abe summed up the state of affairs.

The more Lin shared the company of Etta June Cather, the more she impressed him.

A lot of ranchwomen did not do actual ranch work. They tended to the house and the upkeep of their families. The cooking and preserving, the washing and ironing, the cleaning and polishing, were an occupation in themselves. Preparing a meal could take hours. Doing the laundry could take an entire day.

Etta June was not content to be chained to her domestic duties. She had helped her husband out on the range, and she made it plain to Lin and Chancy that she would do the same with them.

So it was that the next morning she was at the corral to oversee the picking of their string.

The cavvy was not large, but Lin liked

their quality. Hammerheads were absent, none were cold jawed, and all had experience cutting. Lin and Chancy each wound up with three horses besides their own. The supplies they strapped on a pack animal.

The ranch had two branding pens. Neither had been used since Etta June's husband died. It had been only a year, and Lin reckoned the pens would be in good shape. The nearest pen was, but when they reached the second, they discovered the gate was in need of repair.

Lin had brought tools. Etta June helped, and now and again they brushed shoulders. He was disappointed when she squinted up at the sun and announced, "I have to head back soon."

"Will you be out tomorrow?" Lin hopefully asked.

"I can't say. I have a lot to catch up on." Etta June removed her work gloves. "But I will come out every day I can until the roundup is done."

Lin was watching her ride off when a chuckle sounded behind him. "If you are fixing to say what I think you are fixing to say, I do not want to hear it."

Chancy came up next to him. "All I was going to say is that she will make a fine sister-in-law."

"I knew it."

"I have seen how you look at her when you think she will not notice, and I have seen how she looks at you."

"I do no such thing," Lin said. He took a step toward the horses, then stopped. "Wait. What do you mean by how she looks at me?"

"The lady is fond of you, Big Brother. Pretty soon she will throw her loop and it won't surprise me a lick if you step right into it."

"You are mistaken. She is being friendly, is all."

"Keep telling yourself that until you are in front of a parson saying 'I do.' " Chancy laughed.

Lin refused to believe him. But for the rest of the day all he could think about was Etta June. He considered Chancy's notion preposterous. The thing was, though, that deep down he liked the idea. Etta June had a lot of admirable traits. That, and when he looked into her eyes, he did not want to stop.

The next day they began the roundup. There was too much work to do for idle talk.

A lot of the cattle were scattered among the broken slopes that bordered the valley. Flushing them was a chore. Lin or Chancy would work through the thick brush while the other stayed back waiting for cows to break. Another tactic was for one of them to wind along the bottom of a ravine while the other kept pace on the rim.

A lot of the cows meekly let themselves be herded to the branding pens. Those already branded — and they were a majority — were counted and set free to graze. Those not branded — mainly calves, but more than a few cows — had to be roped and then treated to the red-hot end of a branding iron.

The calves were small but they were quick, and roping them took know-how as well as a skilled cutting horse. Usually the calves struggled and bawled, causing their mothers despair, and occasionally a cow would charge to the rescue with lowered horns.

Lin and Chancy worked the orneriest critters together. They would ride up on either side. One would throw his rope over the cow's head and dally the rope tight. With the cow distracted, the other would toss his rope under the animal's rear legs so the loop fastened about its heels. Once the cow was down, the brothers took turns dismounting and applying the branding iron.

That evening, around the campfire, Chancy pressed a hand to his spine and grumbled, "I forgot how rough ranching can be. I am sore and stiff all over. Too bad I cannot take a hot bath."

"Pa would roll over in his grave if he heard you talk like that," Lin bantered. "You are getting soft."

Chancy nodded at their growing herd. "They do not mean as much to me as they do to you."

"They are cows."

"Cows that belong to the filly you have set your sights on."

"You beat a dead horse to death," Lin complained. He refilled his tin cup with steaming hot coffee and sat back.

"You could do worse," Chancy said. "Wed her and this ranch is as much yours as hers."

"Listen to you," Lin said indignantly. "I have not known her a week and you have me married off."

"You are not getting any younger."

"I do not want to talk about it," Lin said. There had been a girl once. The daughter of a neighbor. She fancied him, and he thought she was the prettiest girl alive. Then his father died and his mother took to drink and his every waking minute was spent trying to keep their ranch afloat. He did not get over to see the girl as often. Maybe it was stupid of him, but he figured she would

125

understand and stay true. Instead she became engaged to the son of another rancher.

"Lin?"

"I said I do not care to talk about it."

"Lin!" Chancy said again.

Annoyed, Lin shifted. His brother was on his feet, pointing to the west. "What?"

"Damn it, look!"

Lin shifted again and nearly spilled his coffee.

Twilight had descended, and out of the gathering dark, riding slowly toward them, came a group of riders. Not cowhands or settlers or shootists — but a band of Indians.

CHAPTER 11

Many whites lived in terror of the red race. Whites called them redskins, or savages, or heathens, or, as one newspaper put it, "little better than animals." Indian attacks and atrocities were written up in grisly detail. Reports of Indians on the prowl spawned widespread fear.

Growing up, Lin did not have much to do with Indians. He saw Indians from time to time, but he never got to speak to them or to know them. The newspapers, he noticed, nearly always blamed the Indians for any flare-up. But when he read of Indian women and children being killed in raids on Indian villages, and of how one prominent white referred to them as "gnats that must be crushed," he did not see where his own kind had the right to put on airs.

Still, as the band of warriors approached, Lin could not quash the fear that coursed through him. The warriors bristled with weapons: bows and arrows, lances, knives, tomahawks. It was easy to imagine him and his brother being massacred.

Then Lin noticed that the warriors were not painted for war. Nor were any of their weapons brandished in a threatening manner. Arrows were all in their quivers, the bows were unstrung.

Out of the corner of his eye Lin saw Chancy's hand swoop to his Colt. "Don't!" he said, standing.

"I can drop three or four before they let fly a shaft."

"You stand there and do nothing. I will handle this." Lin stepped past him.

"Don't you remember? There are reports of Crows on the warpath. This bunch is liable to stake us out and skin us alive."

"We don't even know if they *are* Crows." Lin looked at him. "Take your hand off your six-shooter, but be ready to back me if it goes bad."

"Are you loco?" Chancy snapped. "These are redskins. What in hell are you trying to prove?"

"Etta June says she has never had any trouble with the Indians," Lin brought up. "She says her husband was even friendly with some of them."

"Her husband is dead."

"It wasn't Indians that killed him." Lin faced the warriors. He squared his shoulders, held his hands out from his sides and smiled.

The warriors showed no emotion beyond what Lin construed as curiosity.

The one in the lead, a tall warrior in fine buckskins astride a splendid pinto, studied him as Lin was studying them. Ten feet out, the warrior came to a stop and the rest followed suit.

"Welcome," Lin said.

None of the Indians responded. The tall warrior might as well have been a statue carved from wood.

"I do not speak your lingo," Lin went on. "Or sign talk, neither. Do any of you speak my tongue?"

"I speak it," the tall warrior said.

"My name is Lin. My brother and me ride for the EJ Ranch. Are you and your friends passing through?"

"We hunt."

Lin almost asked, *Men or animals?* but instead he said, "Get down and join us if you like. We have coffee on, but there might not be enough for all of you."

The warrior said something in his own language to the others. Climbing down, he came over. He moved with a calm bearing.

Stopping in front of Lin, he said, "You are a friend of Tom Cather?"

"Tom Cather is dead," Lin explained. "A mustang crushed his head. His wife hired us to do the work Tom used to do."

For the longest while the warrior did not speak. Lin began to worry that the Indians might not be as friendly as he had hoped.

Then the tall warrior said, "Tom Cather was my friend."

"I never got to meet him," Lin said.

The warrior gazed toward a knot of grazing cattle. "He gave my people meat."

Lin had it then. Etta June's husband made friends with the Indians by letting them have a cow now and then. "You are welcome to take one if you like. Any more than that, and I must ask Tom's wife. She runs the ranch now."

The warrior looked at him, and Lin would swear there was a hint of amusement in his eyes.

"You work for a woman?"

"Tom's woman, yes." The warrior said something over his shoulder, and many of the warriors grinned. "We will take one cow," he said in English, and white fashion, he held out his hand.

Lin shook. Chancy started to speak, but Lin motioned for him to keep quiet. The warrior climbed back on the pinto and the band faded into the gathering darkness. Only then did it occur to Lin that he had not asked the warrior's name or learned which tribe they were from.

Chancy was staring at him.

"All right. What?"

"You were awful free with Etta June's cow."

"She will understand," Lin predicted. "Losing one is better than losing twenty. They could have snuck in and helped themselves to as many as they wanted."

"You don't think that Injun was lying about her husband giving them meat?"

"There was an honest man if ever I met one," Lin said. "He was telling the truth."

"Listen to yourself," Chancy said. "He was a red, for God's sake."

"Are you sure you are my brother?"

"What the hell is that supposed to mean? I do not have your high opinion of them. They should all be put on reservations. And those that won't go should be exterminated."

Lin sat and picked up his tin cup, saying, "What did they ever do to you? They are people, like us."

Chancy snorted. "Where you get some of your notions, I will never know. I will allow that some of them are decent enough. But most hate us as much as we hate them."

"Speak for yourself. I try not to hate anyone if I can help it."

"You are too easygoing. You always have been. When Pa died you weren't nearly as shook up as Ma and me."

Lin disagreed. He had hurt deep inside, hurt so much that for weeks he barely ate or slept. But he did not make a spectacle of his grief. His father always said that a man should mend in private.

"If they show up again tomorrow and ask for another beef, what will you do?"

"Give them you."

Chancy blinked, put his hands on his hips and roared with mirth. "I believe you would too, you sorry so-and-so. But I am too scrawny. There is not enough meat on me to feed a cat. They would like you better."

On that lighthearted note, they settled in for the night. They did not bother riding herd. The cattle they had collected would not stray far, certainly not off the EJ Ranch.

Unable to sleep, Lin lay on his back staring up at the stars. He was glad the Indians had not caused trouble. Let other whites despise them on general principle. He judged each man on that man's merit, no matter what the color of his skin happened to be.

Lin thought of Etta June. He liked thinking about her. About her face, and those eyes of hers. Others might say she was plain, but to him she was as pretty as a rose. Funny, how he rode into Mason on his way to who knew where, with no prospects to speak of, and now here he was, daring to entertain notions he had no earthly right entertaining.

Life was peculiar. Before his father died, Lin had his future all worked out. He'd reckoned on having a ranch of his own not far from his folks, and marrying and having kids for them to bounce on their knees and spoil. Then calamity struck. His mother could not manage on her own, so he stayed to help. But they were so deep in debt they could never get ahead.

The worst was the night his mother died. Another drunken stupor was to blame. Liquor killed her as surely as if she put a revolver to her head and squeezed the trigger. But then, she wanted to die. She missed their father so much, she refused to go on without him. It took her five years, but she succeeded in joining him in the hereafter. *I miss you, Ma,* was Lin's last thought before he drifted off.

The low of a cow brought Lin back to the here and now. Sitting up, he stretched and yawned and looked around. His brother was buried under his blankets, which glistened with morning dew.

Lin reminded himself to ask Etta June whether she had any spare tarps.

A few prods with Lin's boot roused Chancy.

Etta June had left them some buttermilk biscuits for breakfast. They washed the biscuits down with half a pot of coffee and were soon in the saddle commencing another day's work.

Lin liked ranch work. Yes, it was hard. Yes, the hours were god-awful long. Yes, cattle were not always predictable and could be as stubborn as sin, but with a good horse under him and a rope in his hand, he was the master of any situation that might develop.

About nine that morning his ability was put to the test.

They were working the breaks to the north of the valley when they flushed a bull. So far all the bulls they'd come across were branded. Bulls were costly, and no rancher would let one loose on the range without a brand. This one planted its four legs and snorted, tossing its horns from side to side, as they warily circled, inspecting its hide.

"No brand that I can see," Chancy said.

"Me, either."

"Didn't Etta June say all their bulls had been, so far as she knew?" Chancy mentioned. "Maybe it is not one of theirs. Could be it strayed here from another spread."

"It has been frolicking with EJ cows. That makes it an EJ bull now," Lin said.

Chancy laughed.

"What?"

"All a bull does is walk up behind a cow and ram it in. That is hardly what I would call a frolic."

"To a bull it might be."

"I have said it before and I will say it again. You come up with the darnedest notions."

Lin began to shake out his rope. "We have to do it, Little Brother. Let's drive him to the branding pen."

"I would as soon wrestle a bear," Chancy said. But he reined into position on the other side of the bull. "Ready when you are."

Lin gigged his mount closer. He was astride one of Etta June's cavvy, a claybank so well trained that he could guide it by his legs alone, leaving his hands free for roping. "Get along there!" he shouted. At the same time Chancy let out a yell.

The bull was supposed to head for the valley floor. Instead, it wheeled, lowered its head and charged the claybank.

"Look out!" Chancy hollered.

Lin was not caught unaware. He reined to one side and used his spurs, and the claybank took off as if fired from a cannon. The bull veered and tried to hook the claybank's belly with the tip of its horn, but the claybank was too quick. After a short chase the bull stopped.

Lin reined in a wide circle and joined his brother. "This critter is going to be difficult."

"You don't say," Chancy dryly returned.

"I would rather not risk losing a horse," Lin said. "Come with me." He headed off.

"Where are we going?"

"I have an idea."

"Uh-oh," Chancy said.

Where there was a bull, there was his harem. Lin did not go far before several cows broke from cover and stood staring. "If you were a bull, which one would tickle your fancy?"

Chancy cackled. "There you go again. How in thunder would I know? I like a big bosom and long legs on a female, not an udder and a tail."

"We will take that one," Lin said, pointing at the fattest.

"Take her where?"

"To the bull."

"Oh. I get it. You romantic devil. But what if Mr. Bull is not in the mood for one of your frolics?"

"He is male."

"I would resent that if it were not true."

Lin roped the cow and brought her close to the bull so the bull got a good look at her and could smell her. Then Lin led the cow off, thinking the bull would follow. But it did not move a hoof.

"How about if you sprinkle some perfume on the big-eyed miss?" Chancy suggested, grinning.

"How about if you come up with an idea of your own," Lin said. As a last resort they could rope the bull and force it down to the pen. But it was bound to fight them every foot of the way, and they might lose a horse, or be gored themselves.

"My idea is to leave the critter be. No one is likely to steal him, as mean as he is."

"What will Etta June think if we give up?"

"That we showed good common sense," Chancy said. "Besides, I won't tell her if you don't."

Lin freed the cow, climbed back on the

claybank and moved toward the glaring bull. He held his rope ready for a sidearm throw.

"What in God's name are you up to?"

"If I can get my rope over his horns I will have him."

"If he gets his horns into your horse, he will have you," Chancy warned. "Be careful."

Lin watched the bull's front legs. Sometimes bulls did not give warning before they attacked. They exploded into motion from a standstill.

The next moment, this one did.

CHAPTER 12

Lin reined to the right and the claybank responded superbly. The bull pounded past. Lin applied his spurs to gallop away, and the claybank started to, then stumbled.

Lin glanced down to see what had caused it to lose its footing.

"Behind you!"

The bull had wheeled on the head of a pin and was on them again. Uttering a rumbling snort, it lowered its head.

Lin tried his best. He hauled on the reins and used his spurs but the claybank had not quite recovered its balance. Before it could, the bull's horn speared its belly. The claybank squealed as the bull ripped its horn up and out.

The horn cleaved the claybank like a sword. Shearing through flesh and organs and hide, it opened the horse wide. Out gushed blood and entrails.

"Lin!" Chancy screamed.

Lin felt the claybank give out under him and pushed clear of the saddle. Or tried to. A boot snagged in a stirrup. He wrenched to clear it just as the claybank came down on its side, pinning his leg underneath. He pushed against the saddle but his leg would not move.

Another snort, nearly in his ear, caused Lin to snap his head up.

The bull's nose was nearly touching his. Its nostrils flared; its eyes were pools of fire. Blood and gore dripped from the one horn.

Lin froze. One blink, and he was dead. The bull would do to him as it had done to the poor claybank.

Hooves drummed. Lin thought his brother was coming to his rescue. He did not move his head to look. He wanted to shout, to warn Chancy to stay back. The bull was too dangerous. Then, over its back, the shoulders and head of the rider appeared.

It was Etta June.

Stunned, Lin saw her swing a rope overhead, saw the loop arc toward the bull and slip over its head and horns as neatly as could be. The bull grunted and began to turn.

Another rope came sailing at the bull from behind. Chancy's rope, the loop catching a hind leg but not both.

Both of them reined hard around and the bull crashed down. It raised a fearsome racket and struggled fiercely but could not get back up.

Etta June yanked her Winchester from the saddle scabbard. She worked the lever, then wedged the stock to her shoulder.

"What are you doing?" Lin cried.

The rifle cracked and the bull roared in pain and struggled harder. The rifle cracked again. This time the bull's right eye acquired a hole in the center. The bull's struggles ceased. Its great bulk went limp and its tongue lolled.

Then Etta June was next to the claybank, offering her hand. "Here. Let me help you."

Lin could not take his eyes off the bull. "You shouldn't have. That was a fine animal."

"It nearly killed you."

"An animal worth a lot of money," Lin stressed. For most ranchers her deed was unthinkable.

"I did the same to the mustang that killed my husband," Etta June said. "I do not let anyone or anything hurt those I care for and go on breathing."

Lin was so intent on the dead bull that it was a few seconds before the import of her comment sank in. She had just said she cared for him. "I am obliged," he said, his throat oddly raw. "But I have let you down."

Etta June grasped his hand and pulled. "Don't be ridiculous."

"I have lost you a horse and a bull, both," Lin noted. "I can never begin to pay you their worth."

"Who asked for money?" Etta June said, and grunted. "If you would help, this might go better."

"Sorry." Lin pushed against the claybank, straining mightily, and bit by bit extracted his leg. His boot nearly came off but he got it out, and sat up.

A pool of blood was forming under the bull's head and already flies were gathering.

Chancy strode up, coiling his rope. "That was something," he said to Etta June.

"Why didn't you shoot? Your brother could have died."

"He would have been mad if I did," Chancy said. "I know him, know how he thinks."

Etta June regarded them both. "Let me make this plain. If at any time either of you is in peril because of my stock, you have my permission to do whatever is necessary. I don't care whether it is a bull, a cow, a horse or a chicken. I would rather they were dead than either of you."

Chancy chuckled. "A chicken on a rampage? Now that is something I would like to see." He walked toward his horse.

Lin bent and began brushing himself off. His leg was sore but otherwise he was fine.

"Are you all right?"

"Embarrassed is all."

"I was riding up and saw the whole thing. It could have happened to anyone."

"How did you find us?"

"I saw some cows you had flushed and figured you had to be close by," Etta June said while coiling her rope.

"I am glad you made it out again. I thought you had work to do at the house."

Etta June shrugged. "Truth to tell, I like working the range more than I like housework. But I can't stay as long as I did yesterday." She paused. "I brought a meal in a basket. I left it at the branding pen."

"You are the best boss anyone could have," Lin heard himself say.

"A good boss would pay you. Montfort pays his punchers forty a month. His gun sharks earn more."

Lin turned to the claybank and set to work stripping his saddle and saddle blank. It took some doing, but at last he got the saddle out from under, and straightened. "I will carry these down and get another mount."

"Nonsense," Etta June said. "I will take you. You can ride back up bareback and get your rig. It will save you time."

"If that is what you want."

Etta June climbed on. She offered her hand.

"I have never ridden double with a lady before," Lin said.

"There is a first time for everything," was Etta June's rejoinder. "And it is no different than riding double with a man."

Lin begged to differ, but he dutifully swung on behind her. He had to sit close, so close he breathed in the scent of her hair and her body.

"Hold on to me."

Reluctantly, Lin hooked an arm around her waist. It brought her nearer. He could practically feel her back against his chest.

"Don't be shy," Etta June told him. "I will not break." With that, she flicked the reins.

The movement brought Lin flush against her. He tried to draw back but they were going down the slope at a trot and he could not help but press his body to hers. He grew so hot, he thought he would burst into flame.

"You are a good man, Lin Gray," Etta June said over her shoulder.

Lin winced. He had forgotten about his lie. "I am?"

"You were more worried about my loss than your life. Devotion like that is uncommon."

"You will not think me so devoted when you hear about the cow I gave away." Lin explained about the Indians, concluding with, "I did what I figured you would do. If I was wrong, say so, and I will never let them have another."

"You did right. The last thing I need is Indian trouble." Etta June paused. "We had an incident of our own at the house last night. It scared Beth something awful."

"Were the wolves howling again?"

"No. Nothing like that. I was in bed reading. I had tucked Tom Jr. and Beth in at the usual hour and figured they were sound asleep. Then Beth called my name. I ran to her room and found her at her window. She had been tossing and turning and could not get to sleep, so she got up to look out at the stars. That was when she saw him."

"Him who?"

"She claims a man was skulking about the stable. She could not say who it was, or whether he was white or red, but she was sure she saw him."

Lin remembered the figure in the stable

who pushed the ladder out from under him. Apparently the man had come back — or had never left. Both prospects were troubling. "What did you do?"

"What else? I lit a lantern and took a rifle and went to the stable. No one was there."

"Do you reckon she imagined it?"

"She is only eight," Etta June said. "And for the life of me, I can't think of why anyone would be prowling about my place so late at night."

Neither could Lin, but someone definitely was. "Chancy and me should cut the roundup short and come back."

"Don't be silly. You have only begun. I am perfectly safe. I always lock the doors at night, and the windows are kept latched."

Lin did not share her confidence. Whoever was prowling about must be up to no good. He decided he should do something about it, but not say anything to Etta June.

Over the next several hours the three of them roved the brush and timber, adding a considerable number of cows and calves to the herd. They broke to eat the meal Etta June had brought, which consisted of thick slabs of beef, potatoes and Saratoga chips. Enough coffee was left from breakfast that Lin did not need to heat up a new pot.

Etta June stayed until nearly four. She did

as much work as they did, and as well.

Lin could not get over her comment that she liked him. His gaze strayed to her often — when she was not looking.

Toward sunset Lin and Chancy called it a day. They returned to their camp at the branding pen. After stripping their mounts, Chancy rekindled the fire while Lin sat cleaning his rifle.

"Fixing to use that soon, are you?"

"You will be on your own for a while tonight. I have something to do." Lin told his brother about Beth, and about his own close shave.

"Why didn't you tell me this before?"

"I was going to, but I forgot."

"You think it is the same hombre you tangled with?"

"I will find out."

"We should both go," Chancy suggested. "One of us can watch the house and the other the stable."

Lin had thought of that. But they had something else to consider. He nodded at the string and then at the cattle. "We have them to protect too."

"You think it is a rustler?"

No, Lin did not, but he could be wrong. "It is best you stay here. If I am not back by daybreak, come look for me."

An hour after dark, Lin saddled the buttermilk. He stepped into the stirrups and lifted the reins.

Chancy came up and patted a saddlebag. "Aren't you forgetting something, Big Brother?"

"No."

"If ever there was a time to take it out, this is it," Chancy said. "You can't hide from what you did forever."

"Watch over the horses," Lin said gruffly, and gigged the buttermilk.

The wind was at his back. A sliver of moon cast a pale glow over bunches of cattle. To the north and south, stark peaks were silhouetted against the stars. The highest were cones of white against the black.

Lin held to a walk. It was early yet, and the skulker seemed to like to do his skulking a lot later. He doubted it was an Indian. The band he gave the cow to had moved on; their tracks had gone off to the northwest, deeper into the mountains.

Lin was convinced it was a white man. That the man had not harmed anyone was of little comfort. Whoever it was had no business sneaking around the ranch.

Squares of light appeared to the east. A few windows in the house were aglow.

By the time Lin came within a quarter

mile, only one window was lit. The children had turned in. He rode at a walk until he was about two hundred yards from the stable. Then he dismounted, shucked his Winchester and advanced on foot, leading the buttermilk. He stopped often to listen and probe inky patches near the buildings.

The corral was empty. Lin looped the reins around a rail and crept to the front corner of the stable. The wide doors were closed. Etta June's doing, he figured. He hunkered and scanned the area between the stable and the house. The blacksmith shop, the chicken coop, the outbuildings, all were quiet and still. Nothing moved anywhere.

The night was deceptively peaceful.

Lin leaned against the corner. He would wait there all night if he had to. He glanced at the lit window. Etta June's bedroom. He imagined her sitting in bed in her night-dress, reading. His throat grew tight and he felt twitches where he should not feel twitches. Upset with himself, he closed his eyes.

A sound stiffened him, and Lin opened them again. The soft sound of a stealthy step warned him he was not alone. He strained his ears and heard the sound again. But it did not come from the direction of the

house or from in front of the stable.
The footfalls came from behind him.

CHAPTER 13

Lin glanced back.

A man, moving furtively, was midway along the wall. The skulker kept looking over his shoulder and glancing all around. One hand appeared to be on his hip, but Lin knew better; that hand was on a revolver.

It occurred to Lin that the man must have seen his buttermilk tied to the corral. Which meant the man knew he was there, and must be searching for him. He was surprised the man had not spotted him. Perhaps because he was in pitch-black shadow.

Lin sank lower and gripped his rifle with both hands. He tensed his legs to spring. Scarcely breathing, he waited until the man was almost on top of him and had twisted to glance toward the rear of the stable.

Heaving erect, Lin swept the Winchester's hardwood stock up and around and slammed it against the side of the man's head. The man's hat went flying. The revolver started to rise. Lin hit him again, and then a third time. At the last blow the man's legs buckled and he pitched to his knees. The six-shooter fell with a thud. Both arms went limp and the man oozed to the ground like so much mud.

Lin palmed the prowler's revolver and tucked it under his belt. Bending, he grabbed hold of the man's shirt at the scruff of the neck and dragged him to the double doors.

A glance at the house showed that all the lights were out. *Good,* Lin thought. He did not want to disturb the Cathers — or be disturbed.

Another minute, and Lin was lighting a lantern that hung on a peg. He closed the wide door he had opened and hauled the limp form to the middle of the aisle.

The man was in his mid-thirties or thereabouts. He had short, curly brown hair and bushy eyebrows. There was nothing remarkable about his clothes or his boots, but the gun belt decorated with conchas and the nickel-plated Colt Lin took from him were far from typical. Scowling, Lin poked him in the side. The man stirred but did not come around. Lin poked him again. When that did not have an effect, Lin stooped and slapped his cheek.

Suddenly the man's eyes were open. They were brown and filled with fury.

He swore, about to lunge upward.

Lin was quicker. Taking a step back, he leveled his rifle. "Try it," he warned.

The man gave his head a toss, as if to clear it, then gazed about them. "What do you want with me?"

"I will ask the questions and you will give the answers," Lin said. "We will start with your name."

"Go to hell."

Lin kicked him in the knee, hard.

Clutching his leg, the man writhed in pain and growled through clenched teeth, "You bastard! You rotten bastard!"

"I can do it again if you want," Lin said, training the Winchester on the man's face. "It is up to you."

"Griggs," the man spat. "My name is Griggs."

Lin played a hunch. He had a feeling he had seen the man before. "You ride for Seth Montfort. You are one of his gun sharks."

Griggs hesitated, but only for a few seconds. "Yes. I came up with a bunch from Laramie."

Lin stepped back in case the man tried to jump him. "How long have you been hiring out your gun?"

"What difference does that make?" Griggs angrily asked, but then he answered, "About ten years."

"Killed a lot of people in that time, have you?"

Griggs glared.

"You have been coming here night after night for a while now," Lin said. "Suppose you tell me why." When Griggs did not respond, Lin wagged the Winchester. "Is it worth losing teeth?"

"Damn you," Griggs said. "No, it is not. I will take a slug if I have to, but I will not be beat on. Not for the money Montfort is paying."

"I am waiting," Lin said.

Griggs rubbed his knee and said in disgust, "I am here because of the woman."

"You are interested in Mrs. Cather?"

"Not me, you idiot. Seth Montfort. He is powerful fond of her. Although what he sees in her, I will never know. I have seen prettier fillies."

"I work for her," Lin said. "Insult her again and you will take that slug."

"You are full of threats," Griggs declared.

"If you think I am a bluff, say so and I will prove otherwise."

Griggs glared, then shook his head. "No,

thank you. We have learned a little about you and that brother of yours, and Montfort sent a man to Cheyenne to learn more."

"Explain," Lin said.

"It was Stone. When we met you the other day, he got the notion he had heard of you two. Your first names, anyway. He was in Cheyenne a while back and he heard about two brothers who shot a banker and some others." Griggs looked at Lin and chuckled. "If it is you, you are as stupid as sin."

"Some bankers deserve to be shot."

"Not that, lunkhead. When we ran into you, you gave your real first names. You only made up a last name. The smart thing to do is to make up both. I have been on the run. I know."

Lin couldn't have given Montfort a whole new name, not with Etta June there. He had already told her his real first name. "Tell me more about you sneaking around like a thief in the night."

"I am no thief," Griggs bristled. "I am camped in a wash off to the south. My orders are to keep an eye on you and report to Montfort if you dally with Mrs. Cather."

Lin's surprise must have shown.

"Why do you look so shocked? Seth Montfort has his sights on her. If you were to ask me, I would say he wants her land more than he really wants her, but that is his business. The important thing is that he will not let anyone stand in his way of claiming her, or her land, for his own."

"I'll be damned," Lin said.

"You will be dead if you are not careful," Griggs told him. "Montfort has me come in close to the house each night to make sure you are not sleeping in Mrs. Cather's bed."

"I wish he was here now and not you," Lin said.

Griggs flexed a leg. "So, what now, big man? Do you make worm food of me or let me go?"

"How worthless is your word?" Lin asked.

"That is a hell of a thing to say to a man. I may hire my six-shooter out, but I have my scruples. When I give my word I keep it."

"Then give me yours that if I let you leave you will get on your horse and leave the Big Horns and never come back."

"You have it."

Lin did not believe him. Every instinct he had told him the man was lying. But he stepped aside and motioned. "Off you go. Don't stop at the Bar M on your way to wherever. Let Montfort go on thinking you are spying on us."

"Sure, mister, sure." Griggs stood and

took a tentative step, wincing as he put his weight on the leg Lin had kicked. He stopped and glanced at the Colt wedged under Lin's belt. "What about my pistol?"

"Don't push your luck."

"You intend to keep it?"

"I don't intend to give it back."

Griggs colored and clenched his fists. "I have given my word I will leave the country. But I will not leave without my smoke wagon."

Lin was more amused than annoyed. "I would not argue, were I you."

"I mean it," Griggs said. "I have had that revolver almost as long as I have been in the gun-for-hire trade, and I am mighty attached to it."

"Buy another," Lin said.

Griggs glowered, his jaw twitching. His fists opened and closed.

For a few moments Lin expected him to pounce. To discourage him, Lin raised the Winchester to his shoulder.

"Scat while you can."

Uttering an oath, Griggs limped to the door. He paused to glare and snarl, "You have a reckoning coming." With that, he melted into the dark.

Lin went out. He pushed on the door to close it, then realized he had neglected to put out the lantern. Suddenly he heard a soft sound so close it had to be Griggs sneaking up on him. He whirled, primed to shoot. The person about to reach out to him froze. "You!" he blurted.

"Me," Etta June said. She had a purple robe on over a yellow nightdress, and was holding a rifle.

"What are you doing here?" Lin had hoped to avoid involving her. She had enough on her mind without this.

"I couldn't sleep," Etta June said. "I thought I heard something and looked out my window. I saw you drag that man into the stable."

"So you have been out here the whole time listening?"

"The nerve of Seth Montfort, sending someone to spy on me." Etta June said. "I mean to go to the Bar M tomorrow and have words with him."

Lin did not intend to insult her, but he said without thinking, "Is that smart? Rile Montfort and there is no telling what he will do."

Etta June pulled at the belt to her robe. "I cannot allow this to pass. There is a line that should not be crossed, and he has crossed it."

"What of Tom Jr. and Beth?"

"They are old enough to fend for themselves, but I will count on you to look in on them," Etta June said. "I should not be gone more than five days at the most."

"That is not what I meant," Lin said. "What if something happens to you? How will they get by?"

"Seth acts like he *owns* me. I must set him straight."

"Let me go," Lin said.

"What?"

"I ride for you. Send me with your message."

Etta June shook her head. "I appreciate the offer. But this is personal. It is me he has wronged."

"You have only been back from Mason a few days," Lin pointed out. "Why leave your kids alone again when you don't have to?"

Etta June stared, her eyes mired in shadow. At last she said, "That is not why you want to go in my stead, is it?"

Lin did not say anything.

"You are asking for grief. Seth would not dare lay a finger on me, but he will have no qualms about roughing you up."

"He is welcome to try."

"It is kind of you to offer, but if something were to happen to you it would be on my shoulders."

"Better me than you," Lin said with more heat than he intended.

"Oh." Etta June averted her face. "Oh," she said again, more softly.

Lin waited. He hoped he had not over-stepped himself. The seconds crawled into a minute and he could not keep quiet. "I am sorry if I shamed you."

"You haven't," Etta June said. "Quite the contrary."

Now it was Lin who said, "Oh."

Somewhere in the night a coyote yipped and was answered by another. A moth flew into the ring of lantern light and fluttered about them. A horse nickered in the stable.

"It is a fine night," Etta June said.

"Yes, it is."

"I am a bit scared."

"So am I," Lin admitted.

"It is so unexpected," Etta June said. "And it has only been a year. Part of me thinks it can't be proper, but another part thinks a year is plenty long enough."

"It is your decision."

Etta June turned. "If you go to Montfort on my behalf, it will be the same as —" She stopped.

"I am in your employ," Lin said.

"That is not the same and we both know it. Seth Montfort will know it too." Etta

June put a hand to her forehead. "What has gotten into me? Into us?"

"It would go better if I weren't so tongue-tied."

Etta June shifted her hand to his arm. "I fear what he might do to you. I would rather die than have you harmed."

A lump formed in Lin's throat and he had to cough to clear it. "I am not a babe in the woods. Fact is, Etta June, I am worse than Seth Montfort in one regard." To his knowledge, Seth Montfort had never killed.

"What regard is that?"

Lin could not make his tongue move.

"Do me a favor. Take your brother along. I will feel a little easier if it's both of you."

"Not Chancy," Lin said. "He should stay with the roundup and be close if you need him."

"If you think that best."

"I do."

"When will you leave?"

"Daybreak."

"I will feed you before you go." Etta June held out her hand. "Good night, then. When you get back, come see me first thing."

Lin held her small hand in his big one. "I do this of my own free will, so don't lose any sleep over it."

161

"Be careful, Lin Gray," Etta June cautioned.

Lin Bryce winced.

CHAPTER 14

Cattle, cattle, everywhere.

Lin had never seen so many cattle in his life. The Bar M range was a sea of horns and tails. Seth Montfort's ranch was bursting at the seams. It was easy to see why Montfort needed more land.

Punchers were plentiful too. Lin spied them in groups and riding singly, but always at a distance. Evidently they mistook him for one of their own, because no one challenged his being there.

That night he camped in a dry wash and kept his fire small. The next morning at first light he was under way again. He had ridden about an hour when three punchers appeared to the east. They were moving a small bunch of cows toward a large herd, but when they spotted him, two of them broke away and came toward him at a gallop.

Lin had been expecting this. But he did

not draw rein. He continued in the direction Etta June had said he must go.

The hands swept down on him like a pair of ravens on a nestling. One had peach fuzz on his chin, he was so young. The other puncher was a seasoned veteran with the rawhide skin to prove it.

"Hold on there, mister!"

Lin did no such thing. He smiled and held up his free hand and continued on. Within moments the punchers were on either side of him.

The oldest had his hand on his revolver, but he took it off when he saw that Lin was not wearing a six-gun. "Didn't you hear me?" he demanded.

"Heard you just fine."

"Then why didn't you stop?"

"I have a message to deliver to your boss from my boss and I can't be all year at it."

The young hand piped up with, "Who might your boss be?" He had red hair to go with his peach fuzz.

"Etta June Cather," Lin said.

"What is the message?" the older hand asked.

"That is for Seth Montfort's ears and only his ears," Lin said. "I have my orders."

The older man scratched his grizzled chin. "Mr. Montfort doesn't like strangers on his spread. But since you ride for the EJ, and he is fond of your boss, we will let you pass."

"I am obliged," Lin said.

"We will escort you in," the older man said. "Just so you don't get lost, you understand."

"You are loyal to the brand."

"Loyal as hell," the older man said. "I am Wiley, by the way. My green pard there is Andy."

"Who the hell are you calling green?" Andy immediately demanded.

Wiley chuckled. "As you can see, he is a rooster on the peck. I was too, at his age, but I learned better."

"We all do," Lin said. He liked this one. It was a shame they had to be enemies. "Mind if I ask you a question?"

"So long as it is not about my former wife or that time I got drunk in Denver, you may ask what you please," Wiley replied.

"I reckon you have heard what your boss claims about the Dixon family and Aven Magill," Lin said.

Wiley's grin evaporated. "I have."

"And you are aware of all the gun sharks your boss has hired of late and what he intends to do with them."

"I am."

"My question, then, is this." Lin paused.

"Where do the punchers stand? When the lead starts to fly, will they add to the swarm?"

"You already have your answer. You said it yourself. We are loyal to the brand."

"Even when the brand you are loyal to might be in the wrong?"

Andy had a short temper to go with his red hair. "I will not listen to talk like that, mister. Insult the Bar M and you had better jerk your iron."

"He isn't wearing one," Wiley said, and looked at Lin. "I didn't catch your handle."

Lin told the lie.

"Well, Lin. I can tell a gent who has worked cows when I see one, so as one cow-savvy hand to another, and speaking for the rest of the Bar M punchers, I will say that if a shooting war breaks out, we will do our share."

"That is too bad," Lin said.

"What are you upset about?" Andy demanded. "Mr. Montfort hasn't accused your boss of helping herself to our cows. It is the Dixons and Magill who must answer for their deeds."

"They are her friends," Lin said.

"They will be mounds of dirt if they don't light a shuck," Andy boasted. "Mr. Montfort does not make idle threats."

After that little was said until they arrived. The Bar M had every building the EJ did, only bigger and painted white, plus a dozen more. It looked like a small town. A number of trees and a tilled patch for vegetables provided a splash of green among the white. Punchers were busy at a variety of jobs. The blacksmith was at his forge, his hammer ringing sharply. A portly man in a white apron came out of the cookhouse and watched them ride by.

The house was big enough to accommodate half of Mason. Glass panes testified to the Bar M's affluence.

Lin drew rein at a hitch rail in front of a wide porch. He did not dismount.

"I will get the big sugar," Wiley said, and swung down. Spurs jangling, he went up the steps and knocked on the door. A servant in a white uniform answered, then hurried off.

Andy was giving Lin a closer scrutiny. "I heard Stone talk about you and your brother," he mentioned. "Something to do with bucking a few gents out in gore. Is that true?"

"You will find out soon enough," Lin said. "Your boss sent a man to Cheyenne to find out."

"Stone has a reputation too," Andy said.

"They say he has shot eight men. He is a Texan," he added, as if that explained everything.

Wiley leaned on a porch post and hooked his thumbs in his belt. "Have you ever seen a finer spread?" he asked with an appreciative nod at the hustle and bustle around them.

"I have not," Lin admitted.

"Is it any wonder we are loyal? Mr. Montfort has only the best. The food we eat here is fit for a restaurant. And the bunkhouse has rugs on the floor and an indoor sink."

"Now I have heard everything."

Wiley chortled. "We are paid better than most too. If you ever get tired of the EJ, you might apply here. Openings do not come along often, but they are worth the wait."

The door opened and out strode Seth Montfort. He was without his bowler and suit jacket. Striding to the edge of the porch, he put his hands on his hips. "Mr. Gray, isn't it? My butler told me you have a message from Etta June."

"You have a butler?"

"The message," Montfort said. "I am a busy man."

Lin leaned on his saddle horn. "Very well. I will give it to you straight. Mrs. Cather will not be spied on. She says that the next time you send someone to watch her comings and goings, she will ride over here with a shotgun."

"She threatened me?"

"I will ride over with her," Lin said.

Montfort lowered his arms. "From her I will take abuse, but not from a saddle tramp. You will watch your tongue or I will have you horsewhipped."

"You are welcome to try."

Glancing at Lin's waist, Montfort sneered, "Hell, you are not even wearing a gun. If you will not go around heeled, you should not put on airs."

Andy laughed.

"You are not heeled," Lin told Montfort, "and you put on airs."

"Here, now," Seth Montfort growled.

"There is more to the message," Lin said. "Do you want to hear it?"

Montfort curtly nodded.

"I will give it to you straight," Lin said. "You are no longer welcome on the EJ. Should you or any of your hands be found anywhere on EJ range, you will be asked to leave."

"And if we don't?" Montfort gestured in contempt. "Will you and that hotheaded brother of yours make war on the Bar M all by your lonesome? I don't know why Mr.

Stone thought you might be a thorn in my side. You are nothing but a mouth without a brain. You are a nuisance, and I damned well do not like nuisances."

Lin lifted his reins. "I have given you her message. You would be wise to heed it." He wheeled the buttermilk and started off, but he had gone only a few yards when the air swished and a loop settled over his head and shoulders. He grabbed at it, and the next instant was violently wrenched from the saddle. He landed hard on his back in the grass. Incensed, he went to rise but saw Wiley holding a revolver on him.

Andy had done the roping and was beaming.

"It figures you would take me from behind," Lin said to their boss.

"That will cost you," Seth Montfort snapped. He cupped a hand to his mouth and shouted to several men over near a long, low building. "Mr. Lassiter! Fetch Mr. Stone from the bunkhouse and be quick about it!"

"Will do!"

Montfort approached and stood over Lin. "I warned you. I made it clear I have a particular interest in Etta June Cather. I will not brook interference."

"I have an interest myself," Lin said.

170

Thrusting his legs up and out, he planted both boot heels in Seth Montfort's groin.

Montfort bleated and doubled over. "You bastard!" He would have fallen, only Andy vaulted from the saddle and leaped to support him.

Wiley pointed his six-shooter at Lin's head. "Not another twitch out of you, mister!"

Lin was content to lie there and enjoy the commotion he caused. Punchers and gun sharks came running from all directions, among them one he recognized: Stone. With Stone was a tall bundle of rawhide who wore two Merwin and Hulbert revolvers, tied low. They shouldered through the gathering ring, and Stone walked up to Lin, drew his pistol and jammed the muzzle against Lin's temple.

"Say the word and I will blow a window in his skull, Mr. Montfort."

Seth Montfort could not answer. Bent half over, sputtering and gasping, he was the same color as a strawberry.

"What happened?" Stone asked Wiley, and after the puncher explained, Stone grinned down at Lin. "You have stepped in it now." His gaze flicked to Lin's hips. "And you rode in here not wearing a six-gun? What kind of fool are you?"

"The kind who does not kill for money," Lin said.

The pistolero wearing the two Merwin and Hulbert revolvers went to step past Stone. "Let me have him. I will take him to the blacksmith shop and work on him with tongs and hot coals."

"That is for the boss to decide," Stone said.

Montfort was still a deep shade of red. "The whip!" he wheezed. "I want the bull-whip."

A man ran off.

Lin focused on Wiley. The older puncher did not appear happy at the turn of events. "This is how you treat a hand who was only doing his job?"

Stone gouged the barrel of his revolver hard into Lin. "Shut up, you. You will not speak unless we say you can."

"That will be the day."

"Why don't you wear a six-gun?" Wiley asked.

"What difference does it make?" From Lassiter. "Anyone stupid enough not to go around heeled shouldn't stir up those who are."

"It was me who roped him," young Andy said proudly. "The boss pointed at my rope and I guessed right away what he wanted."

Lassiter eyed him up and down. "Make a lot out of it, why don't you, small potatoes?"

"Here, now," Wiley said. "The boy was only saying."

"When he has bedded down his first man, he can crow," Lassiter said. "Until then, he should not boast before his betters."

Lin was an interested listener. The punchers and the hired killers were not getting along. It was to be expected. Cowpunchers earned their pay the honest way: they worked for it — and worked hard. Gun sharks liked the easy life, and paid for their whiskey and women by putting lead into people. Punchers generally held shootists in low regard, and the feeling was mutual.

Seth Montfort slowly straightened. Twin fires danced in his eyes as he said, "Before I am done with you, Mr. Gray, you will regret the day you were born."

"You talk big when you have the advantage," Lin said. He felt surprisingly calm.

"What would you prefer?" Montfort asked. "That I put myself against you in personal combat? I am not a fighter — not in the sense that Mr. Stone and Mr. Lassiter are. I hire men like them to fight for me."

"In other words, you are yellow."

Everyone stopped talking and moving,

and all eyes swung toward the lord of the Bar M. To call a man a coward was the supreme insult. In most instances it resulted in a flash of firearms and the thunder of shots.

Seth Montfort's lips twitched. "You amaze me. It appears you do not know when to keep your mouth shut. But by all means, keep provoking me. Your comeuppance will be that much sweeter."

As if that were a cue, the hand who had run off returned nearly out of breath and thrust a bullwhip out. "Here you go, boss."

Montfort took hold of the handle and smiled at Lin. "I hope you can take a lot of pain."

CHAPTER 15

A bullwhip had many uses. Mule skinners used them to drive mule teams. Bull whackers used them to keep their oxen moving. Cowmen used them on occasion, although most preferred a rope to a whip.

It was common knowledge that someone skilled with a bullwhip could flay the flesh from his or her victim a tiny piece at a time. Flay the flesh right down to the bone.

Lin never had cause to use a bullwhip himself, but he had seen others wield one, and he had been impressed by how precise the whip could be. He made up his mind that he was not going to lie there and let them whittle him down to a blood-soaked ruin. He would resist to his dying breath.

Accordingly, when Seth Montfort raised his arm to give the whip a practice swing, Lin pushed up off the ground, casting the rope from him as he stood. He had loosened it while he lay there, and no one had noticed. Everyone was watching Montfort.

Lin plowed into the punchers, bowling them aside and knocking several over, making for the buttermilk. He broke clear of the ring and ran faster. Behind him curses and shouts erupted. His hand was on the saddle horn and he was pulling himself up when there was a loud *crack* and a sharp stinging sensation about his neck.

The whip, Lin realized, and snatched at the coils around his throat. His fingers had barely touched them when he was brutally wrenched to the ground. He rolled, felt the whip slide off and rose to his hands and knees.

The punchers and guns for hire were standing well back. Their excited, sweaty faces betrayed their blood-lust.

"Do it again, boss!" Lassiter cried.

Seth Montfort stood with his legs planted wide. He grinned as he moved his arm and the whip slithered like a snake. "Did that hurt, Mr. Gray? I assure you it is only the beginning."

"You might want to have your men hold me down to make it easier for you," Lin taunted, stalling as he girded his legs.

"That will not be necessary," Montfort said smugly. "You see, while I am not all that adept with a pistol or a rifle, I am quite proficient with my leather friend here. I saw one used years ago and got hold of a whip to practice with in my spare time." He snapped his arm and the lash streaked at Lin's face but stopped a few inches short with a loud *crack.*

Reflexively, Lin drew back.

Seth Montfort laughed. "See what I mean? Where do you want me to start?"

"On yourself," Lin said.

Montfort laughed louder. "You have sand. I will grant you that. But courage is never enough when you are bucking impossible odds."

"You sure do like to hear yourself talk." Lin's every muscle was taut.

"And you are one of those who does not know when to keep his mouth shut," Montfort responded. He sidled to the left, moving his arm in slow circles. Suddenly the whip became a blur.

Lin sidestepped, then did the thing he hoped Montfort least expected: he charged him. Shoulders lowered, he hurtled at the rancher, but he had taken only one stride when the whip hissed and his ankles were yanked off the ground. He crashed onto his elbows, wincing from the pain, as the whip crawled toward its holder.

"That's the way, Mr. Montfort!" Andy

hollered.

The faces of Stone and Lassiter were among those aglow with vicious glee at Lin's expense. He was startled to spot Griggs, as well. So much for the man's word. Griggs smiled when Lin saw him.

"Did you really think I would ride off, mister? I owe you."

Lin got his hands under him. Montfort had continued to circle and was now to his left. Lin swung toward him and rose into a crouch.

"I do so enjoy playing with you like this," Montfort said. "I could do it all day, but I do not have the time to spare. I have set wheels in motion that must be attended to."

Lin wondered what he meant by that. The distraction cost him. The whip cleaved the air, and a sharp pain in his cheek caused him to jerk his head back. A warm, wet sensation spread down over his jaw. He touched his cheek, and when he drew his fingertips away, they were streaked with scarlet.

Whoops and cheers rose to the sky. Some of the onlookers urged Montfort to take out an eye or slash off an ear.

"Do you hear them?" Montfort grinned. "Which part of you will it be? Decisions, decisions."

"Go to hell," Lin said.

"You first."

The bullwhip exploded into life. Montfort was going for his face. Lin got his arms up, but the whip sliced through his shirt to his skin, drawing more blood. Lin sidestepped and ducked a heartbeat before the whip sizzled over his head. But he could not avoid them all. Again and again and again the lash came at him, striking his arms, his body, his legs. He could not twist or dodge fast enough. Blood stained his shirt, his pants. He took it for as long as he could. Then he threw himself at his tormentor, hoping to catch Seth Montfort off guard.

The whip was lightning. It coiled around Lin's legs and pulled them out from under him. He grabbed for it, but the whip uncoiled and was gone in a twinkling.

Montfort was having a grand time. "I had forgotten how much fun this is. I just might give Cody Dixon and Aven Magill a taste of the lash too."

Lin tried once more. He made it halfway to Montfort before the whip brought him down. He sought to grab it before Montfort could draw it back, but the thing was uncannily quick.

"You are fine entertainment," Seth Montfort complimented him. "I want to thank you for showing up today."

Lin glanced at the buttermilk, then his saddlebags. Chancy had pleaded with him before he left to strap on what was in them before he rode to the Bar M, but Lin had refused. Chancy could not seem to understand that to Lin killing did not come naturally. He deeply regretted taking the lives of those two men that day the banker came to evict them. It did not help that the men were about to shoot his brother.

Agony in Lin's left shoulder brought him out of himself. The whip had drawn more blood. He dug his fingers into the soil, and coiled.

Montfort, showing off for his men, cracked the whip in the air a few times. He turned toward them, saying, "I will let you take a vote. Should it be his nose or one of his ears?"

It was the opening Lin needed. He leaped at Montfort's back, his arms spread wide to catch him in a bear hug.

"Mr. Montfort! Look out!" someone shouted.

Seth Montfort spun, but he was not completely around when Lin slammed into him. They crashed down. Montfort heaved and kicked and attempted to knee Lin in the groin, and Lin retaliated by ramming his forehead into Montfort's multiple chins. It stunned Montfort; he went momentarily limp.

Lin grabbed for the whip. Montfort did not wear a gun, so it would have to do.

Boots thudded. Hands fell on Lin's arms, shoulders and legs. He fought, but Montfort had been right; the odds were impossible. He was punched and kicked. A blow to the back of his head sent his senses reeling. When the world stopped spinning, he was on his back with half a dozen punchers and shootists on top of him. He bucked but could not dislodge them.

The sun was full on Lin's face, blinding him. He squinted against the glare. Suddenly a shadow fell across him.

Seth Montfort was rubbing his jaw, the bullwhip at his side. "You never give up, do you?"

Lin did not reply.

"I could have you shot, but that might upset Etta June enough for her to go find a federal marshal," Montfort said. "I don't want that. So I will compromise." Montfort stopped and waited as if expecting a question. When Lin did not say anything, he went on. "You must be taught a lesson. One people will talk about for years. But before I give the word, listen well." Montfort squatted. "When you recover, leave the Big Horns and never come back. Take your brother along, or he will suffer the same as you."

Lin broke his silence. "I will not desert Etta June."

Seth Montfort looked at his men, and then up at the sky, and then down at Lin. "You try to be reasonable with some people . . . ," he said to no one in particular. Suddenly he punched Lin in the cheek, nearly snapping Lin's head around. "Get this through your thick skull. She is mine. Her land is mine. Not you or anyone else can stop that from happening. Not even her."

"You have no right," Lin said.

"Why? Because I have not slipped a ring on her finger? Because we have not said our vows? I do not need to. She still has my brand on her." Montfort smiled and nodded. "Yes. That is how it is. I have branded her as I would a cow. To insert yourself as you have done is the same as trying to rustle my cattle."

"Etta June is no cow."

"For all your grit, you are thick of wit," Montfort said, and stood. "Gentlemen," he said, addressing his punchers and leather slappers. "This jackass refuses to listen. An example must be made. Pistol-whip him, if you please."

"Which one of us should do it?" Stone asked.

"*All* of you."

"All?"

"Every last one."

"That many hitting on him, we could damn near kill him," Stone said.

"Your point?"

"I thought you wanted him kept alive."

"Barely alive will do."

Stone hefted his revolver. "I don't much like getting blood on my six-shooter. Can't we use clubs instead?"

"Pistols are the tradition," Montfort said, and laughed. "When you are done, throw him over his horse and send him on his way." He walked toward the house.

"You heard the man, boys," Stone said. "Unlimber your hardware, and we will get to it. Don't hit his throat or his mouth if you can help it. It wouldn't do for him to choke to death."

The faces above Lin were grim. Several men had palmed their revolvers and were wagging them in anticipation.

"Let's get it over with," Lassiter said.

Lin hoped that those on top of him would get off, but none did. The first to hit him was a scrawny puncher on his chest. The barrel caught him across the forehead, and the world swirled madly.

Another blow landed, and another, points of pain in a mist of confusion. Lin nearly screamed when torment racked his knee. His ribs, his elbows, his wrists, his legs. So many blows were raining down, he lost all sense of the number. Pain was in his every sinew — in every bone. He became a welter of throbbing hurt.

Inner darkness nipped at Lin's mind. He struggled to stay conscious. His head rocked to the right and then to the left. The darkness spread, to where all that was left of him was a tiny voice deep inside — a voice growing fainter by the second. *I will kill you all,* the voice said.

No, I will not, Lin thought.

It was his last.

A sound penetrated the darkness.

Sound, and movement.

Lin felt himself sway, felt something pressed against his belly. Gradually it dawned on him that he was lying facedown over a horse. His buttermilk, most likely. He opened his eyes and was overcome with fear; he was blind! The world around him was as dark as the bottom of a well. He blinked, or tried to, and realized his eyes were swollen almost shut.

The sound was repeated. Someone was groaning. With a start he realized it was him.

Lin became more alert.

Pain, pain, everywhere. Such pain as Lin had never known. Pain such as he had never imagined. From head to toe, front and back — pain, pain, pain. It nearly blacked him out again.

Lin tried to move but couldn't. He was able, with an effort, to move his swollen fingers, but his arms and legs were locked stiff. The mystery was explained when he twisted his head. His wrists were tied. Judging by a tightness around his ankles, he could tell that they were as well. He tried to move his arms and legs but couldn't. He suspected that whoever bound him had passed the rope from his wrists, under the horse, to his ankles.

Lin craned his neck to see the sky. Stars glittered in the firmament. The position of the Big Dipper told him that dawn would break in a few hours. He had been unconscious most of the day and night.

He glimpsed trees — a lot of trees. A forest, evidently.

Lin licked his lips. They were puffy and split and caked with dry blood. Someone had hit on him the mouth, after all. That his teeth were still there was a miracle.

Lin willed his mouth to move. In a voice that was a dry croak, he said, "Whoa, boy." The buttermilk was well trained, and ordinarily that would be enough, along with a slight tug on the reins.

The horse did not stop.

Lin wriggled and strained. Excruciating torment shot through his body, and he subsided. He noticed that his saddle scabbard was empty; they had taken his rifle.

Somewhere in the night an owl hooted.

Lin peered about him but could not begin to guess where he was. He figured that whoever tied him had given the buttermilk a smack on the rump and sent it galloping off. He cleared his throat. "Whoa, fella!"

To Lin's delight, the buttermilk came to a stop. But his delight proved short-lived.

Out of the nearby woods came an ominous growl.

CHAPTER 16

The Big Horn Mountains were home to many meat eaters. Mountain lions, bears, wolves, coyotes, a few wolverines — all roamed the range, and all craved the succulent taste of flesh. Normally, though, most of them ran off at the sight or smell of a human. Normally, but not always.

Lin felt the buttermilk tremble slightly and heard it sniff the air.

The creature in the woods growled a second time.

Lin had encountered bears and mountain lions and wolves before. A bear's growl was low and rumbling; mountain lions tended to snarl and hiss; wolves sounded more like big dogs than either bears or mountains lions. He tried to identify the beast in the forest by its growls but, as yet, could not.

The buttermilk nickered and stamped.

"That's the way, boy. Show it you are not afraid," Lin said, both to calm the horse and in the hope his voice would drive the meat eater off.

It had the opposite effect. The thing growled a third time, louder than before, giving Lin the impression that whatever it was, it was closer. It must be stalking them.

The buttermilk pranced a few yards to one side, away from the thing in the trees.

"Easy, boy, easy," Lin said soothingly. Bound and helpless as he was, he was completely at fate's mercy. If the buttermilk bolted, there was no telling the consequences.

A twig snapped, and the underbrush crackled.

Instantly, the buttermilk wheeled toward the sounds.

Lin's wrist, ankles and shoulders protested as the rope pulled tighter. "Easy, easy!"

The crackling grew louder.

Whinnying in fright, the buttermilk raised its front hooves off the ground and stomped them down again.

For Lin, it was like being punched in the gut. He did not blame the horse for being scared. Whatever was out there had to be big. Bigger than a mountain lion or a wolf. That left one culprit: a bear. But the question now became, was it a black bear or a grizzly? The answer made all the difference.

Black bears rarely attacked people or horses. Grizzlies, on the other hand, were as fierce as they were huge, and as unpredictable as could be.

A loud grunt and snort confirmed that it was a bear.

The buttermilk whinnied again and stomped.

Lin had to try something. The bear might attack at any moment. Taking a breath, he hollered, "Go away! Leave us be!"

Something crunched, and a strong odor tingled Lin's nose. The bear was so close, he could smell it.

The buttermilk was quivering nonstop. It began backing away and bobbing its head.

"God, no," Lin said to himself.

The next moment the night was shattered by a tremendous roar, and the horse did what most any would do: it wheeled and fled.

Everything became a blur. A limb scraped Lin's legs. Another gouged his shoulder. The buttermilk was in a panic, racing recklessly through the timber with no regard for its safety, or for Lin's.

Hard on its hooves came the bear, a virtual monster, or so it seemed to Lin as he saw it charge out of the murk toward them.

Most people were unaware that over short distances bears could outrun horses. This bear, despite its immense bulk, was incredibly swift. Within seconds it was near enough to snap at the buttermilk's tail.

It was a grizzly. A living juggernaut of muscle, claws and teeth. Able to crush bone and pulverize flesh with a swipe of its huge paws, or to bite clean through a leg or an arm with a snap of its powerful jaws.

Lin gnashed his teeth in frustration. If the bear caught them, they were as good as dead. Even if he had had his rifle, it might not save them. Grizzly skulls were notoriously thick. Slugs glanced off them like pebbles off a boulder.

The horse galloped faster.

Lin was violently bounced and jolted and jarred. Pain racked his limbs. Queasiness assailed him, and bitter bile rose in his gorge.

The grizzly poured on more speed. Teeth flashing white, it bit at the buttermilk's flank but missed.

"Consarn all bears, anyhow!" Lin fumed. Suddenly the horse veered to avoid a tree, and it felt as if his arms were being torn from their sockets.

The bear was wheezing like a bellows, its paws drumming the ground with the impact of sledgehammers.

Lin had not prayed in so long, he could not remember the last time, but he closed his eyes and prayed now. It was an old habit resurfacing. His mother made Chancy and him say their prayers every night when they were young. She read to them each evening from the Bible and insisted they attend church each and every Sunday. She taught them to believe that the Lord looked after them and protected them from harm. Then their father died, and Lin was not so sure. His mother's slow suicide by drink had raised more doubts, to the point where Lin no longer believed that God looked after anyone. Chancy had gone a step further and now claimed there was no God.

And here Lin was, praying to he knew not whom or what, when he did know that the God his mother claimed would always watch over them had let his father and mother die senseless deaths. But he prayed anyway.

A frightened whinny from the buttermilk greeted a loud gnash of the grizzly's razor teeth.

Another limb slammed into Lin's legs. His wrists and ankles throbbed with torment, and a moist sensation was spreading down both hands. He was bleeding — possibly badly.

Lin raised his head to watch for trees ahead. Even as he did, a thick branch materialized in front of him. He started to jerk his head down.

A blow to the temple nearly ripped Lin's head from his shoulders. The world dimmed and spun. Lin could not tell up from down or front from back. The pain was overpowering.

A black veil descended.

Etta June Cather was hanging out laundry when Tom Jr. and Beth ran up.

"Rider coming, Ma!" her daughter cried.

"Thank you for letting me know." Etta June had instilled in them to always be wary of strangers. They were to trust no one unless she said the person was to be trusted. And when they spotted someone coming, they were to tell her immediately. "From which direction?"

"From Mason," Tom Jr. reported.

Dropping one of Beth's dresses in the basket, Etta June hurried around to the front of the house. The horseman was a quarter of a mile off yet, plenty of time for her to go inside and arm herself with a Winchester. She was waiting on the porch, her children huddled in the doorway behind her, when the man in black drew rein, leaned on his saddle horn and smiled.

"Surprised to see me?" Efram Pike asked.

Yes, Etta June was. Pike had been out to her place once before, and she had made it plain she did not care to have him come courting, and would take it unkindly if he persisted. "What are you doing here?"

Pike pushed his wide-brimmed black hat back on his head. "If you were any colder, I would swear it was winter."

"I am a busy woman, Mr. Pike. Unlike some people, I work for a living."

"Meaning me?" Pike said, and laughed. "Gambling is work, Etta June, no matter what you think."

"It is Mrs. Cather to you. Now, I will ask one more time. What are you doing here?"

"I came to see one of your new hands," Pike replied. "Chancy Gray, as he calls himself."

"Neither he nor his brother is here at the moment," Etta June said. "And I do not appreciate having my help disturbed at their work."

"You are a caution," Pike said amiably. "But I would not think of disturbing him."

"Then you have come a long way for nothing."

"Not if you will do me a favor," Pike said.

"Why should I?"

"It is the Christian thing to do, and last I heard, you tend to swear by the Good Book. Or am I mistaken?"

Etta June's lips pinched together. "What is it you would ask of me?"

"Pass on word to Chancy," Pike said. "Some gents with a lot of money have drifted into Mason and are looking to have a poker game. I thought Chancy might want to sit in."

"When is this game to be held?"

"When is he due back?" Pike rejoined.

"I daresay not for a week or more," Etta June said. "We are in the middle of branding."

"Let him know the game will take place whenever Chancy can make it into Mason." Pike touched the edge of his hat brim. "It was a pleasure, Etta June, as always."

"Hold on," Etta June said. "These gentlemen with money — they will wait that long just for him?"

"They aim to stick around Mason a while," Pike answered.

"Why did you invite only Chancy and not Lin? They are brothers, you know."

"Because I like the younger but not the older," Pike said. "Chancy reminds me of me about ten years ago. The older one thinks he is better than everyone else, and sticks his nose where it does not belong."

"You are referring to the incident at the general store when he came to my rescue?"

"I would never hurt you, Etta June. You know that. He had no call to butt in like he did."

"It is unbecoming to hold a grudge," Etta June said.

Pike snickered. "None of my grudges are petty. I am a good hater. When someone rubs me wrong, I never forget." He smiled and reined his bay around and tapped with his spurs.

Etta June lowered the Winchester. "Strange," she said softly.

The screen door banged, and out came her children to stand on either side of her.

"What is strange, Ma?" Beth asked.

"That business just now," Etta June said. "You would think Mr. Pike would want Chancy to come sooner rather than later."

"Mr. Pike sure was in good spirits," Tom Jr. mentioned. "I never saw him smile so much."

Her brow puckering, Etta June said, "Come to think of it, neither have I. His disposition is generally grumpy."

"Could be he was happy to see you," Beth offered.

Etta June placed a hand on her daughter's shoulder. "Could be, little one. But I was not happy to see him."

"You don't like Mr. Pike, do you?"

"No, I do not," Etta June confessed. "I have had nothing to do with his kind all my life, and I will not start now."

"What do you mean by his kind?" Tom Jr. wanted to know.

"Is he a bad man?" Beth asked.

Etta June stared after the dwindling figure. Tendrils of dust were rising from under the bay. "Not bad the way an outlaw is bad — no. He doesn't rob banks or hold up stages or kill people. He plays cards."

"Cards are bad, then?" Beth said.

"No, not at all," Etta June answered. "So long as it is for fun and not money. But Mr. Pike plays cards for that very reason. His nights are spent gambling and drinking and passing remarks unfit for our ears."

"So is he bad or not?" Beth said. "I am confused."

"Mr. Pike is not entirely bad, and he is not entirely good," Etta June clarified. "He is somewhere in the middle. I am sorry I cannot make it more clear. Even for adults it can be confusing."

"Is Chancy a good man?" Tom Jr. inquired.

"I would say yes — deep down. But he is young and has not had his mettle tested. It is uncertain which road he will take."

"And Lin?"

"Yes, he is very good. As good as men come."

"As good as Pa?"

Etta June hesitated. "Yes, I think so. Your father, bless his soul, did not have a dishonest bone in his body. Lin is very much like him. More like him than anyone I have met."

Beth tugged on Etta June's dress. "Do you like Lin, Ma?"

"I think of him as a friend, yes."

Tom Jr. said, "Is that all?"

Her cheeks coloring, Etta June said, "Whatever do you mean, Thomas? What more could there be?"

"Remember a while back when you told us we might have a new pa one day? That night you were so sad, we found you crying?"

"I wish you would forget that. I have," Etta June said. "And I was speaking in general terms. Perhaps I will remarry one day. But whether my new husband is Lin Gray or someone else, who can say?"

Tom Jr. gazed to the south. "He should be on his way back from Mr. Montfort's by now, shouldn't he?"

"I hope so," Etta June said.

"Are you worried Mr. Montfort will try to hurt him?"

"Enough questions. Both of you have chores to do, and I have the laundry to finish. Off you go." Etta June shooed them indoors and closed the door after them. Turning, she moved to the edge of the porch and clasped her arms to her middle. "Yes, I am very worried," she said softly.

CHAPTER 17

Lin was in a bad way. A very bad way. He would be conscious for short spells, then be dragged down into inner darkness by throbbing waves of pain and dizziness. He lost all sense of time. He lost all sense of direction. He lost all sense of where he was.

He felt close to death's door; closer than he had ever been; closer than he ever wanted to be. Each time he passed out, he feared it would be his last.

Deep down inside, Lin clung to the hope that the buttermilk would take him back to the EJ Ranch. A slim hope, since the horse had not been there long enough to regard it as home.

Eventually, hunger and thirst came to rival the pain. Lin's throat was parched for water; his belly craved food. He was so infernally weak that when he was conscious, he could barely lift his head.

A jumble of days and nights passed.

Sometimes when Lin came up out of the inner darkness, the sun was baking him alive. At other times he was shrouded in cool night.

The buttermilk plodded on, mile after endless mile. Once Lin heard the crunch of the buttermilk cropping grass. Another time, water was flowing under him; clear, sweet, wonderful water, so tantalizingly close, yet he could not reach it no matter how he strained.

He nearly went mad.

Lin tugged and pulled, but the rope would not loosen. All he succeeded in doing was to set his wrists to bleeding again. The whole time, the buttermilk drank noisily, which made his own thirst worse.

As if all that were not enough, Lin was in constant dread of running into another meat eater, or hostiles or badmen. The buttermilk had been lucky to escape the grizzly. It might not be so lucky at the next encounter. As for hostiles, they would delight to find a helpless white man they could torture to their hearts' content. Outlaws would no doubt help themselves to his effects and the buttermilk — after disposing of him, of course.

Then his dread became reality.

Lin was drawn out of the inky well of

limbo into the bright glare of day by the buzz of voices. They were faint at first but grew louder. He could not understand what they were saying. It seemed to be gibberish. Suddenly it struck him that they must be Indians, and his blood ran cold.

The buttermilk had stopped. Lin prayed the Indians would not spot them and would go on by. But the voices became excited, hooves thudded and the last thing he remembered was a hand falling roughly on his back.

Suddenly Lin was aware again.

He was lying on his back on something soft, and he was delightfully warm, and his body felt almost pleasant. He thought he must be dreaming. Then the pain returned — his wrists the worst, but points of pain everywhere.

The voices returned too. Only now Lin understood them.

"I think he is coming around," someone said. A woman, and she sounded familiar.

"Who could have done that to him?" a man responded.

"You know as well as I do."

To Lin's dismay, the softness and warmth and pleasant feeling faded, and once again he was adrift in nothingness.

The sound of humming brought him back.

Lin was still lying flat, still warm and comfortable. He opened his eyes as far as they would open. He was on a bed, and there was a roof over his head. A woman in a green dress was over by a dresser, rummaging in a drawer. Her back was to him, but he thought he should know her. He had to swallow a few times before he could croak, "Etta June?"

The woman spun. "My word! You gave me a start, Mr. Gray."

"It can't be . . . ?" Lin said.

Sue Dixon nodded and came to the side of the bed. She gently touched his arm. "How do you feel?"

"Awful."

"I must fetch Ma. We have been terribly worried. For a while we were not sure you would make it."

"How long?" Lin croaked.

"Sorry?" Sue bent down. "I can't quite hear you."

"How long have I been here?"

"Let me see." Sue held up fingers while counting to herself. "My goodness. It has been twelve days."

"Dear God," Lin breathed. "How did you find me?"

"It was not me. It was my brothers. They

were out looking for strays." Sue backed away. "Lie there and rest. I really must fetch Ma." Turning, she hastened out.

Lin could not get over it. Twelve days! Etta June and Chancy must think he was dead. He had to get word to them. He had to find out whether Etta June was safe. The thought startled him. He was as concerned for her as he was for his own brother.

Someone shouted. A commotion ensued, and into the bedroom rushed Patricia Dixon with Sue. A man was in tow. Broad with muscle, ruggedly built, he wore work clothes and scuffed boots. He stayed at the foot of the bed, his big arms folded, while the women came up on either side.

"Mr. Gray!" Pat exclaimed happily. "You are back among us at last! I daresay you gave us quite a scare."

"I have your sons to thank, I understand," Lin said.

"You can thank them when they get in this evening," Pat said. She placed a hand on his shoulder. "What would you like? Water? Milk? I have been able to get some soup into you to keep you alive, but I am afraid you have lost considerable weight. You would not recognize yourself."

"Let me see," Lin requested. He went to sit up, but she pressed him down.

"Nothing doing. You are too weak yet. Cody, the mirror in the dresser, if you please."

That last was addressed to the man, who walked to the dresser, opened a drawer and came back with a hand mirror, which he held in front of Lin, without comment.

Lin gaped. The image that stared back at him was a horrible mockery of his usual self. His eyebrows were swollen and discolored, his cheeks split, his lips puffy and split. There were welts and bruises everywhere. He glanced at the blanket that covered him almost to his neck. "The rest of me?"

"Almost as bad," the man said, and held out a calloused hand. "I am Cody Dixon. This is my house."

Lin brought his hands out from under the blanket and discovered that his wrists were heavily bandaged. It hurt to move them, but he shook, noting that Dixon was considerate enough not to squeeze too hard. "I am obliged."

"My wife tells me she met you at Etta June's — that you and your brother have hired on at the EJ."

"Did you get word to them?" Lin eagerly asked. "Do they know I am alive?"

Cody Dixon frowned. "I am sorry. I could not spare one of my sons, and I will not let the women go off by themselves. Either we all had to go, or no one."

"I don't understand," Lin said.

"Seth Montfort has given us a month to get off our ranch, or he intends to hang us as rustlers."

"I should have shot him."

"You can appreciate the fix I am in," Cody Dixon said. "It will be a cold day in hell before I let that son of a —"

"Cody!" Patricia said sharply. "There are ladies present."

The rancher smiled sheepishly. "Sorry. But just thinking about his gall makes me mad." He turned back to Lin. "We have seen riders on our range. Montfort's hired killers, I suspect. They always ride off when we go near them. But you can see why I can't send anyone to Etta June's. They are liable to be bushwhacked."

"Susan and I could try," Pat said. "Montfort wouldn't dare harm women."

"I would not put anything past him," her husband disagreed.

"Why not let me?" Susan said. "I can ride as good as any man. I will sneak away in the middle of the night and by daybreak be far from here and Montfort's men."

"What if they are watching the trails?" Cody Dixon shook his head. "No. No one is going anywhere, and that is final." He looked at Lin. "Again, I am sorry. But if you want Etta June and your brother to know you are alive, you will have to ride to the EJ yourself."

"We are not being neighborly," Pat complained.

"We are alive, and I intend to keep us that way."

To nip their argument, Lin said, "It is all right. I will get some food into me and head out tomorrow."

"Tomorrow?" Pat repeated. "I am afraid you will not be fit to ride for four or five days, if then."

"We will see," Lin said.

"What I want to know," Cody Dixon said, "is who put you in this state?"

Briefly, Lin told them. Yet even brief was too much; it left him tired and feeling drained.

"Did you hear him?" Cody Dixon demanded of his wife and daughter. "Montfort has lost all reason. He will carry out his threat to string me and the boys up unless we get to him first."

"Don't start with that again," Patricia said.

Cody Dixon explained for Lin's benefit. "I had a brainstorm. Instead of waiting for Montfort to come after us, we go after him.

A bullet to his brain and we are safe."

Her face a mask of worry, Pat clasped her husband's hands. "They call that murder. And I do not consider it safe when the law might come after you."

"Better Montfort than us," Cody insisted. To Lin he said, "She won't let me do it. Says she will walk out on me if I do."

"It is wrong to kill," Pat said.

"Not if it is done to protect those you love," Cody countered. "No judge would send me to the gallows for that." He appeared to have more to say but glanced at Lin, gestured helplessly and strode out.

Pat stared at the empty doorway. "We have been spatting," she said quietly. "We never used to." She followed her husband.

That left Susan, who shifted her weight from one leg to the next and back again before asking, "How is your brother?"

"The last I saw him, he was fine," Lin said. But a lot could have happened in the past two weeks. Chancy might have gone to the Bar M looking for him. If Montfort did to Chancy what Montfort had done to him — Lin grew so mad he had to resist an urge to punch the bed.

"Are you all right?" Sue asked. "You are red all of a sudden."

"I am alive," Lin said. "Thanks to your

family." An obligation he could never repay.

"We would have done the same for anyone." Sue chuckled. "Well, maybe not for Seth Montfort."

Lin laughed and wished he hadn't. It hurt too much.

"So, what would you like? Soup? Eggs and a slice or two of bacon? Water, milk, coffee or tea?"

"Those eggs sound good," Lin said. A rumble from his stomach showed how famished he was. "And coffee to wash them down."

"How many?"

"Four, if you can spare them," Lin said.

"Oh, please. We get thirty a day out of the chicken coop. There are always plenty." Sue whisked from the room, saying, "It won't take long to heat up the stove."

Lin smiled, and regretted it when his swollen lips flared with pain. Closing his eyes, he gave silent thanks for being alive. Now he would get to see Etta June again. He very much looked forward to that. The talk they had before he left had persuaded him miracles could happen. How else to explain the fact that a fine woman like her liked him?

He must have dozed off, because when he opened his eyes Sue was bearing a silver tray into the bedroom. The aroma of the food set his mouth to watering.

"Here you go. I also brought toast and jam, and added sugar and cream to your coffee. I hope that is all right."

Lin put his hands flat on the bed and slowly sat up. "You will make some man a fine wife one day."

Blushing, Sue carefully set the tray across his legs. "Does that hurt? I can feed you if you would like."

"I can manage," Lin said. The blanket had slid down around his waist, exposing his bare chest. He reached to pull the blanket up, and happened to glance under it. "Dear God."

"What?"

"I am —" Lin stopped.

"Naked? Yes, I know. Your clothes were an awful mess. Ma said the only thing to do was to burn them."

"But who — ?" Again Lin could not say the rest.

"Undressed you? Ma did." Sue laughed. "She wouldn't let me stay in the room."

"Your mother." Lin was aghast. He could not recollect the last time eyes other than his own had beheld him without a stitch on.

Sue laughed harder. "Oh, please. She has

seen my pa and my brothers without clothes plenty of times."

"I am not your pa or a brother." Lin pulled the blanket as high as it would go and still stay up. "Did she have to take my drawers too?"

"They were so stained with blood and whatnot, they were past saving," Sue explained.

Whatnot? Lin thought to himself, and shriveled inside.

"Don't fret none. My brother Ty is about your size. You can wear some of his things when you are fit enough to dress." Sue gazed out the window. "Ty is short for Tyler. He is twenty-two. My other brother, Henry, is a year younger than me. He is eighteen. We call him Hank." Suddenly she stiffened and moved quickly to the window, her hand to the pane.

"What is it?"

"Riders coming," Sue answered, and dashed to the doorway. "And coming in fast."

CHAPTER 18

Chancy Bryce had been through two of the worst weeks of his life. He was worried near sick over Lin. His brother should have been back from the Bar M days ago. Something had happened. Something terrible.

Chancy could think of only one reason his brother had been gone so long. Lin must be dead.

Chancy's natural impulse was to ride hell-for-leather to the Bar M and find out. But he couldn't. Not and keep his word. Lin had made him promise that under no circumstances was he to leave the EJ. "I want you to swear by Ma and Pa," Lin had insisted.

His brother was smart. It was the one oath Chancy would never break. He had loved his parents — loved them more than anything. He would not dishonor their memory by lying in their name.

Then there was Etta June Cather. She

would not stop reminding him that she needed him there, that if he left, she and her children would be at Seth Montfort's mercy.

So Chancy stayed. But he hated it. He hated twiddling his thumbs when he should be off avenging his brother. He stuck it out as long as he could. He did work around the house and the stable, staying near Etta June and her children as his brother had instructed.

But it was hell.

Pure hell.

Chancy did not understand why Etta June was so dead set against him going. He had a hunch she cared for Lin. Yet she refused to change her mind.

She was another example of why, if Chancy lived to be a hundred, he would never savvy women.

Two weeks went by. Two whole weeks. Chancy came to the end of his tether, marched up to the house and loudly knocked.

Etta June came to the door herself, wiping her hands on her apron. "Goodness gracious. Are you trying to break it down?"

"I can't wait any longer," Chancy told her. "I must find out about my brother."

Etta June came out on the porch. "Listen

to me. Go to the Bar M and you will die. I know that as surely as I know anything."

Chancy patted his Colt. "I am not helpless."

"I did not say you were. But Montfort has a lot of leather slappers at his beck and call. You cannot kill them all."

Her logic was a wall Chancy could not break down. He was mad at her for that. He was mad at Lin too, for making him give his word. Hell, he was mad at the world.

Maybe Etta June sensed that. Maybe that was why she said, "What you need is to get away for a bit. Forget your worries and do what you like best."

"What are you talking about?" Chancy doubted she knew what that was.

"The invite you had to go play poker," Etta June reminded him.

Chancy had almost forgotten about Efram Pike's visit. It had surprised him considerably — Pike riding all the way out from Mason just to offer him a seat in a card game. "You want me to go?"

"If it will take your mind off Lin for a while," Etta June said. "If it will keep you from going off to the Bar M and getting shot to pieces."

Chancy liked the idea. A night or two of cards and drink were exactly what he needed. But he shook his head. "I can't. I promised Lin I would stay close to you and the kids."

"He cannot hold it against you if you go at my bidding," Etta June said. "We will be all right for a few days."

"I don't know," Chancy said.

"No one has been skulking about the ranch," Etta June said. "And the Indians are gone. We will be perfectly safe."

"You could talk rings around a tree," Chancy said.

"I am only thinking of you. But I do have my reservations."

"Reservations how?"

"Something about Pike's invitation bothers me. I can't help but wonder if he is up to no good."

"Why would he want to harm me? He was as friendly as could be when I met him." Chancy grinned. "Friendlier than you were."

Etta June smiled. "You have yourself to blame. You showed a deplorable lack of manners."

"I am sorry about that."

"Apology accepted."

Chancy gave voice to his last objection. "But what if Lin shows up while I am gone?"

"If he is hurt, I will tend him."

"If he is hurt, Seth Montfort will pay."

"You are wasting daylight," Etta June said.

Chancy gazed toward the east end of the valley and the range he must cross to reach the settlement. "I would be gone five days at the most."

"We have them to spare," Etta June reiterated. "Saddle your horse. I will get some food for you to take."

Chancy gave in. He was back in fifteen minutes and accepted the bundle she gave him. "This is awful kind of you. You must want me out of your hair."

"Not at all. I just pray we are not making a mistake. Be careful, Chancy. Have your fun, but don't trust Efram Pike."

"You would make a fine mother hen." Chancy chuckled and gigged the zebra dun. When he was well out, he glanced back and she was still there. The children were at her side. They waved, so he did likewise.

Chancy almost turned back. It did not seem right, leaving them alone. But it had been her idea. She had practically booted him in the britches to get him to go. He faced to the east and brought the zebra dun to a canter.

Lin hated being helpless. He tried to slide

out of bed, but he was too weak. He had to lie there and listen to the commotion outside and hope the Dixons were not in danger.

The aroma of the food made his mouth water. He ignored it for as long as he could. But his rumbling stomach would not be denied. He picked up a fork.

Eggs had never tasted so delicious. The toast was exquisite. Lin resisted an urge to wolf the food down in great gulps. He chewed slowly, taking his time, savoring every mouthful.

Presently hooves pounded, going away from the house. Footsteps in the hall alerted him that someone was coming. "Sue?"

"No, me," Patricia Dixon said, whisking into the bedroom. "How are you holding up? Is there anything else I can get you?"

"What was the ruckus?"

"My sons saw some riders camped up in the timber. Montfort's men, most likely. My husband has gone off with them to pay the camp a visit."

"How long will they be gone?"

"Overnight. In the meantime, we are on our own. If there is anything you want — anything at all — give a holler."

The door closed behind her. Lin sank back against the headboard and pondered while he ate. He must regain his strength quickly so he could help when Seth Montfort moved against the Dixons.

Lin raised the blanket and looked down at himself again. So many bruises. So many welts. Half his body was black and blue. They had beaten him within a whisker of his life.

It was peculiar how things had worked out. Chancy and he had fled Cheyenne with a posse nipping at their heels. They had shaken their pursuers off and headed for parts unknown where they could start over. Lin's aim had been to push on into Montana or even Canada. But here they were, caught up in a budding range war in the Big Horns. If blood was spilled, it would draw attention. A federal marshal might show up, which was the last thing he wanted.

Lin sipped the piping-hot coffee and thought about the banker, Pettigrew. He had practically begged the man to give them more time. Another couple of months — that was all they had needed. They would have sold some cattle and had enough money to make good on almost all the money they had owed. But Pettigrew would not hear of it. Pay up in full or be evicted. When Chancy had argued that Pettigrew was not being fair, Pettigrew had said that his bank could not continue to support a no-account family like theirs.

No wonder Chancy had shot him in the shoulder.

That was bad enough. But then the three men Pettigrew had brought along had gotten involved. Chancy had had his back to them and had not seen them go for their six-guns. Lin had. They had been fixing to shoot his brother, so he had done the only thing he could to save Chancy's life: He had gunned down all three. Two had died, but the third one and Pettigrew had lived.

Sometimes Lin wished they hadn't, so no one could point the finger of blame at Chancy and him. A jury could not convict without proof or a witness. He and his brother would not be on the run.

Lin finished eating, pushed the tray aside and sat back to digest his food. He felt wonderfully sluggish. He closed his eyes, not intending to doze off, but he did. The scrape of a plate caused him to snap his head up. "Eh?"

Patricia Dixon was about to bear the tray off. "Oh. I am sorry. I did not mean to wake you."

"That's all right," Lin said. "If there is one thing I have had plenty of, it is rest."

"You need more. You are far from healed up."

"I wish I were. I would look after you and your daughter until your husband got back. It is the least I could do."

"I am beginning to see what Etta June sees in you," Pat Dixon said.

"Excuse me?"

"Surely you know by now that she has taken a shine to you. I saw it that night we stayed for supper."

"She is a fine woman," Lin said.

"The finest. You came along at just the right time. For a year now she has grieved over her Tom. She has cried herself to sleep at night so many times, she has run out of tears."

"Should you be telling me this?"

"You deserve to know. She will never forget him, but she is over him. She is ready for a new man in her life."

"We are getting ahead of ourselves," Lin said.

"I know; I know. The heart cannot be rushed. All I am saying is that you do not need to worry her heart is already filled."

Pat smiled and left.

Settling back, Lin draped an arm over his eyes. He was so tired, he could not keep his eyes open. He fell asleep thinking of Etta

June's face and eyes and the touch of her hand on his.

A sound woke him. Blinking, Lin gazed about him in confusion until he remembered where he was. Outside the window the world was a somber gray, and the room was dark with the approaching twilight.

Lin was thirsty, but he did not holler for a drink. He had imposed on the good graces of the Dixons too much as it was. Granted, he was not to blame, given the condition he was in. Nevertheless, he was uncomfortable having them wait on him and nurse him. He had hardly ever needed nursing. He could count the number of times he had been sick on one hand and have fingers left over.

Shifting to make himself comfortable, Lin stared at the ceiling. He imagined he saw Etta June's face floating in the air and smiling down at him. He sure did miss her.

A noise from the front of the house perked Lin's ears. He sat up. He would swear it had been a low cry. Nerves, he reckoned, and listened without hearing anything more.

"I am downright silly," Lin chided himself. But it was almost *too* quiet. Pat and Sue were not ghosts. They should make *some* sounds. The house might as well be a tomb.

Lin figured they were outdoors doing last-minute chores. The chicken coop had to be shut for the night. All the horses had to be put in the corral or the stable.

Garden implements and other tools had to be put away. Sinking into the pillow, he willed himself to relax.

Lin might have dozed off a third time, but just then the house resounded with a loud crash. Pushing himself up, he listened for voices. But the house remained quiet. Worried now, he carefully swung his legs over the edge. "Pat? Sue?" he called out.

No one responded.

The continued silence compounded Lin's unease. Something was wrong. Holding the blanket tight about his waist, he attempted to stand. He was almost erect when a wave of dizziness washed over him. His legs became mush, and he had to sit.

"Pat? Sue?" Lin tried again. "Can you hear me? Is either of you there?"

This was a fine note, Lin bitterly reflected. Here he was, as naked as on the day he came into the world, with neither a rifle nor a pistol, his body weak and battered, and the women might be in trouble. He pushed to his feet and took a step, and regretted it when the dizziness returned.

Sinking back onto the bed, Lin simmered with frustration. He decided to try one more time. Taking a deep breath, he bellowed as loud as he could, "Mrs. Dixon! Where are you?"

Spurs jangled in the hallway.

The next moment, the doorway was filled by the last person Lin expected. The smug sneer and the two Merwin and Hulbert revolvers tied low sparked vivid memories of being hit again and again and again. "You!" he blurted.

Lassiter grinned and placed his hands on his revolvers. "Are you as happy to see me as I am to see you?"

CHAPTER 19

Seth Montfort was dining on grouse roasted to perfection, vegetables so soft they melted in his mouth and freshly baked bread smeared thick with butter, the way he liked it.

Seth loved food. He had loved it since he was knee-high to a foal. He loved food almost as much as he loved running a ranch, and he loved running a ranch more than anything. It was akin to being a general in an army. He gave orders, and people did his bidding. He liked that sort of power. He liked power, period.

Seth liked cows too, but only as a means to an end. Bigger herds meant larger profits, and larger profits made him almost as happy as running a ranch and eating food.

People liked to joke that Seth probably had the first dollars he ever made, and they were right. He hoarded his money. He was a miser and proud to be one. To his credit, when he had to spend his money, he spent it on the best it could buy.

Seth's ambition was to be as rich as John Jacob Astor and to own the largest ranch in northern Wyoming. If that meant gobbling up his nearest neighbors, so be it.

Seth never had liked the Dixons. They were low-born Appalachians who lived hand to mouth and had no more vision than a tree stump. Aven Magill was little better: an old grump who would as soon shoot trespassers as order them off his property.

Then there was Etta June Cather. From the moment Seth set eyes on her, he had been smitten. For a while he had wondered why, since she was not all that beautiful. Her breeding could not begin to compare to the social circles in which he had moved before he left Connecticut for the West. She was, in short, ordinary. But he still wanted her. And her land. Especially the land. The EJ had better graze and more water than either the Dixons' spread or Magill's.

Seth wanted it, and he would have it.

Seth fantasized about owning that land, and about Etta June. His fantasies involving her always brought a smile. They were the kind men did not repeat aloud. They always started with her wearing clothes and ended with her not having a stitch on.

Thinking of her now, Seth forked a piece of roast grouse into his mouth and smiled as he chewed.

"You sure are a happy cuss these days."

Seth's smile became a frown, and he stared down the long table at Isaac Stone. It was his custom, from time to time, to invite underlings to share a meal. Tonight he had invited Stone and one other.

Seth had a second reason for inviting him. He had put Stone in charge of the leather slappers he hired, and he deemed it prudent to keep a close watch over them. "What was that?"

Stone forked a piece of grouse into his mouth, but he did so with his fork turned the wrong way, then chomped with his mouth open. "You seem happier since you gave the Dixons their warning. I reckon once you have the Big Horns all to yourself, you will go around with all your teeth showing all the time."

"An overstatement," Seth said, "but you are quite observant."

"I have to be," Stone responded. "Men who make their living like I do don't last long if they aren't."

"I always thought that killing was a simple matter of squeezing a trigger," Seth said.

It was Stone's turn to frown. "Not everyone can squeeze that trigger. Some can't snuff out another life if their own depended on it."

"How is it you wound up in the profession you are in?" Seth idly inquired. Not that he cared, but he was always curious about why people did what they did. To understand someone was to have power over them.

"You could say I sort of fell into it, just like most folks fall into whatever they do."

Seth set down his fork. "Can you be more specific?"

"It is personal," Stone said testily.

"I do not mean to pry. If it is something you would rather not talk about, I respect your wishes."

Stone stared down the table. "I will say this for you, Montfort. You are a puffed-up rooster, but you always treat us fair. I respect that."

Seth did not know whether to be insulted or flattered. "I am not barnyard fowl. But yes, I make it a point to be honest with those who work for me, in whatever capacity."

"Since you brought that up," Stone said, "some of your punchers resent me and my curly wolves being here."

"That is to be expected, is it not? Cowhands have little love for assassins." Seth paused. "And they are *my* curly wolves, Mr. Stone — not yours."

"Don't get prickly," Stone said.

"You are a fine one to talk. All I did was ask how you got started in your trade."

Stone shrugged. "How does anyone start? I threw lead. My pa and a neighbor were squabbling over water rights. In some parts of Texas, water is more valuable than gold. Without it, a small spread like ours would have turned to dust." Stone stabbed a piece of potato but did not raise it to his mouth. "Our neighbor had four boys. They took over the water hole and would not let my pa anywhere near it. When Pa objected, they shot him. He didn't die, but he was in bed for a month."

"What did you do?"

"What in hell do you think I did? I killed every last one of the sons of bitches. The neighbor, his sons, the mother, the daughter."

"You murdered their women too?"

"It would not do to have anyone run to the law," Stone said.

Seth Montfort smiled. "I was right in picking you over the rest. You comprehend the intricacies involved."

Stone snorted. "I am not sure what you

just said, but if it was what I think it was, I savvy what you are up to, yes."

Seth looked at his other guest. "How about you, Mr. Griggs? You are unusually quiet this evening. Do you savvy what I am up to?"

Griggs was about to sip coffee. "You want to rid yourself of the other ranchers. Any jackass could figure that out."

"There is one I would rather not rub out if I do not need to," Seth said. "Or haven't I made it clear she is to be spared unless I say otherwise?"

"There is not a gent on this spread who does not know," Griggs assured him.

Seth placed his hand on the table and slowly drummed his fingers. "I also thought I made it clear that the job I gave you was crucial. Under no circumstances were you to be caught."

"Hey, now." Griggs set down his cup so hard that coffee spilled over the rim. "I did exactly as you told me to do. I never showed myself except late at night, and then only to make sure he was not in her bed."

"Yet you were caught."

"He was waiting for me. Somehow he knew."

"The somehow is not hard to figure out. You were careless. I expected better."

"I did my best," Griggs said sullenly.

"Is that what you call it?" Seth fingered his butter knife. "And after Lin Gray caught you, what happened?"

"I have already told you."

"Tell me again," Seth said.

Griggs glanced at Stone, who ignored him. "He asked me what I was doing there. I told him my horse had run off and I was hoping to borrow one to get back to the Bar M."

"And he believed you?"

"Why wouldn't he?" Griggs retorted.

Stone pushed his chair back and lowered an arm to his side. He snickered as if something were funny, then looked at Griggs and said, "You have brought this on yourself."

"Brought what?"

Stone glanced at Seth. "You pay me extra to keep your pistoleros in line, so I reckon I owe you the truth. Griggs here is lying to you. There is more to his story."

"The hell you say!" Griggs exploded, and shoved his chair back. "I will not be accused without cause."

"I have cause," Stone said. "I overheard you talking to Lassiter out behind the stable. You asked him if you could borrow his spare revolver since Lin Gray took yours."

Griggs rose out of his chair. "You damned busybody." His hand hovered near the six-shooter Lassiter had lent him.

Seth Montfort smacked the table. "Sit down, Mr. Griggs!" To Stone he said, "What else did you overhear?"

"Just that Lin Gray, or whatever his real name is, made Griggs tell him the truth. That you sent Griggs to spy on the Cather woman."

"Damnation," Seth said.

Griggs had not sat back down. "You had no call to do that, Stone. Why make trouble for me?"

"Didn't you hear me?" Stone rejoined. "I work under Montfort, and you work under me. By lying to him, you throw dirt in my face."

Seth Montfort glared at Griggs. "So what Mr. Stone has told me is true? You told Lin Gray the truth. Do you have any idea of the trouble you have caused me?"

"I had to tell him," Griggs said. "He is snake mean, that one, when he wants to be."

"He is not the only one," Stone said.

Seth sighed. "I am disappointed in you, Mr. Griggs. Collect your belongings and go. You are fired."

"I will be glad to!" Griggs declared.

"No," Stone said.

Both Seth and Griggs looked at him.

"No?" Griggs repeated.

"You lied to Montfort. You lied to me. Now you stand there ready to draw on me and you think you can just ride off?" Stone rose, his right hand close to his holster. "You have another think coming."

"Not in the house!" Seth said.

"Here is as good as anywhere!" Griggs cried, and went to draw.

Stone's hand flashed. The dining room rocked to the boom of a shot, and Griggs was punched back by an invisible fist. He collided with his chair, and both crashed to the floor, a chair leg breaking with a snap. Griggs' own legs thrashed, and his body broke into convulsions.

Stone calmly stepped around the end of the table, stood over Griggs and thumbed back the hammer. "Any last words?"

Griggs' mouth moved, but all that came out was blood. Whining, he sought to draw.

"Save me a bunk in hell," Stone said, and squeezed the trigger.

Shouts rose, both in the house and outside. Feet drummed as Seth Montfort came down the table and regarded a spreading scarlet ring. "I did not want shooting in here."

"He left me no choice."

"Assign men to bury him. You may keep his effects and his horse, or sell them and pocket the money."

Stone started to replace the spent cartridges. "I would have done that anyway, but thanks."

"I am grateful that you were honest with me," Seth said. "But do not take too many liberties. And when Mr. Lassiter returns, I want a word with him over his."

"His what?"

"The liberty he took. He should have told me what Griggs told him and not kept it to himself."

"He told me," Stone responded.

"I just heard you say to Griggs that you overheard them talking out behind the stable."

"I lied." Stone fished a cartridge from his cartridge belt and slid it into the cylinder. "Lassiter asked me not to let on that he told me, and I gave my word I wouldn't."

"I see. So you lied to Griggs to keep your word to Lassiter. I must say, your morals are as fluid as water."

Stone twirled the revolver into his holster. "There you go again. Talk so I can understand you."

"We are remarkably alike," Seth said. "We do what we have to and don't give a tinker's damn about the consequences."

"Do you still aim to talk to Lassiter?"

"I certainly do," Seth replied. "It was remiss of him not to report to me. I do not expect loyalty, Mr. Stone; I *demand* it. If he is no more loyal than that, I am better off without his services."

"Don't be hasty," Stone advised. "Next to me, Lassiter is the best short-trigger man you have. He's a bloodthirsty cuss too. The only thing he likes more than spilling blood is forcing himself on a filly."

"Surely you do not mean to suggest he is partial to rape?"

Stone laughed. "Surely I do. He can't keep his hands off them. In Texas he was run out of three towns for taking liberties, as you would call it."

"Thank you for informing me. I will make it a point not to let him anywhere near Etta June from now on."

"Oh, Lassiter would never touch Mrs. Cather. He knows she has your brand on her. But every other female in these parts had better watch out if Lassiter gets them alone."

"He can't control himself. Is that it?"

"Let me put it this way. Single or married, it makes no difference to Lassiter. To him all women are ripe fruit, and he can't wait to take a bite out of them. But the worst part is what he does after he is done with them."

"After?"

"You do not want to know," Stone said.

CHAPTER 20

Lin Bryce was dumbfounded. He had sensed something was wrong, but he never expected *this*.

Lassiter came toward the bed, stopping just out of reach. "So, this is where you got to."

"How — ?" Lin blurted.

"You are wondering what I am doing here?" Lassiter uttered a cold laugh. "It's simple. After we beat you and threw you over your horse and sent you on your way, Montfort got to thinking. He figured it would upset his precious Etta Sue if you were to show up at her ranch more dead than alive. So he sent me and some others to catch up to you and finish what we started."

Lin's blood was racing and he had broken out in a sweat. He struggled to regain his self-control, saying, "It took you this long to find me?"

"Hell, I didn't even know you were here. A thunderstorm wiped out your trail," Lassiter said. "We came for another reason."

"What have you done with Pat and Sue Dixon?"

"The others are keeping them in the kitchen," Lassiter replied. "With the husband and sons gone, I can take my time."

Lin did not like the sound of that. "This is Montfort's idea? Barging in here and mistreating them?"

"No, it is not," Lassiter said. "It is my notion. I have been a long time without a female."

"You wouldn't," Lin gasped.

"Why not? They are handy."

"Seth Montfort wouldn't like it." Lin grasped at a straw.

"Who is to tell him? You? Hell, you look fit to keel over if you get out of that bed."

"Leave them be," Lin said. "They have never done you any harm."

"What does that have to do with anything?" Lassiter retorted. He turned to go. "I could shoot you, but that would be too easy. Lie there and worry about what I am going to do to you while I go have fun with the females."

Lin struggled to sit up. "Damn it! Don't!" he exploded. His arms shook so violently, he nearly pitched onto his face.

All Lassiter did was laugh.

"No!" Lin cried, but the killer was gone. Panic swelling, he glanced around the bedroom. He needed his saddlebags — needed what was in them. But he had neglected to ask the Dixons where they were. Over in a corner was a closet. *Maybe there,* he told himself, and balanced on the edge of the bed.

Dizziness struck again. Lin swore; the women needed his help! Desperate, he placed one foot on the floor, and then the other. Now came the test. With a quick shove, he made it to his feet but swayed like a reed in high wind. He took a shambling step. Then another. He smiled, telling himself he could do it. But no sooner did he think he could than his legs gave out and he fell hard onto his chest and shoulder.

Lin got his hands under him and crabbed forward. Pain rippled through him in waves, each as strong as the last.

Somewhere a woman screamed.

Stark fear filled Lin. Not for himself, but for the two sweet souls who had treated him so kindly. He moved faster, but his best was still painstakingly slow.

A bark of laughter froze Lin in place.

Just outside the room stood another of

Montfort's assassins, a scruffy killer with a Starr revolver crosswise on his hip. "Here he is, Reb. Pretending to be a snake."

The man entered, followed by the one called Reb, a lean rail in a worn gray coat, carrying a Loomis short-barreled shotgun. Belted about his waist were a Le Mat and a long knife.

"I don't like this, Harry," Reb said in a thick Southern accent.

"We are paid to kill. It is what we do."

Reb nodded at Lin. "I don't mind doin' him. It's the other. Lassiter ought not to molest the women. It ain't right."

"Since when did you give a damn about right and wrong? You have been on the wrong side of the law since after the war."

To Lin's amazement, Reb offered the same objection he had. "Seth Montfort won't like it none — us actin' on our own."

"Could be he will," Harry disagreed. "Could be it will make Cody Dixon so mad, him and his sons will ride to the Bar M to kill Montfort and we can get rid of them as easy as can be."

"I don't cotton to abusin' women," Reb persisted.

"Go tell that to Lassiter if you are so fired up," Harry said. "But I get that nine-shot smoke wagon of yours after he bucks you out in gore."

Another scream caused Reb to half turn toward the hall. "Damn him to hell."

"Make up your mind," Harry said. "If you are going to get yourself killed, go do it. If not, lend a hand here." He pointed at Lin. "Roll this hombre over. Lassiter wants us to finish beating him to death." He put a hand on the butt of his Starr.

Reb stooped and hooked a forearm under Lin. "Why not just shoot him? Or I have my knife."

No, Lin had it. As the Southerner lifted him, Lin drew the long blade and plunged it into Reb below the ribs, thrusting it to the hilt. Reb stiffened and sucked in a breath, his eyes widening in surprise.

Harry, who was behind Reb and had not seen Lin stab him, said, "What is it?"

Lin twisted the knife. Reb grunted and sagged, his whole body going limp. Grabbing the shotgun, Lin threw himself to the right, onto his shoulder. He cocked the twin hammers as he dropped.

Startled, Harry swore and jerked his pistol. Lin let him have one of the barrels full in the gut. The blast lifted Harry off his feet and sent him staggering against a wall. A red smear marked his slow slide down. He half sat, half lay, his lifeless eyes fixed on the emptiness that had claimed him.

On a hunch, Lin patted the pockets of Reb's coat. He found what he was looking for: extra shells. Helping himself to a handful, he crawled toward the doorway. He reached it just as boots thudded down the hall. Poking his head out, he saw two more gun sharks hurrying toward him. The one in the lead was looking back and saying something to the other one.

Lin set down the shells and raised the shotgun. He fired at the same instant the man turned.

The buckshot caught him in the face and made a mess of his head; he was dead before he hit the floor.

Lin ducked back to reload. The danger now was that the second killer would rush him, but apparently the man sought cover instead. A wary peek showed the body and an otherwise empty hall. But a door on the left that had been closed was now open a crack.

Lin centered the shotgun on the crack at the same height as the latch, and unleashed both barrels at once. A sharp cry was drowned out by the boom. Lin's ears rang as he hastily reloaded. He peeked out again. The door had a hole in it the size of a melon. There was no movement inside.

"You in the room yonder!" Lin hollered. "Throw out your hardware and I will let you live."

No one responded.

"Do you hear me?" Lin tried again. It could be a trick. But he did not have the luxury of waiting the other man out. He must get to the women; he must get to them right away. Accordingly, using the wall for support, he made it upright. For a few harrowing seconds his legs once again threatened to give out, but they didn't. Taking one painful step after another, he moved toward the buckshot door.

The only sound was a peculiar sucking. A push on the door revealed the source.

The killer was on his back, half his throat blown away. Somehow he was still alive. But even as Lin set eyes on him, the man stiffened, exhaled and was no more.

Lin continued down the hall. He still had Lassiter to deal with — maybe more. He wished he had his saddlebags, but the shotgun would suffice.

The hallway forked. Lin debated which way to go and bore to the right. The screams had come from that direction.

Ten yards more and Lin came to a wide doorway without a door. He smelled coffee and the lingering aroma of cooked eggs.

Leveling the shotgun, he poked one eye past the jamb.

It was the kitchen. In the center stood a round table, to the right an oak counter and cupboards, and to the left a large stove and a stack of wood. Lying near the table, bound wrists and ankles, and gagged, was Patricia Dixon. Her tear-filled eyes fixed on him in mute appeal.

Lin gave the room another scrutiny. On the far side, a door to the outside hung open. No one else was there. He started to enter, then drew up short in shock. He had forgotten; he was buck naked. He looked down at himself, and then at the woman who had so tenderly nursed him back to the land of the living, and he shambled in, holding the shotgun over the part of his body that no one should ever see. "I am sorry," he said.

Pat wagged her arms and tried to talk, her words muffled by the gag.

"Where is Lassiter? And your daughter?" Lin pried at the knot with his fingernails and it came undone.

"He took her!" Pat sobbed. "Go after them! Stop him!" She raised her bound wrists to her mouth and tore at the rope with her teeth.

Lin shuffled to the open door. In the

distance was Lassiter, leading a horse by the reins. Slung over the second animal was a figure in a dress. "Damn."

"Can you see them? Stop him!"

"I wish I could." Lin leaned against the wall. He was about done in. The exertion had taken everything out of him. "I am sorry."

"Stop saying that." Pat got her wrists loose and bent toward her ankles. "If you can't ride, I can. I will go after them myself."

"He will kill you," Lin said. "Both of you."

"He will try. But that is my little girl he took. I have to do it." In a maternal frenzy, Pat tore at the rope and the knot parted. Rising, she darted to the door. A sob escaped her. She whirled and disappeared down the hall, only to return half a minute later carrying a Winchester.

Lin held out an arm to block the doorway. "Give me five minutes and I will go with you."

"I can't wait that long!" Pat pushed his arm aside and charged on out, sprinting madly for the corral.

"My saddlebags!" Lin shouted. "Where are they?"

"In the stable!"

Lin marshaled his strength and walked out into the harsh glare of the midday sun. He had spent so many days abed, the brightness hurt his eyes. He blinked and squinted and held a hand up to shield them. "Pat?"

She had the gate open and was vaulting onto a sorrel. In her anxiety, she did not bother with a saddle blanket or saddle. She slapped her legs and flew out of the corral.

"Pat!"

She paid him no heed. Bareback, she galloped in pursuit.

Lin headed for the stable. The more moving he did, the less the bruises and welts pained him. He broke into a stiff-legged run, each step easier. Thankfully, the stable doors were open. The stable itself was bigger than the stable at the EJ Ranch, with a third again as many stalls. As luck would have it, the buttermilk was in the very last stall on the right.

Lin's saddle blanket and saddle were draped over the side. He looked for his saddlebags but did not see them. Setting down the shotgun and the shells, he opened the stall and brought out the palomino.

At the rear of the stall were his bedroll — and his saddlebags.

Lin sank to his knees. In one bag were his spare shirt and pants. In the other was the thing he had not touched since the shooting affray. He opened the one containing his

clothes. The shirt had seen a lot of wear and
the denims were torn, but they were all he
had. He dressed as quickly as he was able.
He did not have a spare belt, but the pants
fit tightly enough to stay on. Nor did he
own spare socks or extra boots. He would
have to go barefoot.

Lin reached for the other saddlebag but
did not open it. Instead, he swung both bags
over his shoulder and hurriedly saddled the
buttermilk. He tied the saddlebags and
bedroll on, then reclaimed the shotgun and
the shells.

It felt good to be in the saddle again. Lin
brought the horse to a gallop. Pat Dixon
had long since vanished into the thick
timber to the south.

Lin imagined that Lassiter would head for
the Bar M — or would he? — given that he
did not have Seth Montfort's permission to
do what he was doing.

Dust motes hung suspended in the air at
the point where Patricia had plunged into
the trees. Lin slowed, threading in among
them. Following her trail proved to be no
chore at all; she had crashed through the
undergrowth like a cow elk gone amok.

Lin hoped she did not catch up to Lassiter. Not before Lin caught up to her. In
the emotional state she was in, she would

be easy to pick off. He kept fearing he would hear a shot.

The minutes dragged. Lin considered firing into the air to get Pat's attention, but Lassiter might hear too.

Lin glanced at the saddlebag he had refused to open. Maybe he should reconsider. What difference did it make *how* he killed Lassiter so long as he killed him? Principles were fine and dandy, but they could be carried too far. Chancy certainly thought he was being pigheaded, but the man Chancy shot had lived. Lin would give anything to be able to go back and relive that day. He would not let his brother —

Abruptly, up ahead, that which Lin dreaded, happened. A shot cracked. A horse whinnied. Then a woman screamed in terror.

It sounded like Pat Dixon.

Lin rode for all he was worth.

CHAPTER 21

Lin almost missed her. He was racing pell-mell through the wood, intent on the terrain ahead, when a splash of color at the edge of his vision drew his gaze to a form sprawled in a twisted heap. Instantly, he reined toward her, and was out of the saddle before the buttermilk came to a stop. He forgot the condition he was in. His momentum nearly threw him to his hands and knees.

Her mouth was moving, but no words came out. The slug had cored her high on her bosom, and the hole was oozing red.

Kneeling, Lin set the shotgun down and gently cradled her head on his leg. "You should have waited for me."

Patricia Dixon shuddered. The pink tip of her tongue rimmed her lips and she whispered, "He was waiting for me. Shot me from ambush and rode off laughing with my Sue."

"If it is the last thing I ever do," Lin vowed, "he is not long for this world."

Her hand fumbled at his clothes — at his arm — and found his hand. She squeezed him, hard. "Save her. Please."

"I will try."

"Go," Patricia urged.

Lin watched more blood ooze from the bullet hole. "I can't leave you quite yet."

Her fingernails dug into his hand. "You must! I can't bear the thought of him, and her." A tear formed at the corner of her eye. "I'm begging you, Lin. I know why you won't go. But she is more important than I am."

Lin had to cough in order to say, "It won't be long."

"Dear God," she said weakly, and sobbed. "My husband and my sons! They will go after Montfort. You mustn't let them."

Lin did not know how he could stop them.

"I mean it," Pat said. "They will get themselves killed, and one death is enough."

Lin looked away. It was that, or lose control.

"Please don't stay. Save my sweet baby." She stopped and made a choking sound.

"Maybe you shouldn't talk," Lin said.

"So what if I hurry it along?" Pat replied. "I would rather it was sooner if it gets you on your horse."

"I just can't. I am sorry."

Pat shifted her head toward him and wanly smiled. "It is too bad she is more fond of your brother than you. But then, you have Etta June."

"I do not have anyone yet," Lin said.

"I told you she fancies you." Pat placed her other hand on his. "You could do worse. She is as fine a woman as you will come across." Pat paused. "Now will you go? It could take me half an hour to die."

"I will wait," Lin said.

"No, you won't."

And just like that, she rolled away from him. Lin's surprise rooted him in place for the time it took her to snatch up the shotgun. Too late, he guessed her intent. "Don't!" he cried, and lunged, but she had pressed the muzzles to her chin and thumbed back one of the hammers.

Their eyes met.

"Please," Lin said.

Pat squeezed the trigger. The buckshot blew half her head off. One moment her face was whole and seamed with pain and love, and the next what was left of her brain was bulging through the cavity in her skull.

Lin's stomach churned. He turned away, thinking he would be sick, but all that came up was bile. Steeling himself, he spat it out and turned back. Her remaining eye stared at him accusingly.

Flesh and bone and blood were spattered all over. Over her, over the ground, over him, over the shotgun.

Picking up the gun, Lin wiped it as clean as he could on leaves, then replaced the shell. "You shouldn't have," he said to the corpse.

The buttermilk had shied at the shot but had not bolted. Talking softly, Lin got close enough to snag the reins. He forked leather and rode on. After he dealt with Lassiter, he would come back and bury Patricia, then bear the sorrowful news to her husband and her sons.

Her death shook him. Lin found it impossible to concentrate. The image of her face, or what was left of it, filled his mind's eye. He shook his head, but it would not go away. "Damn me," he said, and lashed the reins.

Trees and limbs and brush flowed past on either side. The buttermilk vaulted logs, avoided boulders, skirted impenetrable thickets. Lin had never ridden so fast in heavy timber, or so recklessly. He was determined to catch up before the unthinkable happened. He owed that much to Pat. Her sacrifice must not be for nothing.

Lin cast about for signs. There should be tracks, broken brush. Pockmarks in a small clearing showed he had not lost them. Now and again he rose in the stirrups and scanned the woods but did not spot them. He began to regret staying so long with Pat. He would hate to fail her.

The sun climbed. The buttermilk tired. Lin was forced to stop and give the horse a rest. He needed one himself. He was pushing too hard. The chase was taking a toll.

Five minutes were all Lin could spare. He climbed back on and jabbed his heels. They had gone a short way when he stiffened.

A horse was coming toward him. Lin recognized it as the animal Lassiter had thrown Susan on. Only she was not on it now. He reined to intercept it, and the animal halted of its own accord. It was lathered with sweat, and hung its head.

Lin did not know what to make of it. Either the horse had thrown Sue and run off, or her absence was more sinister. He left it there. It would only slow him.

The sun was hovering over the western horizon when Lin crossed a rise and descended a boulder-strewn slope toward more woodland. The buttermilk whinnied and bobbed its head. Drawing rein, Lin searched for the cause.

A bare foot jutted from behind a boulder lower down.

"Lord, no," Lin breathed. He clucked to the buttermilk, and the horse grudgingly obeyed.

Lin slid down. Wary of a trap, he scanned the vicinity. The double click as he pulled back the twin hammers was reassuring.

He was almost afraid to look. He stepped over the foot, and this time what came up was not bile. Wheeling, he doubled over and was violently sick. He could not bring himself to look again, but he had to.

"God, no."

It was worse than anything Lin had ever beheld. He could not imagine how anyone could do what Lassiter had done. Slumping, he bowed his head.

He felt numb inside. Both women, dead.

Lassiter had done the killing, but Seth Montfort was to blame. The owner of the Bar M had hired him.

"You are both on my list," Lin said out loud.

As he girded himself for the grisly task ahead, it occurred to Lin that part of the blame was his. He'd had a chance to kill Montfort, and hadn't. He could have killed Lassiter too, now that he thought about it.

If he'd worn his pistol instead of stuffing it in his saddlebags, the women might still be alive.

Lin pressed a hand to his forehead and closed his eyes. How could something like this happen? He had tried to do right — tried to do as his conscience guided him — and it had all turned out wrong. What sort of world was it where something so bad could result from a man trying to do good?

It did not make any kind of sense at all. If this was what happened when someone did the right thing, why bother trying? Turn the other cheek, the Good Book said. He had done his best to live that creed, and look at the consequences.

Lin was the first to admit he was not a deep thinker. He never could understand why things were the way they were. But now he was more confused than ever.

The hoot of an owl brought Lin's brooding to an end. It would be dark soon. Unless he wanted the remains to lie there all night, and draw every wolf, coyote, bear and mountain lion that smelled the blood, he had better get busy. Rising, he gathered up rocks and small boulders. He had nothing to dig with, so he would do the next best thing.

It took forever, but at last Lin stepped

back and stared at the mound. Folding his hands, he said to the sky, "I suppose I should say some words. She was a good woman, Lord. She tended me when I had one foot in the grave. If that doesn't earn her a place in heaven, I don't know what would." He stopped, afraid that might offend the Almighty. "It is your decision, I know. If I were you, that is what I would do. But you do what you want." He searched his mind for a suitable quote. All he could think of were a few lines from the Old Testament. He was not sure he had them in the proper order, but he said them anyway. "There is a time to laugh and a time to weep, a time to heal and a time to kill, a time to be born and a time to die. Amen."

Lin stepped to the buttermilk and wearily climbed on. It was a long ride back to the Dixon ranch. The smart thing to do was make camp and go back in the morning. But he had Pat to bury yet.

"Damn stupid world," he said.

Stone was in the bunkhouse when word came to him. He bent his steps to the ranch house and discovered his employer in a rocking chair on the porch. "You sent for me?"

"That I did," Seth Montfort said. "It has

been too long. Lassiter and the others should have been back by now."

"Maybe they lost the trail."

"Could be, but Reb is a good tracker. He can track an ant over solid rock."

Stone let the exaggeration pass. "What do you want me to do?"

"Pick two men. One of them should be Frost. He can track almost as good as Reb. Find out what happened to Lassiter."

"I don't see the need, but you are paying me."

"I cannot help thinking of that day you tangled with Lin Gray. I particularly remember the look on his face. He is a tiger when aroused."

"But he was in no shape to lick Lassiter when he left," Stone noted. "Hell, he was in no shape to lick a kitten."

"Be that as it may, my gut feeling is to send you to find them. If by some miracle Lassiter is dead and Lin Gray is still alive, do whatever is necessary to remedy that mistake."

"Consider it done." Stone turned to go but stopped on the top step.

A rider was galloping toward the house as if he and his horse were on fire. Both were covered with dust. They came straight for the porch, and the rider drew rein. Leaning on the saddle horn, the rider bobbed his chin at Seth Montfort. "I am back, boss."

"I can see that, Williams."

"I went clear to Cheyenne, like you told me. About rode this animal into the ground, but I found out what you wanted to know."

"Do not keep me in suspense."

"Lin Gray is not Lin Gray. His real name is Lin Bryce. His brother is Chancy Bryce. They are wanted by the law. It seems a bank was set to foreclose on their ranch and they did not like it. The younger brother shot the banker, and Lin Bryce shot three men who were protecting the banker. Two of them are in the Cheyenne cemetery."

"You don't say."

"There is more. The banker is not happy about being shot. Word is, he hired quick-draw artists to plant the Bryces, permanent."

"Even better," Montfort said.

"There is more. The banker complained to the governor. He demanded a marshal be sent. Since he is rich and powerful, he had his way. A federal lawdog was due in Cheyenne any day."

"I like this more and more," Montfort said.

"I don't," Stone declared. "The last thing we need is a federal marshal nosing around.

Some of the leather slappers you hired will have to make themselves scarce."

"Let them. One way or another, I will be rid of Lin Bryce, and that is what matters."

"You are forgetting his younger brother."

"I forget nothing, Mr. Stone. It is why I am sitting here and you are not. The younger one is of no consequence."

"He shot that banker."

"But it was Lin Bryce who killed the two guards. Lin Bryce who fought you. Lin Bryce who rode over here as brazen as you please to warn me to stay away from Etta June." Montfort shook his head. "No, it is the older brother we must worry about. The younger will pose no problem."

"I hope you are right."

"Surely you have noticed by now that I nearly always am? But your advice is duly noted. Now, be so kind as to be on your way before the hour is out. If you find Lassiter, join forces, and if he has not disposed of Lin Bryce, handle it yourself."

"Neither of the Bryces will ever bother you again," Stone promised.

"Good." Seth Montfort gazed out over his ranch and began to rock. "Take an ax with you."

"What the hell for?"

"I want you to bring me Lin Bryce's head."

"You're serious?"

"Never more so. I have been thinking about Etta June. She betrayed my trust. Worse, she has apparently taken up with a man she hardly knows. Since she cares for him so much, I think it only fitting that I give her his head as a parting gift, you might say."

Stone laughed and slapped his leg. "You sure do beat all."

Seth Montfort smiled. "I do, don't I?"

CHAPTER 22

Mason lay quiet under the stars. No one was out and about. Light glowed in windows and voices wafted on the breeze.

A dog lying between buildings stirred as Chancy rode past but did not growl or bark. Chancy drew rein at the hitch rail in front of the saloon. A row of horses was already tied off. He had to tie the zebra dun at the very end.

Chancy took off his hat and swatted some of the dust from his clothes, then jammed it back on and ambled inside. The portly bartender was cleaning glasses. Two men from the settlement were nursing a whiskey bottle at a table. In a far corner sat Efram Pike, playing solitaire. Chancy sauntered over. "I got your message and here I am."

Pike glanced up and returned Chancy's smile. "I was beginning to think you would not make it."

"I suppose those gents you told Mrs.

Cather about have lit out?" Chancy said as he hooked a chair with a boot and slid it out so he could sit.

"You are in luck. They are still here," Pike informed him. "They should stray in shortly, and the fun can commence."

Chancy sat back and gestured. "Thank you for the invite. I am so sick of rounding up cows, I could kick one."

"Ranch work does not appeal to you?" Pike asked sarcastically.

"*Any* work does not appeal to me," Chancy said, and they laughed. He called out for the bartender to bring them a bottle. "This place reminds me of a watering hole in Cheyenne I was fond of. I spent many a night there drinking and gambling."

"How about your brother? Did he drink and gamble too?"

Chancy frowned. "Lin takes life more serious than I do. He can have no fun at all and be content."

"Not me," Pike said. "Which is why I refuse to break my back punching cows when I can earn twice as much shuffling cards. Throw in whiskey and women, and life is as good as it ever gets."

"When did you take up gambling?" Chancy idly inquired.

"About five years ago. I was down to

Denver at the time. Helped bring a herd up to Kansas and kept drifting. I was down to my last few dollars and sat in on a game and won big. That was when I got the notion."

"What in God's name are you doing here in the tules when you could be living high on the hog in a big city?"

"I ran into a lick of trouble and had to make myself scarce," Pike explained. "But I will not be here much longer. I expect to have enough money soon to see me to San Francisco. I hear it is wide open. Money falls into a man's lap."

"I have always had a hankering to see California," Chancy mentioned. He sipped his whiskey. "What do you know? It is not watered down. There is an honest barkeep left in the world."

Pike chuckled. "Honesty has never paid as well as living for yourself. It is only popular with Bible thumpers."

"Etta June believes in the Bible, and you are fond of her, as I recollect," Chancy said.

"I like her for her body, not her Bible. She is plain of face, but a man can always close his eyes and imagine."

"She will never let you in her bed. Not Seth Montfort, either, although he takes it for granted she will."

"Let's talk about something else," Pike said harshly.

"Sorry." Chancy downed more whiskey and set down his glass. "I hope these gents get here soon. I do not have all night to win their money."

"Oh? In a hurry to get back to the EJ, are you?"

Chancy nodded. "It is my brother. He has gone missing. I wanted to go look for him, but Etta June talked me into coming here instead."

"Gone missing how? Did he ride off after strays and never come back? Or did he go up into the mountains to hunt?"

"He went to have a talk with Seth Montfort."

"By his lonesome?"

"I wanted to go with him, but he refused to take me," Chancy said bitterly. "Told me he could handle it himself. But I suspect he was afraid my temper would get us killed."

"He might be dead anyway," Pike said.

Now it was Chancy who said irritably, "Let's talk about something else. I will find out soon enough. I aim to go straight to the Bar M from here."

"It is too bad none of their punchers are here tonight," Pike said. "You could ask them about him."

"If Seth Montfort has harmed Lin —" Chancy left the thought unfinished.

"What will you do?" Pike challenged. "It is you against — what — fifteen guns? More if you count Montfort's hands."

"That does not scare me."

Just then, three men in slickers and wide-brimmed hats filed into the saloon. The man in the lead was big and broad and wore twin Remingtons. He made for the corner table. "Pike," he said in greeting, and looked at Chancy. "Who is your young friend?"

"The one I told you about," Pike answered. "One of the Gray brothers. This would be Chancy."

"I am Lute Bass," the man said. He offered his hand and pumped with vigor. "I am right pleased to make your acquaintance."

"I hear you are powerful fond of poker," Chancy said.

"I am powerful fond of money. Cards are one way to get it, but not as reliable as other ways." Bass pulled out a chair across from Chancy and bellowed for the bartender to bring another bottle. "These are my pards," he said to Chancy. "The beanstalk with the Sharps is Rufus. He used to run buffalo, but the buffs have almost all died out."

"That they have," Rufus said with regret.

"I would shoot a hundred a day or better and live high on the hog."

Lute nodded at the third man, who was rubbing a salt-and-pepper beard. "This here is Mort. Don't let your boots stray near his chair, or you will have tobacco juice on them. He could not hit a spittoon if his life depended on it."

"How do you do, boy," Mort said, adjusting his holster as he sat so his revolver was in ready reach.

"I am a man, thank you," Chancy said. He did not like how they all grinned at that, even Pike.

"Of course you are," Lute Bass said.

Chancy took another swallow. "Are we here to play cards, or what?"

"Of course we are," Lute Bass said.

Pike produced a pack and began to shuffle. "When do I get that hundred dollars you promised me?" he asked Bass.

"When it is done and not before."

Chancy assumed they were talking about cards. "Those stakes are too high for my poke. You will have to come down some if you want me to play."

"We want you," Lute Bass said.

"So, what is it you do, exactly?" Chancy made conversation. "By those slickers I would judge you to be cattle buyers or some such."

"We are manhunters," Lute Bass said.

Chancy noticed that Rufus had placed the Sharps on the table so the muzzle pointed at him and that Mort had his hand under the table. His mouth suddenly went dry. "Are you hunting anyone in particular?"

"That we are," Lute Bass said. "We are hunting you."

Lin Bryce sat in the dark kitchen with his sixth cup of coffee in front of him. He had found his boots in a closet in the bedroom the Dixons had placed him in, and his feet as well as his belly were nice and warm. He wanted something stronger to drink, but he did not think it right to help himself to another man's liquor without asking first.

On the table in front of him were the Loomis shotgun and his saddlebags. His saddlebags were open, but he had not taken anything out.

The night was half over. Lin had been sitting there since before midnight. He was worried sick about Chancy and Etta June, but he could not leave until he was finished here.

Lin had considered writing a note but decided against it. The news must come from him in person. He owed Cody Dixon that much. He owed him a hell of a lot more.

He figured the three of them would not return until morning, and he was debating whether to have another cup or to try and catch some shut-eye, when the rumble of hooves proved him wrong. It was not long before boots clomped at the front of the house, and voices mingled.

"Light a lamp. And try to be quiet so we don't wake your ma and your sister."

A light blossomed out in the hall. Three shadows came to the wide doorway and stopped.

"You!" Cody Dixon exclaimed. "What the devil are you doing out of bed? My wife said you need three or four more days of rest."

Lin swept an arm at the chairs. "You might want to have a seat. All of you."

They looked at one another. The sons were mirror images of the father, except the older had sandy hair and the younger had caterpillars for eyebrows.

"What is this about?" Cody Dixon asked. "If it is to thank us, there is no need."

Lin would rather chop off an arm or leg than do what he had to do. "Did you find the riders your boys saw?"

"No, we did not," Cody said. "But it was

not for lack of trying. We found their tracks and followed them to a stream. I reckon they took to the water to throw us off. They could be anywhere by now."

"They came here," Lin said.

"What?"

"They lured you off so your women would be alone. Three of them are lying out back waiting to be buried. I did not have the time, or I'd have done the burying myself."

The full import was slow to sink in. Cody Dixon absorbed it first, and shot to his feet. "Pat and Sue! Where are they?" He turned toward the door.

"Gone," Lin said.

"Gone where? To Etta June's? To Mason? Did you send them away so they would be safe? I will be forever in your debt. They are everything to me."

"They are dead, Mr. Dixon."

Cody Dixon paled and reached for the table to brace himself. Tyler and Hank were speechless with shock.

Lin related the events at the house, and the aftermath. He left out the worst parts. "I am sorry," he concluded. He was saying that a lot lately. "I did my best, but I could not save them."

"Lord, no," Cody breathed. His eyes were closed and his whole body was shaking.

"No, no, no."

Tyler and Hank were fighting back tears, and Hank was losing the battle. His voice broke as he asked, "What do we do, Pa? What do we do?"

Tyler spoke up, his voice breaking. "We fetch their bodies. They should be buried here, not up in the high country."

"I would not do that, were I you," Lin advised.

"You are not us, mister," Tyler said. "They are our mother and our sister. We will bury them proper."

Cody had opened his eyes and was red in the face. For a few moments Lin feared he would explode in rage and go rushing out to slay Seth Montfort. But the father kept his head. "By the time we got up there they would be starting to rot. It is better we leave them be and treasure our memory of them than see them bloated and ripe."

"Oh, God," Hank said.

"The important thing now," the father went on, "is to deal with Montfort. He is to blame. He must pay."

"Let's ride to the Bar M and do it!" Tyler urged.

"And play right into Montfort's hands?" Cody shook his head. "His men would shoot us to pieces before we got close enough. Besides, according to Lin here, the man we want even more than Montfort is this Lassiter. He has made me a widow and you motherless."

"Then, let's go after him." Tyler was quick to agree.

"We will at first light," Cody said. "Provided Lin can give us an idea of where to pick up his trail."

All eyes swung to Lin. "I have a better idea," he said. "Instead of wearing yourselves out trying to find Lassiter, why not have him come to you?"

"How do we do that?" Tyler scoffed. "Send him an invite?"

"In another week or so, Montfort will carry out his threat to drive you out or hang you," Lin said. "He will bring his assassins along, and Lassiter is bound to be with them."

"There will be too many for the three of us," Cody said. "I do not want to lose my boys too."

"The four of us," Lin amended. "Five if you count my brother, Chancy, and six if I can persuade Aven Magill to lend a hand."

"You and your brother would do that for us?"

"I would do it for my own sake," Lin said. To make amends for not saving Pat and

Sue, and to have a personal reckoning with Seth Montfort. "My brother might do it to back me. As for Magill . . ." He shrugged.

"I like your idea," Cody Dixon said.

Lin finished his coffee in a gulp. "I will leave for the EJ at first light. If all goes well, I should be back in four or five days with my brother and Magill and all the ammunition Etta June has to spare."

"We have plenty," Tyler told him.

"I have an old keg of black powder down in the root cellar," Cody mentioned. "I hear tell that if you rig a fuse, you can blow a man — or a lot of men — to kingdom come."

"Then, we are agreed," Lin said, looking from one to the other. "We will make our stand here."

"I did not ask for this range war, but I will by God end it," Cody Dixon vowed. "Now, if you will excuse me." He rose and moved toward the hall. "I have held in my grief too long, and it is not seemly that anyone else see."

Both his sons drifted after him, leaving Lin to ponder the coming battle, and to voice aloud a heartfelt, "God help us."

CHAPTER 23

Chancy tilted his glass to his mouth, then smacked his lips and said, "You don't say."

Lute Bass' eyebrows met over his nose. "You are taking it awful calm, boy. Or do you think I am joshing?"

"I told you before," Chancy said. "I am no boy."

"Don't you want to know who hired us? Or why? Or how much we are being paid? Those are the usual questions."

Chancy glanced at Rufus and the Sharps pointed at him, then at Mort with his hand under the table, and he shook his head. "It doesn't much matter, now, does it?"

"That is damn sensible of you," Lute Bass said. "But I will tell you anyway. We were hired by that banker you shot, Pettigrew. He was not content with siccing the law on you. He doubts you will be hung, and he wants you dead. You and your brother, both."

"It is a good thing you found me first and not Lin."

"Why is that?"

"Because if I was Lin, you would already be dead," Chancy said. He drained his glass and put it down.

"Big talk, boy. And yes, we have heard how he is supposed to be greased lightning and hits what he aims at, but folks say the same about me. And Mort and Rufus are no slouches."

Chancy looked at Efram Pike. "This is why you came out to the EJ? To get me here so they can kill me?"

"A hundred dollars is a lot of money when you do not have more than ten to your name," Pike said. "Nothing personal. I like you. But I like the idea of San Francisco more."

"Maybe you should change your handle to Judas." Chancy began to refill his glass, pouring slowly. "I reckon I should treat myself to one more before you start throwing lead."

"I have done my job and am out of it," Pike said.

Lute Bass sat back. "Go ahead, boy. We will not begrudge you a last drink. But no tricks, hear? That Sharps is the same as a cannon. It will blow you near in half."

Chancy glanced at the rifle and inwardly smiled. Rufus had neglected to pull back the hammer. "I don't suppose I can talk you out of this?"

"You can flap your gums until you are blue in the face and it will do you no good," Lute Bass confirmed. "When we take a job, we always see it through. That is part of why we are paid more than most manhunters."

"What is the other part?"

"We are like that outfit that wears the red coats up in Canada. We always get our man."

"Must make you proud."

"Now, now," Lute Bass said. "Let's keep this civil. Or are you going to be one of those who spews insults and carries on?"

"I will do as my brother says to do, and stay calm," Chancy said.

"The more I hear of him, the more it is a shame I have to kill him." Lute Bass fingered his glass but did not lift it. "Where is he now, by the way?"

"I have plumb lost him," Chancy replied.

"Listen. I have a proposition for you. How would you like to live a little longer?"

"Little as in minutes?"

"Little as in days. You do something for us, and we will not kill you here and now," Lute said.

Chancy laughed. "You want me to do a favor for vermin who have been paid to feed me to the worms?"

"There you go again with the insults." Mort broke his silence. "The next will be your last."

"That it will," Rufus confirmed.

Lute Bass motioned at them. "Take it easy. He can save us a lot of effort if he will cooperate."

"What is it you want me to do?" Chancy stalled.

"Did you have any schooling? Can you write? Some of those we hunt can't do more than make an *X* for their name."

"I can scribble some, although it looks more like chicken scratches," Chancy said. "Our ma thought it important we learn the alphabet."

"Good," Lute Bass said. "We will get paper and ink, and you will write what I tell you."

"If it's a letter to Pettigrew asking him to call you off, I am all for it," Chancy said. He casually slid his right hand to the edge of the table.

"It will be to your brother," Lute Bass said. "Asking him to come to Mason right away."

"You are ridiculous," Chancy said.

"If you do it, you get to live until he shows up. Wouldn't you like that? The two of you bucked out together rather than one at a time?"

Chancy chuckled while sliding his other hand to the table's edge. "You should sell ladies' corsets."

Rufus bleated like a sheep. "That was a good one, Lute. I could see you doing that too."

Bass' eyes grew flinty. "I am doing you a favor, boy. In return, you do us one. That is fair, isn't it?"

"Fair for you; stupid for me," Chancy said. "What kind of scum do you take me for? Betray my own brother? If you are not drunk, you should be." He planted both his boots flat on the floor and braced himself.

Efram Pike was laying a black eight on a red nine. "I don't suppose you could take this to another table and let me play my solitaire in peace?"

"If you want your hundred dollars, you will shut up until we are through," Lute snapped.

"I won't be talked to like that."

"I will talk to you or anyone else as I damn well please," Lute Bass declared. "We are conducting business, and you pester me with a trifle."

Pike slapped the deck down. "I might need your money, but I do not need to put up with you. Give me the hundred and go somewhere else."

"No tinhorn tells us what to do," Lute Bass said coldly.

"Listen to the pot call the kettle black," Pike said. "As man killers you three would make great store clerks."

"Be careful," Lute Bass said.

"I will have my money and I will have it now," Pike demanded. "If not, I will send all three of you to an early grave."

"The hell you say."

The moment Chancy had been waiting for had come. All three manhunters were looking at Pike. Tensing, he heaved upright, upending the table as he rose. Then he clawed for his Colt.

Etta June, seated on the top step of her porch, was gazing up at the stars, when her youngest came out and sat beside her. "You are supposed to be in bed, Elizabeth."

"I can't sleep, Ma."

"Why not?" Etta June draped an arm across her shoulders. "Something you ate?"

"No. I am worried about Mr. Gray."

"I am worried too." Etta June kissed her

daughter on the forehead. "It is sweet you care."

"Do you care for him, Ma?"

"The questions you ask."

"What?" Beth snuggled against her. "Tommy says he might be our new pa."

"It is too soon to talk like that," Etta June said. "I would have to know him — or any man — a good long while before I commit to that."

"He is nice, isn't he?"

"Very nice. The nicest I have met since your father passed on. But nice is not always enough. When you are a grown woman, you will understand."

"Tell me, Ma. I want to understand now."

Etta June stroked her daughter's hair and leaned back. "A husband and wife are more than two people agreeing to live together. They need to be in love."

"Like I love you and you love me?"

"Like that, but different. I love you with all my heart, and I loved your father with all my heart. But I do not love you like I loved him."

"I am confused, Ma," Beth admitted.

"I was too, at your age. It wasn't until I met your father that I understood."

"Why?"

"Because until I met him, I had no idea

what the other kind of love is like. Oh, I knew about it in my head, but I had never felt it in my heart. His smile, the way he talked, everything about him, kindled the new love inside of me until it burned like the brightest flame."

Beth giggled. "You make it sound like you were on fire."

"In a way, I was. You will be too one day, when the right man comes along. You might think you won't. You might think it will never happen to you — that you are different from every female who ever lived. But you are not. It happens to all of us whether we want it to or not."

"I have no say at all?"

"Not where love is concerned, no," Etta June said. "You can fight it. You can hide in a shell, but it will drag you out."

"Now I am scared," Beth said.

Etta June smiled and squeezed her shoulder. "It is nothing to be afraid of. It has happened to every woman since the dawn of time. Think of it as a seed deep inside you, and when the right moment comes — when the right man appears — that seed takes root and buds."

Beth laughed and patted her tummy. "I have a seed inside me now? Wait until I tell Tommy."

"I would rather you didn't. This is just between us. Mother to daughter, and no one else."

"One of our special talks?"

"Yes, one of those."

They fell quiet, staring at the heavens, until Beth stirred and said, "I am not sure I want to grow up."

"We have no choice," Etta June said.

"You keep saying that. But didn't you tell me once we always have choices?"

"Back when we had our talk about right and wrong, yes," Etta June said. "I told you to think of life as a path. Every now and then you will come to a fork, and you must decide which path to take."

"How do we know which is the right one?"

"Sometimes we don't. Sometimes we must guess. Sometimes we pick the wrong one through no fault of our own."

Beth looked up at her, worried. "I wish I could stay as I am now forever."

"Life does not let us."

"Who made things this way? God?"

Etta June stared at the sparkling points in the sky. "So the Good Book says. 'In the beginning, God created the heaven and the earth,' " she quoted.

"So God made women and God made

men and God made love. Is that how it goes?"

"You learned about Adam and Eve, remember?"

"They were in a garden, and they were bad, and God was mad at them."

"They took the wrong path," Etta June said.

"Will God be mad at me if I take the wrong one?"

Etta June cupped her daughter's chin. "Your brother never asked questions like these."

"You don't want me to ask them?"

"You can come to me anytime, about anything. I may not always know the answers, but I will share all I know, and you can use it for what it is worth." Etta June rumpled her hair. "Now, let's get you back into bed."

Beth hugged her tight. "I want to stay with you. It is nice out here, and I am not tired yet."

"Very well," Etta June said reluctantly. "I don't often let you stay up past your bedtime, but I will make an exception tonight."

"Tell me more about Mr. Gray. About what it is about him that you like so much."

Etta June sighed and gazed across the valley into the night. "Some things are hard to put into words. It is like when you see a real pretty flower. You want to tell everyone how pretty it is, but words are not enough to describe the prettiness."

"Is there no way, then?"

"Not unless you are an artist and can paint or sculpt, and even then —" Etta June stopped. "I will be honest with you. I should not be saying this, but the moment I set eyes on Lin, something deep down inside of me stirred. It is why I asked him and his brother to come work for me. I want to get to know him better, to see if the stirring continues."

"Now you sound like you are a stew, Ma."

Etta June chortled. "Kids say the darnedest things. But what it boils down to is this. Tell your brother that if I do decide Lin will be your new pa, I will let you know well in advance."

"Why isn't he back yet? Tommy says Mr. Montfort might have hurt him — hurt him bad."

"I need to have a talk with your brother tomorrow."

"Is Tommy right?"

"I don't know, little one." Etta June shivered, but she was not cold. "All we can do is wait and pray Lin makes it back to us alive."

"If he doesn't, will you be sad?"

"Very sad."

"As sad as you were when Pa died?"

"I have changed my mind. I am getting you to bed."

"Aw, Ma."

CHAPTER 24

As Chancy Bryce drew, he whirled toward the door. For once he was doing what his brother always said he did not do often enough: he was using his head. The three manhunters would disentangle themselves from the table and the chairs at any moment. He could shoot them, but he might take a slug or two himself. So he was getting out of there.

Chancy was halfway across the room when a revolver blasted and lead buzzed his ear. He twisted, saw that both Lute Bass and Mort were partway to their feet and snapped off a shot at Mort, who was taking aim to shoot again. Whether he hit him, Chancy could not say, but both ducked behind the table, gaining him the precious seconds he needed to plunge on out into the cool night air.

The hitch rail was only a few yards away. Chancy bounded toward the zebra dun. He was almost to it when inside the saloon the big Sharps boomed, the window shattered into shards and the top of the zebra dun's head exploded in a gory shower.

Stunned, Chancy stopped in his tracks as his horse crashed to the ground. He had been fond of that dun. He had ridden it for years.

His only recourse was to steal one of the other mounts tied to the rail. He would have too, but boots pounded inside, galvanizing him into whirling to the west and racing down the street. A pistol cracked, but the shot did not come close.

Chancy smothered rising panic. He was outnumbered and on foot. But he was still breathing and he was unhurt, and he had an ally in the dark. The three killers could not shoot what they could not see. He reached the last of the buildings and kept running. A score of yards out, the ground suddenly seemed to give way under him. He stumbled, tried to recover his footing and sprawled onto his hands and knees. Pain shot up both legs.

He had fallen into a small hollow, a depression no bigger around than a small room. Scrambling to the top, he removed his hat and peered over.

Figures were moving toward him.

"Where did he get to, damn it?" Lute Bass snapped. "I was sure he came this way."

"He has to be around here somewhere," Mort said. "We should spread out and hunt him down."

"I will watch the street," Rufus said. "Odds are, he will try for a horse, and when he does, I will do him like I did his animal."

"Doubling back is what I would do," Lute Bass agreed. "I will take the south side of the street; Mort, you take the north."

They separated and turned back toward the settlement.

Chancy sank flat and jammed his hat back on. For the moment he was safe. But he could not stay there all night. Once they were convinced he was not hiding in Mason, they would scour the surrounding prairie. They would find him.

Chancy was under no delusions about the outcome. He was a fair hand with a Colt, but he was not Lin, and something told him all three of the manhunters were uncommonly good at dispensing death.

Lin. Chancy wished his brother was there. Then again, maybe it was best he wasn't, since Lin still refused to go around heeled. Chancy could not understand why. If Lin had not shot those men, they would have shot Chancy. In the back. For Lin to keep kicking himself over it was pointless.

Suddenly Chancy stiffened. A boot had crunched. He thought they were all back in Mason, but one must be somewhere close. Slow footfalls came nearer. He stared at the top of the hollow, waiting for a silhouette to appear. The instant it did, he would fire.

To his great relief, the steps faded.

Chancy waited a couple of minutes, then crept from concealment. He figured to circle around to the other side of Mason, sneak back in and help himself to a mount. Rufus was keeping a lookout, but he would deal with the buffalo runner when the moment came.

A twig cracked under Chancy's foot. He froze, hoping none of them heard, but one did. Footfalls pattered, coming in his direction. They slowed, then stopped. Chancy swore he could hear breathing. Every nerve in his body tingled.

Then someone swore, and the footsteps moved away.

It had sounded like Mort.

This time Chancy stayed put a good fifteen minutes before he began circling Mason. When he was past the last of the buildings, he cat footed to the east end of the street. It was deserted save for the horses. Everyone was wisely staying indoors to reduce their risk of taking a stray slug.

The sight of the zebra dun lying in a pond of blood set Chancy's blood to boiling.

A figure stepped into the street at the far end: Rufus, cradling his Sharps. He crossed to the other side and disappeared between buildings.

Chancy hunkered and sought some sign of the others, but they did not show themselves. His patience frayed. He never did have much to spare, and he was tired of the cat and mouse.

The wind gusted. A flapping noise drew Chancy's attention to clothes on a line behind the last house on the left, on the other side of a rickety picket fence. Wash hung out to dry had been left there until morning.

An idea blossomed. Chancy moved toward the fence. It was so low, he easily stepped over. Among the articles hung to dry were a man's homespun shirt and pants. He took the shirt down and held it to his chest. It was much too big. He raised it over his head to slip it on over his own shirt, when without warning the door opened and a rectangle of light splashed over him.

"What the hell?" a man demanded loud enough to be heard in Montana. "What do you think you are doing, mister?"

Chancy dropped the shirt and ran. Without breaking stride, he vaulted over the fence and wheeled to the north.

The night abruptly rocked to revolver shots. Chancy felt a jarring blow to his left shoulder. *He had been hit!* He spun, saw a form rushing toward him and replied with two shots of his own. Whoever it was either fell or went to ground.

Chancy resumed running. A wet sensation spread down his back and arm. Pain flared. He gritted his teeth to keep from crying out. A bellow from Mort spurred him to run faster.

"Over here! He is over here! I think I winged him!"

Chancy fled for his life. He ran and ran, losing all sense of distance and time. He grew sweaty all over. His breaths came in great gasps. A new pain in his side hurt worse than the wound. When he finally glanced back, the lights of Mason were fireflies. He touched his side. His shirt was soaked with blood.

Chancy plodded on. He became dizzy — so dizzy he thought he would be sick. His limbs grew weak. It was all he could do to hold his head up, and presently even that was beyond him.

The night seemed to fade into blackness.

His last thought, as consciousness deserted him, was that this was not how he wanted to die.

A golden crown framed the horizon when Lin Bryce forked leather and headed east. After an hour he left the grassland behind and wound up a trail into heavy timber. The morning air was crisp, birds were warbling. Occasionally deer bounded off with their tails held high. Squirrels scampered in the upper terrace.

All was as it should be. Lin had no reason to suspect he was in danger. Then a hornet nearly stung his cheek, and a heartbeat later the flat *crack* of the shot rolled down over him. He was out of the saddle before the echo died, diving onto his shoulder and rolling up into a crouch behind a pine.

The buttermilk pranced a few yards but stopped when Lin softly called to it.

The forest had gone quiet. Not a single bird chirped.

Lin scoured the slope above for the shooter. He had an idea who it might be.

The stock of a Winchester Cody Dixon had lent him jutted from his saddle scabbard. Lin fought an impulse to try for it. The ambusher was probably waiting for him to do just that.

Lin glanced at his hip and frowned. When would he learn? he asked himself. He still had not taken what he needed out of his saddlebag. Chancy would call him an idiot, and Chancy would be right.

Suddenly a rifle boomed and slivers of bark stung Lin's face. The bushwhacker had changed position. Lin flattened and crawled to a log.

A taunting laugh confirmed his hunch. "Did that one nick you?" Lassiter hollered.

Lin wanted to keep him talking. "I expected you to be back at the Bar M by now!"

"We have unfinished business, you and me!" Lassiter's voice came from a different spot. He was on the move. "You shot my pards!"

Peeking over the log, Lin shouted, "Liar!"

"What?"

"I know the real reason you want me dead!"

"Is that so?" Lassiter had stopped moving. "I am curious to hear it."

Lin suspected he was in a stand of spruce eight feet away. "You think if you kill me, Seth Montfort won't find out what you did to Pat and Sue Dixon."

"Are you saying he will?"

"I am not the only one who knows. So do

Cody Dixon and his sons."

"I figured you would tell them." Lassiter was moving again, but slowly. "I will deal with them after you are out of the way."

"You will try." Lin was bluffing. He was unarmed. He needed that rifle, or better yet, his six-shooter.

"I am going to enjoy killing you more than I have ever enjoyed killing anyone!" Lassiter shouted.

Lin crawled toward a thicket. For a few harrowing seconds he was in the open and his skin crawled with the expectation of being shot. But he made it unscathed, and crouched. He began to work toward the buttermilk, and the rifle in his scabbard.

That no more shots rang out puzzled him. Lin paused every few yards to scan the vegetation. Lassiter was there somewhere, but where?

The buttermilk began nipping grass.

Lin came to a large bush. Another fifteen feet and he would have the Winchester. He sought sign of movement above him, but there was none. Balancing on the balls of his feet, he hurtled forward. Two, three, four strides he took, his hand rising toward the scabbard.

The undergrowth near the buttermilk parted and Lassiter stepped out, his rifle jammed to his shoulder. "Stop or die!" he commanded.

Lin stopped, his fingertips tantalizingly close to the saddle.

"You make it too easy," Lassiter said. "Spread your arms wide."

Scowling, Lin held them out from his sides. "Damn me for a fool," he complained.

Smirking, Lassiter said, "You took the words right out of my month."

"Go to hell."

"Temper, temper," Lassiter said, and laughed.

"Tell that to your friends who wound up in an early grave at the Dixon ranch," Lin responded.

Lassiter sighted down the barrel. "I would not remind me of that again, were I you."

"So, what now?" Lin asked, squaring his shoulders. "You finish me off and go your merry way?"

"I am in no hurry," Lassiter said. "I am like a cat. I like to play with my prey before I kill it."

"I know," Lin said. "I saw what you did to Sue Dixon."

"She was fine, that one. Fought like a wildcat, just like I like them to do. I still have the scratches to prove it."

"You are a miserable bastard," Lin said.

"It was too bad I had to shoot the mother. I would have liked to do the same to her as I did to her girl."

"A miserable, rotten bastard."

"You are repeating yourself," Lassiter mocked him. "Forget about me and start thinking about yourself. Which leg? Which knee? That sort of thing."

"Which what?"

"You will die slow," Lassiter said. "A piece at a time. I will shoot you in the knee or an elbow and then maybe in the hip, and when you are down and helpless I will go on shooting until you are dead or I am bored."

"If you think I will beg for my life, you are mistaken."

"They all say that, but only a few have the grit not to," Lassiter replied. "Not that it matters. I go on shooting them anyway."

"What about my horse?" Lin asked.

"It is a fine palomino," Lassiter said. "But I am partial to my own animal. I will sell yours and use the money to stake me in a poker game."

A glimmer of hope rose in Lin. He knew something Lassiter did not — something that might save his life. "Be sure you get what my horse is worth. He is no hammerhead."

"Can he fetch sticks?" Lassiter asked, and

cackled.

"No, but he knows other tricks," Lin said.

Lassiter glanced at the buttermilk. "Suppose you show me? But be careful. This rifle has a hair trigger."

"Watch," Lin said. He whistled and made a fist and pumped it three times, as if striking the ground, and the buttermilk proceeded to stamp a front hoof three times. Lin whistled again, then bobbed his chin up and down, and the buttermilk bobbed its head.

"Will you look at that?" Lassiter said by way of praise. "You sure have trained him good." He took a step toward the horse. "What else can he do?"

"There is one trick that is better than the rest," Lin said. "It took a week before he could do it right."

"I would like to see it." Lassiter took another step.

Lin recalled the day his father gave the buttermilk to him — recalled how proud he had been. He remembered the hours and days he spent afterward teaching it to stamp and bob its head, and one other trick.

"What are you waiting for? Show me."

Lin pursed his lips to whistle. The next few moments would determine whether he lived or died.

CHAPTER 25

The smells confused him.

Chancy figured he would wake up in the place that was all fire and brimstone and reeked of sulfur. But he smelled tobacco and a lilac fragrance and a tart odor that made him think of pickles in a pickle barrel.

The fog that shrouded his mind faded. Chancy opened his eyes and was more confused than ever. Instead of stars or the daytime sky, he was staring at rafters in a low ceiling. Glass tinkled, and Chancy turned his head.

Abe Tucker was filling a jar with hard candy. The store owner had an apron on and wore a frown. He was muttering under his breath as he worked.

Chancy had to try twice to talk. Moistening his mouth, he croaked, "Am I in your store?"

"Land sakes!" Abe bleated, and nearly dropped the jar. "Don't scare a body like that! I didn't know you had come around."

Chancy was on his back on the counter, a blanket covering him to his chest. He tried to sit up but lacked the strength. "What in God's name am I doing here? Help me down."

The store owner scooted to his side. "Nothing doing, son. You lie there and take it easy. You lost an awful lot of blood. It is a wonder you are alive."

"But how did I get here?" Chancy wanted to know. The last he remembered was being shot and running off across the prairie.

"They brought you," Abe said sourly.

"They who?"

"Who do you think? The three assassins that banker hired to find you and your brother."

"You know about that?"

"Everyone does by now. They did not make a secret of it." Abe paused. "Somehow they heard I have mended a few folks, so when that buffalo hunter tracked drops of blood to where you were passed out, they brought you here."

Chancy looked down at himself. His shirt was gone and his shoulder had been bandaged. "I am surprised I am still alive."

"You are not the only one," Abe Tucker declared. "It is my understanding they are being paid a lot of money to turn you and your brother into worm food."

Chancy looked anxiously around. "Where are they now?"

"Where else? They went to the saloon for a drink. I expect them back anytime now."

Once more Chancy attempted to rise, but all he could do was raise his shoulders. "What on earth is the matter with me?"

"Didn't you hear me say you lost a lot of blood?" Abe replied. "And when I say a lot, I mean if you had lost another drop, you would be buzzard bait. That you are still breathing is the closest thing to a miracle I have ever come across."

"Help me to a horse," Chancy said. He would have Tucker tie him on if need be.

"No."

"I beg your pardon?"

"You heard me. Where would you go? You can't ride — the shape you are in. And there is no place I can hide you that they wouldn't find you. Your best bet is to lie there and regain your strength." Abe lightly patted Chancy's good shoulder.

"Damn you, old man. They are out to kill me. If you do not help, I am as good as a goner and my brother, besides."

"If I do help and they catch us, I am a goner, too." Abe shook his head. "I am sorry. But I will do what is best for you whether you think it is best or not."

The front door opened, and in strolled Lute Bass and his companions. Bass swaggered along the aisle as if he owned the world. He chuckled when he saw that Chancy was awake. "Have a nice nap, did you, boy?"

"Give me my Colt so I have a fighting chance," Chancy said. "I would rather die a wolf than a sheep."

Lute Bass folded his arms across his chest. "You are getting ahead of yourself. We want you alive for the time being. So long as you don't give us cause to regret it, alive is how you will stay."

"Why so generous?" Chancy asked suspiciously.

"You are more use to us alive than dead. For the time being, anyhow," Bass amended.

"You aim to use me for target practice?"

Lute Bass chortled. "Now, there's a notion. But no. We aim to use you as bait."

Chancy did not like the sound of that. "Bait for who?" The answer came to him on its own, and shock brought him up on an elbow. "No! You can't."

"Who is to stop us?" Lute Bass asked.

Mort and Rufus laughed.

"Your brother will not ride in of his own

accord," Lute Bass said. "He must be persuaded, and there is no better persuasion than the life of someone he cares about. We expect him by the end of the week."

"One of you is going to fetch him?" Chancy asked. That would whittle the odds for him.

"How dumb do you take us to be?" Lute Bass rejoined. "I have already sent the saloon owner's son."

"My brother won't believe him," Chancy predicted. "He will think it is a trap."

"It *is*," Lute said, smiling. "But to make sure your brother believes we have you, we sent your shirt along. The bullet hole and the blood will convince him where words could not."

Chancy was horrified. His brother would come racing to his rescue and be met by a hailstorm of lead.

Lute Bass had turned to Abe Tucker. "That reminds me. Friday morning we are closing this fleapit down."

"My store?"

"No, jackass. The entire damn town. Everyone is to stay indoors or go for a picnic up in the mountains. We don't care which, so long as no one is on the street."

Abe sputtered, found his voice and exclaimed in outrage, "See here! You can't tell us what to do. We won't stand for it."

Lute stepped to the jar Abe had been filling and helped himself to a piece of hard candy. "You do not exactly scare us with your bluster, old man. Nor do the good people of Mason. Three are women, withered prunes who could not harm a fly, and the men are like you, rabbits who have crawled into a hole and pulled the dirt in after them so the world will leave them be."

"If I were twenty years younger —" Abe shook a bony fist.

"You would still be a rabbit," Lute said. "The thing for you to keep in mind — the thing for you to hope — is that me and my pards do not decide to go rabbit hunting after we are done with the Bryces."

"You wouldn't."

Rufus was rubbing a dirty hand over a corset on display. "There is not a creature west of the Mississippi I have not killed. If Lute says we rub you out, then by God you will be rubbed."

"Do not provoke us, old man," Mort threw in.

Abe Tucker subsided and walked toward the back, muttering. He slammed the door after him.

"Feisty cuss." Lute Bass grinned and faced Chancy. "Now, then. Back to you. We have rounded up all the horses, so don't get any fool notion about riding off on one."

"We didn't round up yours," Mort corrected. "It is still lying over by the saloon. The biggest mound of flies you ever did see."

"And it is commencing to stink," Rufus said. "Give it another day or two and the people in this town will want to kill you their own selves."

"You shot my animal," Chancy said. He yearned to have a pistol in his hand so he could avenge the zebra dun.

Lute Bass grinned. "That he did. And you and your brother are next on our list."

It was a common enough trick. Once, in Cheyenne, Lin saw a man perform it with four horses at once.

Lin whistled and raised an arm over his head. The buttermilk obediently reared, its forelegs swinging out and up.

Lassiter was standing so close, he had to jump back to avoid being struck. In doing so, he forgot to keep his rifle trained on Lin. It was the opening Lin needed. Springing, he grabbed the rifle with both hands and tried to tear it from Lassiter's grasp. But Lassiter clung on, cursing furiously, and kicked viciously at Lin's knee. Lin sidestepped, shifted and swung the rifle in a half circle. Lassiter, caught off guard, held on, but stumbled and almost fell. Instantly, Lin drove forward, bowling the sadistic monster over. They both went down, Lin on top. His full weight smashed onto Lassiter's chest even as Lin drove a knee into his gut.

Lassiter's grip weakened. With a powerful wrench, Lin tore the shotgun free, then brought its stock down on Lassiter's head. Once, twice, three times, he struck, and at the third blow, Lassiter went limp.

Lin slowly stood. He stared at the rifle, a Henry with a shiny brass receiver, then threw it aside. Turning, he walked to the buttermilk. For a moment he hesitated, but only for a moment. Opening a saddlebag, he reached in and slid out a bundle wrapped in a towel. He unwrapped the towel and placed it in the saddlebag.

"So it has come to this," Lin said softly to the object he was holding, a coiled gun belt with a holster and a Colt. A perfectly ordinary belt, a perfectly ordinary holster. No fancy studs or conchas, no etching. Nothing distinguished it from thousands of others of its kind.

The Colt in the holster was the most common model available. It did not have nickel plating and was not engraved. The grips were plain wood, not pearl or ivory. The only difference between this Colt and others was that the barrel had been shortened from seven and a half inches to four and three-quarters. It was a .45-caliber.

Lin thought back to when he turned sixteen and his parents let him order the Colt and holster through the mail. It took forever. Thereafter, he spent every spare minute practicing: shooting, twirling, loading as fast as he could. He discovered he had a talent he never suspected. Even his father had been impressed, so much so that he had sat Lin down and warned him about the dangers of resorting to a revolver in the heat of anger, or to show off. Lin never forgot some of that advice.

"Those who live by the gun die by the gun, son. Don't ever kill if you can help it. Once you do, it is hard to stop. You have the power of life and death in your hand. Use that power wisely."

Lin strapped the belt around his waist and secured the buckle. He adjusted the holster so it was high on his right hip, the grips even with his elbow. Sliding the Colt out, he ran a hand over it, then verified the cylinder was loaded. He gave it a few tentative spins, forward, then backward, then flipped it into the air and caught it by the grips, thumbing back the hammer as he did. He let down the hammer, spun it a few more times and twirled the Colt into his holster and patted it.

"I can avoid you no longer."

Lassiter groaned.

Lin turned to the buttermilk, and his canteen. He opened it and stood over the killer. "Time to die," he said, and upended the canteen.

The water got into Lassiter's nose, into his mouth. Sputtering and coughing and flailing his arms, he sat up. "What the hell?"

Lin stepped back and let the canteen drop at his feet. "Rise and shine," he said.

Blinking and wiping his face with a sleeve, Lassiter growled, "You knocked me out, didn't you, you son of a bitch?"

"Your head is not as hard as I thought it would be."

Lassiter touched a bump and winced. "You about caved my skull in."

"I wasn't trying to kill you," Lin said.

"What now?" Lassiter snapped. "You shoot me with my own —" He stopped, looking puzzled, and glanced about them. "Wait. What did you do with my rifle?" He spotted the Henry gleaming brightly in the grass. "Why is it over there?"

"I don't need it to do what I have to do."

Lassiter looked at Lin — at his waist — and his eyes widened. "I'll be damned. I must be seeing things."

"You aren't," Lin said.

"And here I thought you didn't even own a six-shooter." Lassiter began to rub the bump, then stopped. "Why haven't you drawn your pistol?"

"I am waiting for you."

"You are what?" Lassiter glanced down at his own holsters, at the Merwin and Hulbert revolvers. His face mirrored amazement. "I do not believe it. You have not disarmed me."

"I would never shoot an unarmed man," Lin said quietly, "or murder a defenseless woman."

Lassiter looked up. He had it, then. "Do I get to stand?"

"You do."

Chuckling, Lassiter rose and shook himself. "Of all the boneheaded stunts, this beats all. I will be telling this one for years."

"No, you won't," Lin said.

Lassiter flexed the fingers of both hands. "Mister, I have not shot all those I have killed in the back, if that is what you believe."

"Back or front, it makes no difference."

"For a cowhand, you think awful highly of

305

yourself." Lassiter lowered his hands next to the Merwin and Hulberts. "Anything else to say before I put windows in your skull?"

"Just that I am sorry," Lin said.

"For what?"

"For killing you."

"I am not dead yet."

"You will be," Lin said matter-of-factly.

Their eyes locked.

The moment had come.

CHAPTER 26

Lassiter was no longer amused. "Enough of this!" he snarled, and his right hand stabbed for a revolver. He had not quite touched it when his elbow exploded.

Crying out, he gaped at the smoke curling from the muzzle of Lin's Colt.

Lin twirled the Colt back into its holster and let his hand drop to his side. "You have one more."

"This can't be!" Lassiter blurted in disbelief.

"Are you any good with your left?" Lin asked.

"You will find out," Lassiter declared, and went for the other revolver.

In a blur, Lin drew and shot him in the left elbow, and then twirled the Colt into his holster.

A bawl of rage and pain keened from Lassiter. He glared at his ruined elbows — at the dripping blood and the bits of flesh.

"You have shot my arms to ribbons!"

"I am just starting." Lin calmly drew and, without deliberately aiming, shot him in the right knee.

Howling in agony, Lassiter fell. He tried to clutch his shattered kneecap, but his arms would not work as they should. "Damn you!" he fumed. "Damn you to hell!"

"That was for Pat Dixon," Lin said. "This is for Susan." Lin shot him in the other knee.

Screeching and swearing, Lassiter thrashed wildly, his teeth clenched against the torment.

Lin watched while replacing the spent cartridges. By the time he was done, Lassiter lay still, cursing without stop. "How does it feel?"

"Do you think this is funny, you son of a bitch?"

"Not at all," Lin assured him. "I did not think what you did to Sue Dixon was funny, either." He placed his thumb on the Colt's hammer. "It is good you are as tough as you are."

"Belittle me all you want," Lassiter hissed.

"I meant it as a compliment."

"Why good, then?"

"Because it will take you a long while to

die," Lin said, and shot him in the right thigh.

More thrashing and swearing ended with Lassiter lying spent and caked with sweat and blood. "Enough," he gasped. "Kill me and be done with it."

"No."

"Is this your idea of justice?"

"It is my idea of vengeance."

Lassiter tried to sit up but failed. "Listen. I have close to four hundred dollars in my saddlebags."

"Good for you."

"It is yours if you will mount up and ride off," Lassiter offered. "What do you say?"

"You are a wonderment."

"Then you will do it?"

"Was Sue Dixon alive when you rode off? Her mother does not count because you only shot her."

"You miserable, rotten, stinking —"

A flick of Lin's thumb, a squeeze of his finger, and a .45-caliber slug cored the killer's other thigh.

Lassiter flopped about like a stricken fish out of water, subsiding only when he was too exhausted to move. Blood seeped from the six holes in his body. "End it, damn you," he rasped.

"You do not like it as much when the boot

is on the other foot, do you?"

"What kind of damn-fool question is that?" Lassiter practically screamed. "I have never been in so much pain."

"That is nice to hear. I was afraid it would not get worse after the first couple of times."

"How much more do you intend to do?"

"I have a spare box of ammunition in my saddlebags," Lin said. "It is nearly full."

"Oh, God."

Over the course of the next half hour, Lin shot Lassiter in one ankle, and then the other; in one shoulder, and then the other; in one wrist, and then the other; in one shin, and then the other. After each shot, Lassiter bucked and blistered the air with oaths, but each time he bucked a bit less and blistered a bit less, so that after Lin shot him in the second shin, Lassiter did not buck or blister at all, but lay a quivering wreck.

"Please," Lassiter begged.

"No."

"You are inhuman."

"You have no room to talk."

"I hate you. I have never hated anyone as much as I hate you."

"That will persuade me." Lin finished reloading and twirled the Colt into his holster.

Lassiter's tear-stained face rose a few

inches. "Answer me true. How much more? When will you end it?"

"You have ears; you have fingers; you have toes."

"I am serious, damn it."

Lin smiled. "So am I."

Lassiter swallowed. "I was wrong about you. You are no cowhand. You can't be. How come I never heard of you? People like us — the word gets around."

"We are nothing alike," Lin said.

Lassiter looked down at himself. "Now it is you who are wrong. We are exactly alike, you and me."

"I was raised on a ranch. My whole life was cows and work. You are the fourth man I have shot."

"God," Lassiter said, and laughed. "Done in by an amateur."

"I do not like to shoot people," Lin said. "I do not like to kill." His voice hardened. "I am a peace-loving man driven to do that which he does not want to do by those who think God gave them the right to ride roughshod over everyone else. You, Stone, those other gun sharks, Seth Montfort — none of you care who you hurt. You prod and push and take human life like people are flies, and expect to get away with it. But this time you have pushed and prodded too hard, and taken your last human life."

"A nice speech," Lassiter said. "But there is only one of you. Before this is done, Seth Montfort will piss on your grave."

"I have changed my mind," Lin said, and shot him between the eyes.

For a while he stared down at the body; then he sighed and slid another cartridge from the loops on his belt. "One down and a small army to go."

Chancy was dozing when the front door creaked and boots clomped.

Seth Montfort and Stone and three others cut from the same coarse cloth came down the center aisle. To say they were surprised to find him there was an understatement.

"What is this?" Montfort asked, plucking at the blanket. "You have opened a hotel as well as a store?"

Abe Tucker was leaning on the other side of the counter. "Don't get me started."

Montfort regarded the bandage and smirked at Chancy. "Got yourself shot, did you? Well, it will make things easier." He snapped his fingers at Stone. "Be so kind as to finish him off."

At that, Lute Bass stepped out of the shadows, his big hands on his Remingtons. "No, you don't. I need him alive."

Stone was about to draw, but he stopped and said, "Lute?"

"It has been a spell, Isaac," Lute Bass said. "I did not know you were in this neck of the woods."

Seth Montfort glanced from one to the other. "You know this man, Mr. Stone?"

"We are in the same trade," Stone answered. "We have worked together a few times." He introduced them.

"I am pleased to meet you, Mr. Bass," Montfort said, shaking. "And I will be even more pleased if I can add you to my payroll."

"I would let you if I was not working for someone else," Lute Bass said, and nodded at Chancy. "Me and a couple of others have been hired to make wolf bait of this one and his older brother."

"You don't say."

Stone looked down at Chancy and laughed. "Damn, boy. You have stepped in it up to your knees. If not us, it will be them. If not them, it will be us."

"Go away and let me rest," Chancy said.

"Yes, go away," Abe Tucker said irritably. "It is bad enough my store has been turned into a hospital."

Seth Montfort made a clucking sound. "Is that any way to talk to a paying customer? I am on my way to visit Etta June and need to buy a present. Do you still have that china bowl she admired some months back?"

"I do."

Montfort turned to Lute Bass. "I will not dispute your claim to the boy and his brother. You are doing me a service, and I am grateful. After you are through with them, look me up."

"I might just do that," Lute Bass said.

Abe Tucker came around the counter. "Do you want to see that bowl or not? I cannot stand around all day listening to people jaw."

"You have become a grump in your old age," Seth Montfort said.

"No, I have always been one," Abe retorted. "And people who waste my time only make me grumpier." He moved toward a shelf lined with dishes and bowls, and Montfort followed.

"Someone should take that old coot out and treat him to a few lashes from the bullwhip," Stone remarked. "He will learn to be sociable real quick."

"Since when do you care about sociable?" Lute Bass asked, and laughed.

"Now that I think about it, not ever."

The two walked toward the front. Stone's current companions tagged along, leaving

Chancy alone on the counter. He glared at the whole bunch, his trigger finger twitching. Abe Tucker did not have a monopoly on grumpiness. Chancy was fit to spit nails. He wanted out of there, shoulder wound or no shoulder wound.

Unknown to Lute Bass, Chancy's strength was returning. He was not his normal self yet, but neither was he puny and helpless. Given half a chance, he would slip away from Mason, borrow his brother's revolver and return to settle accounts. But he had to keep his head and not make his move until he was sure he could get away.

Unfortunately, Chancy did not have a lot of time. Lin was due to show up the next day. Unless Chancy warned him, his brother would ride right into the trap Bass had set up. Ride in, but not ride out.

Chancy blamed himself. If he had kept his temper when the banker, Pettigrew, came to call, they would not be on the run. If only Pettigrew had not been so eager to throw them off their land. If only Pettigrew had not been so insulting. The final slur, for Chancy, had come when Pettigrew commented that their father had not planned wisely in the event of his death, leaving his poor wife to drink herself into an early grave.

Outraged, Chancy had shoved Pettigrew and told him to shut up. Pettigrew had told him to keep his hands to himself. When Chancy had pushed him again, Pettigrew had reached under his jacket. Chancy had assumed the banker was about to draw a pocket pistol or a derringer, and he had done what any man with common sense would have: He had whipped out his Colt and shot Pettigrew in the shoulder.

Lin liked to say that it was smart of him to shoot the banker in the shoulder and not the head or the heart, but the truth was, Chancy had shot him in the shoulder by mistake. Chancy had aimed at Pettigrew's chest, intending to shoot the man dead, but Pettigrew had turned to run.

It was then that the banker's protectors had sprung to his aid and gone for their hardware, forcing Lin to shoot all three. Lin had not wanted to kill them, and now he could not forgive himself. As far as Chancy was concerned, they had gotten their due.

An argument between Abe Tucker and Seth Montfort drew Chancy out of himself. They were haggling over the price of the china bowl. Apparently Montfort, the richest man in all the Big Horns, was also the most miserly; he was trying to talk Tucker down five dollars.

It occurred to Chancy that if anyone knew what had happened to his brother, it would be Montfort. Accordingly, when the dickering ended and the pair returned to the counter, Chancy set right in. "My brother came to see you a while ago, didn't he?"

"That he did," Montfort confirmed.

"Why isn't he back at the EJ yet?" Chancy asked, amending it with, "At least, he wasn't when I left to come here."

"You have seen the last of your brother," Seth Montfort declared.

Chancy rose onto his elbows. "What do you mean? He went to your place to deliver a message. What did you do to him?"

"When he left he was still alive."

"Then why did you say that?" Chancy demanded.

"If he is not at the EJ by now, obviously something must have happened to him." Montfort motioned at Tucker. "Put the bowl for Etta June on my account. And wrap it, if you please."

"Want me to shine your boots too?"

"You try my good nature, old man."

Chancy could not shake a terrible feeling about Lin. "How do I know you didn't have my brother shot for trespassing?"

"Give me more credit than that, would you, boy?" Montfort said in contempt.

"Would I want word to get back to Etta June and have her run to the law? No, I would not. I made it a point to see that he left my place in one piece."

"I don't believe you."

"And I don't give a good damn what you believe." Montfort snatched the china bowl from Tucker. "On second thought, forget the wrap. I will not stand here and be insulted by this good-for-nothing. I am leaving." Wheeling, he stalked out.

Abe Tucker snickered. "You sure riled him, son."

Newfound vigor was coursing through Chancy, courtesy of his anger. "I have just begun to rile."

CHAPTER 27

With the big sugar gone, the bunkhouse was noisier than usual.

Seth Montfort was strict about the rules he set down. His punchers were to do as he demanded, or they could pack their war bags and find work elsewhere.

There were a lot of rules. "No drinking" was first and foremost, anywhere on the Bar M, at any time. "No gambling" was next on the list. "No women" was third, with an exception for married punchers, whose wives could come visit from time to time so long as they did not stay the night. That none of his hands were married did not stop Montfort from making the rule.

Other rules had to do with how they should dress, and how they should act, and how they should talk. The "no swearing" rule was loosely enforced because even Montfort realized his hands could not help it. The bronc buster was one example; he regularly swore up a storm when he was thrown. But Montfort never punished him. To the contrary, Montfort complimented him on his "colorful mix of every oath known to man."

Of all the rules, the one the punchers disliked the most had to do with what they considered to be none of their boss's business: cleanliness. Montfort required that each hand take a bath once a month — whether the hand wanted to take a bath or not. To the punchers this was outrageous. They did not understand why Montfort made a fuss over a little dirt and stink. Some regarded baths as harmful to their health. It was common knowledge that too much bathing made a person sickly. As one puncher put it, "If I turn puny, it will be his fault."

On this particular night, with Montfort gone, several of the punchers broke out flasks. A card game was started, and two men went into a corner to throw dice.

Most of the hands, though, refused to break the rules. They had given their word, and breaking it was the one thing they never, ever did. So they sat and talked. Or wrote letters — those who could write. Or read books — those who could read.

Those who broke the rules and those who

did not all had one thing in common. They wanted nothing to do with the three new men who had been given bunks at the far end of the bunkhouse. The new men were not punchers. They were gun sharks Montfort had recently hired. They were left behind, as he told them, to "keep an eye on things." As Montfort explained it, he would not put it past the Dixons to show up and cause trouble. Indeed, Montfort was hoping they would, thereby giving him an excuse to dispose of them and take possession of their land.

The hired assassins sat by themselves, playing poker. The rules were supposed to apply to them, but they were not the least bit loyal to the brand. They were loyal to the dollar. So long as they were paid, they would do what they were hired to do.

The hubbub of voices rose to the roof. Despite the presence of the pistoleros, the punchers joked and laughed and told tall tales, as was their wont. A puncher named Oliver was in the middle of a story about his visit to a house of ill repute and his encounter with a gilded lily who he claimed was as big as a boxcar, when the front door opened and in walked a tall, broad-shouldered man with hair the color of straw.

All conversation ceased. Men froze in the

act of turning a page or sipping from a flask or even opening their mouths to speak.

The broad-shouldered man stood blocking the only way out and did not say anything. He wore an ordinary Colt, his big hand next to the holster.

Finally Wiley, who was near the door, cleared his throat and gruffly asked, "What in hell are you doing back here, mister?"

"I am looking for your boss," Lin Bryce said.

"He has gone to Mason and then to see that filly he is interested in," Wiley returned. "I do not know when he will be back."

"That is too bad," Lin said. "I was hoping to end it tonight." He scanned the rows of bunks, and his gaze settled on the three men by themselves at the far end. Taking a few steps, he called out, "You there. Unless I am mistaken, you are not cowhands."

The three put down their cards. They rose and came down the aisle, two in the front, the last trailing. Bar M punchers moved out of their way to clear a path.

"No, we are not," said one of the foremost assassins. He was short and stocky and favored a cross-draw.

Lin said, "You do not have the look of men who do an honest day's work for an honest dollar."

The three swapped glances. When they were twenty feet from Lin, they stopped, and the man at the rear stepped up to stand shoulder to shoulder with the other two.

"Mister," said the short killer, "I cannot believe how stupid you are. Didn't pistol-whipping you teach you anything?"

"It taught me not to be pistol-whipped," Lin replied.

"You were stupid to come back, but I thank you," said another. "We will be paid extra for blowing out your wick."

Wiley was quick to interject, "Mr. Montfort does not want to upset Etta June Cather, remember?"

"She will not be upset if he is not involved," the short killer said. "We are doing this on our own. You are all witnesses that Montfort had nothing to do with it."

"He hired you," Wiley said.

"Do not prod us, you old goat," the short man warned. "You have your job, and we have ours." He turned to Lin. "You are a mess, mister. You look as if you were stomped by a bull. I bet you are so stiff and sore, you can hardly move."

"You will find out directly."

"Three to one," the short man said. "Odds we can live with."

"Or die by."

323

"You have sand, mister," said the second quick-draw artist. "Or is it that you are so dumb you don't know when you have stepped in it?"

"I have not been too smart," Lin conceded. "I should have finished this when I was here before. I will not make that mistake twice. I might be slow, but I learn my lessons."

The short man grinned. "I reckon you never learned the one about baiting a wolf in its lair."

"Start the dance whenever you are ready," Lin said.

The second assassin gestured. "It is too bad Stone and Lassiter are not here. They are keen on doing you themselves."

"Stone will get his try," Lin said. "Lassiter already had his."

The short man blinked. "What?"

"Lassiter and the three who were with him," Lin said. "They will not be coming back."

"You curled up the toes of all four?"

Lin nodded.

"You are a damned liar!" declared the second man. "I have seen Lassiter practice, and there are few as fast."

"There is always someone better," Lin said.

The short killer tensed. "Hogwash. You are trying to put fear into us, and it will not work."

"Whether you are afraid or not, the end will be the same," Lin informed him. "If you care to make peace with your maker, I suggest you do so."

The third man snorted. "Will you listen to him? As brazen as brass. Let's fill him with lead and see how brazen he is."

The punchers on bunks near the three assassins were quietly moving back to reduce the risk of taking a stray slug. Wiley, though, stayed where he was, saying to Lin, "For what it is worth, I did not beat on you when the others did. Some of us cannot abide Montfort's antics of late."

"That is good to hear." Lin swept the rest of the hands with a steady gaze. "Stay out of this, and none of you will come to grief."

Young Andy, who was on a bunk next to Wiley, shot to his feet. "I don't much care for the airs you put on."

"Hush, pup," Wiley said.

"I will not," the young puncher declared. "Our boss made it plain this jasper is not welcome on the Bar M. I think we should lend the lead chuckers a hand and throw him off the ranch."

Before Wiley could respond, the short

shootist said curtly, "We do not need your help, boy. Yours, nor any of this cow crowd. And we are not tossing him off the spread. We aim to bury him on it."

"Stay out of it," said the second killer.

"None of you are worth a damn with a gun, anyhow," remarked the third.

The insult did not go over well. Cold glares were fixed on the three curly wolves, and a puncher Lin had not seen before took a step toward them.

"I will listen to no more bluster. I have worn a six-shooter since I was old enough to strap one on. I might punch cows for a living, but that does not mean I cannot shoot the head off a prairie dog at ten paces if I am so inclined."

"Prairie dogs do not shoot back," said the short killer. "Now, hush, and let us earn our pay." He faced Lin and squared his shoulders. "All right, mister. Whenever you are ready."

Lin sighed. "Can't you just ride off? I would rather not kill you if I can help it."

"Sprout a yellow streak all of a sudden?" the man mocked him.

"I have no hankering to spill more blood, is all. Maybe the keepsake I brought will persuade you to change your minds."

"Keepsake?" the man repeated. "What in

hell are you talking about?"

Lin reached into a shirt pocket. "Here," he said, and tossed what he took out in a high arc.

The gun shark caught it in both hands, took one look and recoiled in shock. "What the hell!" He dropped it as if it were a hot coal, and it fell to the floor with an audible *plop.* "It is an ear!"

Everyone stared. Adam's apples bobbed, and several men looked fit to be sick. One covered his mouth.

Wiley glanced from the ear to Lin and back again. "Whose is it?" he quietly asked. "As if I can't guess."

"Lassiter's."

A cowpuncher laughed.

The three hired guns did not find it anywhere as amusing. They spread out, and the short one shook a fist at Lin.

"This is supposed to convince us to spare you? Are you loco? He was our friend."

"I doubt Lassiter was anyone's friend," Lin said.

The man looked at the ear. "I get what you are up to. You figure you can scare us. But it won't work. There are three of us, and you can't drop us all before one of us drops you."

"Yes, I can," Lin said.

One of the killers splayed his fingers over his revolver. Another tucked at the knees.

"I will ask you one more time," Lin said. "Walk out and ride off, and you can go on breathing."

The man on the left, the finger splayer, spat on the floor. "To hell with this nonsense, and to hell with you."

"Now!" the short man shouted.

The trio went for their six-shooters.

Lin drew and fanned his Colt three times. Fanning was an iffy proposition unless the fanner knew exactly what he was doing and could hit what he was shooting at. Lin seldom missed.

Each of the gun sharks was jolted by the impact of a .45-caliber slug coring his forehead. Hats, hair and bits of bone and brain sprayed over the floor and bunks and some of the punchers. None of the three cleared leather. Life faded from their wide eyes as their bodies plopped to the floor. The short man twitched, then was still.

Lin began reloading.

"God in heaven!" a puncher exclaimed.

"I saw it, and I still don't believe it!"

Wiley moved to the crumpled forms and felt the wrist of each. "They are dead, sure enough."

"What do we do?" asked a cowhand at the back.

"There are eleven of us."

Wiley looked sharply at him. "And how many are willing to die? I am not, but you go right ahead if you are of a mind to."

"We were hired to ride herd on cows, not swap lead."

Young Andy stepped to the center of the aisle. "Listen to me, all of you! We should do what Mr. Montfort would want us to do, and he does not want this gent on the Bar M."

"Be quiet, infant," Wiley said.

"I will not. I have as much right to speak as you or anyone else. And I am loyal to the brand even if you are not."

"How dare you, boy," another puncher said.

Andy said loudly, "Either we shoot this bastard or we keep him here for Mr. Montfort to deal with when he gets back."

Lin slid his Colt into his holster. He did not expect them to stop him. So he was mildly surprised when he started to turn and one of the cowhands barked a command.

"Stay right where you are! We have not decided what to do with you yet."

"I have decided," Wiley said. "He is free

to light a shuck."

"You are not the boss," Andy disagreed. "We do not have to listen to you." He lowered a hand to his holster.

Lin did not have a quarrel with any of them. He said so, adding, "Don't do this. Let cooler heads prevail, and all of us will live to see the dawn."

"You are slick with a six-gun, and you are slick with words," young Andy said. "But there are more of us than you have pills in the wheel. Unbuckle your gun belt and let it drop."

Wiley took a step toward him. "Damn it, kid. Leave it be."

"Am I the only one here with a backbone?" Andy asked, and answered his own question by swooping his hand to his revolver.

CHAPTER 28

They left Chancy alone in the evenings. They assumed he was too weak to go anywhere. So Lute Bass and Mort and Rufus would leave him there, and after Abe Tucker locked the door, they drifted over to the saloon.

They figured his wound would keep him on that counter until they were ready to take him off it and stake him out in the street as bait for his brother.

They figured wrong.

The general store had been dark and quiet for only a couple of minutes when Chancy slowly sat up. He was not fully recovered, but he had more vigor than they suspected. Enough that he could slide his legs over the side and carefully ease down until he stood panting slightly and leaning against the counter to keep from falling.

By now Chancy knew where practically everything in the store was to be found, and he made straight for the shirts and selected one that fit. Getting it on took some doing since his shoulder protested any and all movement. But by gritting his teeth, he succeeded. Next he found a hat to his liking. They had taken his Colt and his gun belt, but Tucker kept half a dozen revolvers in stock and had a few gun belts on pegs on the wall. Ammunition was stacked on a shelf.

Chancy started for the door, then stopped. Tucker fed him twice a day but never enough to suit him. He was always hungry when he was done eating, yet Tucker refused to give him more.

"I have to pay for your food out of my own till," the store owner complained. "You do not get to make a pig of yourself."

Selecting a can of beans, Chancy opened it and went to the front and warily watched the street as he ate. The zebra dun still lay where it had dropped. No one had bothered to strip off his saddle and saddle blanket, perhaps out of fear of Lute Bass and his friends.

Chancy's anger resurfaced, boiling hotter than ever. They had killed his horse and they had shot him, and he would be damned if he would let them use him to lure in Lin. He had decided to buck out as many of them as he could before they brought him down.

Chancy and Lin had been close growing up. They did chores together; they played together. It was not until their pa died that they drifted apart, largely because Chancy took to spending too many nights in Cheyenne, neglecting his share of the work. Chancy knew it was wrong, but he couldn't help himself. He was mad at the world and he resented everyone and everything in it. His temper, always quick to flare, became quicker.

Chancy regretted shooting the banker, Pettigrew, but he did not regret it that much. Only to the extent that thanks to Pettigrew, Lin and he were on the run. But what was done with was done with.

Chancy focused on the here and now. He spooned out more beans and thoughtfully chewed.

Most every male in Mason was at the saloon by now. So far as he knew, no punchers were there; Montfort was long gone. Nor, to his knowledge, had any strangers shown up. It would be him against the three killers. Hopefully, no one would interfere.

Chancy finished eating and set the can and the spoon on top of a pile of towels. He moved the shade and peered out again.

Stars had blossomed. Many of the windows glowed with light.

Turning, Chancy went down the aisle, past the counter and down a short hall to the back door. He worked the latch and poked his head out. No one was in sight. Slipping out, he left the door ajar and moved with his back to the wall to the corner.

A gap between the buildings was plunged in shadow. He crossed to the saloon.

The back door was not bolted. The first room he came to had a stove and a sink and enough empty liquor bottles to fill a Conestoga. Drawing the Colt he had helped himself to, he crept down a short hall. Voices reached him, mixed with laughter and the tinkle of chips.

Chancy swallowed. He had never killed anyone before. For all his cockiness, he was not like Lute Bass and Bass' ilk. He was not a coldhearted killer.

Steeling himself, Chancy stalked forward. His shoulder hurt, but otherwise he was feeling fine. Just shy of the light that spilled into the hall from the main room, he halted.

Seven men were present, not counting the bartender. The three he was interested in were at a table indulging in cards. None were looking his way.

334

Chancy raised the Colt. He had a clear shot at Mort's back and at Rufus but not at Lute Bass, who sat on the other side of the table, across from Mort, and it was Bass who Chancy wanted most of all.

Chancy debated whether to wait for Mort to move or to shoot whom he could. He centered the Colt smack between Mort's shoulder blades. All he had to do was squeeze the trigger. He curled his finger around it and grimly smiled. *Here goes,* he thought to himself.

But his finger did not tighten.

Chancy swore under his breath. Again he gave the mental command, and again his finger would not do as he wanted. It seemed to have a mind of its own. But the truth was, Chancy could not bring himself to shoot someone in the back. In the front, yes, like Pettigrew, but not like this.

Chancy was mad at himself. He tried a third time. But his hand shook so badly, he could not hold the revolver steady enough to aim. "Damn me," he said under his breath. "I am next to worthless."

Unexpectedly, Mort stood. "I better go check on the boy. We do not want him sneaking off on us."

Chancy hated being called a boy. He almost shot Mort then and there.

"Sit back down," Lute Bass said in that deep voice of his. "He is in no shape to go anywhere."

"I would not be so sure," Mort said. "And a lack of backbone can do wonders."

"Meaning he might crawl off on us?" Lute Bass said.

Chancy burned inside. Now they were saying he was a coward. He never could abide slurs, and these rankled.

"Yellow is as yellow does," Rufus said. "He is a miserable little worm, and worms should be squished."

Before he could stop himself, Chancy stepped into the open. "Who are you calling a worm, you wretch?"

Lin almost felt sorry for the young puncher. Almost. But it did not stop him from drawing and putting a slug into Andy before the cowhand could draw and put one into him. He did not shoot to kill but shot him high in the shoulder.

Andy staggered back, letting out a yip, and would have fallen had Wiley not leaped to catch him.

"He . . . he . . . he shot me!" the young hand bleated, and went limp.

"He's dead!" a puncher roared.

"No, he is not!" Wiley said. "He fainted."

The smoking Colt in Lin's hand dissuaded anyone else from trying Andy's stunt. But many of their faces betrayed fury and resentment. It was one thing for Lin to shoot the shootists; it was another for him to shoot one of their own. "You all saw," Lin said. "He forced me."

"You better skedaddle, mister," Wiley advised. "I am on your side, but Andy is one of us."

"No one drills a Bar M hand and gets away with it!" declared a beefy cowhand near the wall on the right.

Lin began to back out. He had no quarrel with these men. "Don't come after me."

"We better not catch you on the spread come morning."

"You won't." Stopping in the doorway, Lin said, "Give your boss a message. Tell Montfort that if it were up to me, this would end here. But the deaths of the Dixon women are on his shoulders, and I will not —"

"What's that?" Wiley broke in. "Pat and Sue Dixon are dead?"

"Lassiter killed them."

"Oh, hell," Wiley said.

"They were fine ladies," said another. "They always had a smile and a kind word for me."

"For everyone," a third man chimed in.

"What about Cody Dixon and his sons?" Wiley asked.

"Alive and out for blood," Lin informed him, thinking it prudent to add, "They do not hold any of you to blame — only the gun crowd and the one who hired them."

"This is not good," a hand said.

Yet another puncher nodded. "I don't know as I want to belong to an outfit that kills women."

"But it wasn't us. It was those hired killers."

"Hired by the same gent who hired us."

"Hell, hell, hell," Wiley said.

Lin had more to say. "If your boss steps foot on the EJ, he will not step foot off it. As for the Dixons, it was all I could do to keep them from coming here to avenge Pat and Sue. They still might."

"I would not blame them," Wiley said. "And I would not stand in their way. They have a right to vengeance."

"That they do," a lanky puncher agreed, and turned toward a bunk. "This is the last straw for me. I will be gone at first light. Anyone who wants to tag along is welcome."

"I'll go with you," said someone across from him. "I hear a spread down to the Green River country is hiring."

"But Mr. Montfort! We can't up and

338

desert him."

"The hell we can't!"

The argument grew heated. No one noticed when Lin slipped out into the cool of the night and hurried to the buttermilk. Gripping the saddle horn, he forked leather. He reined around to ride to the north but did not use his spurs. His gaze had drifted to the ranch house — to Montfort's home and hearth, the crowning glory of Montfort's years of toil.

"Dare I do it?" Lin asked aloud. He gigged the buttermilk and rode around to the rear. No one tried to stop him. The punchers were still in the bunkhouse.

Dismounting, Lin tried the back door. It opened without a sound. Inside, it was quiet, but he doubted the house was empty. The servants were bound to be there.

The first room Lin came to was the kitchen. A lamp was lit and a pot of coffee was on the stove, so he was right about the servants. He began opening drawers and cabinets. A stack of towels caught his interest. He heaped them on the floor at the base of a wall.

Holding the lamp aloft, Lin went into the parlor and set the curtains on fire. Flames were climbing toward the ceiling, and tendrils of smoke were coiling in the air when he bent his steps back to the kitchen. Hunkering, he soon had tongues of red and orange licking at the towels.

"That should do it," Lin said. He rose and started for the back door, but he had taken only a couple of steps when a battering ram slammed into him low in the back. The next moment he was on his stomach with a weight on his hips and a knee gouging him in the spine. He twisted, and a fist caught him on the jaw.

It was the servant in the white uniform who had answered the door the day Lin was pistol-whipped.

Lin heaved up off the floor and the man tumbled but came up on the balls of his feet with the swiftness of a cat. Lin pushed to his knees, saying, "I don't want to hurt —" He got no further. A fist to his temple jarred him.

The man could hit.

Lin raised an arm to ward off another blow. He tried to stand, but a kick to his leg nearly upended him.

The manservant circled. He had curly black hair and dark eyes that glittered like coals. "I can't let you," he said.

"My fight is with Montfort," Lin said.

"I am in his employ. He depends on me."

"Let's talk this out," Lin suggested. "I am

armed and you are not. What chance do you have?"

Lin barely jerked aside in time when the man's foot flicked out. He threw a punch, but the other skipped lightly out of reach.

"You are slow, mister."

"Rub salt in it, why don't you?" Lin set himself, but he could not stop the servant from darting in close and landing two lightning jabs. Neither hurt all that much, but Lin had bigger concerns. At any moment punchers might come out of the bunkhouse, see the house on fire and spread the alarm. Lin would be up to his neck in outraged hands. "This is pointless."

"Not if I stop you from burning down the house."

"The parlor is already on fire."

"You didn't!" the servant bleated, aghast.

"Run for help if you want," Lin said. It would give him a chance to escape out the back. "I will not try to stop you."

The servant glanced at the towels. They were ablaze, and soon the flames would spread to the floor and the walls. "You have ruined my livelihood. Montfort will fire me over this."

"Then he is not worth working for." Lin figured the man would stop fighting and get out of there.

341

Instead, the servant darted to a drawer and wrenched it open so hard, a large knife and a spoon spilled out. The man did not stoop to pick up the knife. He reached into the drawer, and when he turned, he was holding a meat cleaver. "I will see you bleed."

"Think again," Lin said, and patted his Colt. "Take my advice, and fan the breeze."

"If you are going to use it, you better use it now."

"Be sensible."

"How is this for sensible?" the servant asked, and attacked, swinging the meat cleaver as if he had gone berserk.

CHAPTER 29

The three manhunters were rooted in surprise long enough for Chancy to take a couple of steps to the right so he had a clear shot at Lute Bass. "Not so much as a twitch!"

The bartender had become a statue. The other customers were likewise frozen.

Lute Bass recovered his composure first to say, "Here I thought you were as weak as a kitten, boy."

"You thought wrong," Chancy said.

The bartender found his voice and bellowed, "Here, now! I will have no more tables upended or anyone shot!"

"Anyone who wants to be a Good Samaritan is welcome to try," Chancy said, wagging the Colt.

No one did.

Rufus shifted in his chair. His Sharps was propped against his leg, and his hand was on the barrel. "Big talk, boy, but me and my pards do not impress easy."

"You will have to prove yourself to us," Mort said.

"Get rid of your six-shooters and the buffalo gun," Chancy said. "Place them on the floor one at a time; then raise your arms."

Lute Bass leaned on his elbows. "That is not going to happen, boy. We are calling your bluff. If you have sand, we have not seen much evidence of any." He sat up. "It was a mistake coming here. You should have stole a horse and lit a shuck."

"Don't do anything stupid."

"Or what?" Lute Bass laughed, then looked at his companions. "What do you say, gents? Should we show this simpleton that he has bitten off more than he can chew?"

"Don't!" Chancy said. He had not counted on this. He should shoot them now — shoot them where they sat before they could resort to their artillery. But once again he could not bring himself to do it. As a man killer he was downright pitiful. All that time he had spent strutting around with his pearl-handled Colt, it had never occurred to him that he might be one of those people who could shoot other people only in self-defense. He began to wish he *had* lit a shuck.

An unlikely ally reared his head in the

form of the bartender. This time he was addressing Lute Bass. "I told you before, I do not want my place shot up. Take this outside."

"Polish your glasses and leave us be," Bass said.

But the bartender was not intimidated. "I have a scattergun under this bar, and I am not afraid to use it."

"We will pay for any damage," Lute Bass said, "and give you an extra fifty dollars, besides."

The owner stepped back from the bar. "In that case, feel free. All I ask is that you try to spare my mirror. It takes forever to order a new one. I had to send clear to St. Louis the last time."

"We cannot make any promises, but we will try." Lute Bass grinned at Chancy and slowly unfurled from his chair. "Now, then, boy. With that out of the way, we can have our little affray."

"Don't you care that you might die?" Chancy asked, racking his brain for a way out of the predicament his stupidity had put him in.

"We all go sooner or later. Fretting over it gets us nowhere."

Rufus nodded. "We are none of us masters of our fate. When our time comes, it comes, and there is nothing we can do."

Mort gestured impatiently. "Enough of this jabber. Let's bed this kid down and be done with him."

"I do not die easy," Chancy said with as much conviction as he could muster. "I will take all of you with me."

"A regular badman, are you?" Lute Bass said, smirking.

All three laughed.

Chancy's mouth went dry, but his palms were sweating. "I shot Pettigrew, or have you forgotten?"

"You winged him," Lute Bass amended. "And you did not finish him off after. A real killer would have."

They knew, damn them, Chancy realized. But he continued to bluff. "That does not prove anything."

"Only that you are not a natural-born killer like me and my pards," Lute Bass said. "You are a boy playing at being a man. You are soft and pretending to be hard."

"I am sick of all this talk," Mort growled. "Let's do him and get back to our drinking."

Chancy regretted coming so far into the room; they could easily drop him before he reached the hallway.

"Nothing more to say, boy?" Lute Bass asked.

"I thought you wanted me alive as bait for my brother." Chancy clutched at a last straw.

Bass' grin made him think of a rabid wolf. "We can stake you out dead. If we blindfold and gag the body, he will have no cause to suspect you are not breathing."

"Until it is too late," Rufus stressed.

Lute Bass slid his hands close to his Remingtons. "Ever wondered what it will be like? Dying, I mean?"

"No," Chancy admitted. Dead was dead to him. He used to believe in heaven and hell, but then his pa died a senseless, horrible death, crushed to bits under that horse. It showed him that either there was no God, or the Almighty had a cruel sense of humor. "I don't feel sorry for you one bit," he said.

Lute Bass' brow knit. "What is there to not feel sorry for?"

"When my brother comes after you, there is no place in Wyoming you can hide."

"In the first place, if what Montfort told us is true, your brother might not be alive. In the second, I am not scared of him or any other mother's son. Let him come after us. We are counting on it. And I welcome the challenge."

"And if Lute doesn't get him," Rufus said, patting his Sharps, "I will put a bullet in his back from a thousand yards out."

Mort smacked the top of the table. "Talk, talk, talk, talk, talk! Damn you girls, anyway." His hand dipped and came up holding his revolver.

Chancy shot him. It happened so fast, he had no time to think. He saw the revolver rising. He pointed and fired. At the blast, Mort rocked in his chair and looked at his chest in amazement.

"Mort?" Rufus said.

"The kid has killed me!" Mort exclaimed. Blood trickled from a corner of his mouth, and he was racked by a violent fit of coughing that ended with him falling forward.

Lute Bass and Rufus galvanized to life, Bass going for his Remingtons, Rufus snatching up his Sharps.

Chancy had begun backing toward the hallway. He snapped off another shot, not really aiming, and was as astounded as anyone at the result.

Rufus' head snapped back. His mouth opened and closed, but no sounds came out other than a sucking noise. Bit of broken teeth and blood came dribbling over his lower lip. He started to rise, but his legs gave way and he pitched from his chair to the floor.

The slug had gone in the front of Rufus' mouth and blown out the rear of his skull.

Lute Bass appeared to be in shock. Both of his friends down, mere seconds apart.

Chancy whirled and ran. He was almost to the doorway when a revolver boomed and lead bit into the jamb. Another blast filled the saloon, but he was in the hall and racing madly for the kitchen. His shoulder throbbed, but he did not care. The important thing was to go on breathing.

Chancy did not look back until he was at the rear door. To his consternation, Lute Bass had not come after him. He hurtled out into the night and turned to the right. He had no place in mind to go to. He was running blind.

Chancy flew past three buildings. He rounded a corner and sagged against a wall, out of breath. He was shaking. Shamed by his behavior, he smacked his chest. He was not as fearless as he thought he was, and the revelation was disturbing.

The only good thing about the whole mess was that two of the bastards were dead. Chancy smiled. Maybe he was not completely worthless, after all.

Suddenly a revolver cracked and slivers

peppered his cheek.

Lin threw himself back just as the cleaver flashed past his face, the razor edge missing his eyes by the width of a cat's whiskers. Searing pain and heat flared up his legs, and he glanced down to discover he had stepped on the burning towels. He sprang clear, smoke rising from his pants, and for a moment forgot about the manservant. A reminder came in the form of a stinging sensation in his left hand.

Out of the corner of his eye, Lin saw the man raising the cleaver to split him down the middle. He skipped to one side and glanced at his hand. A sick feeling came over him, and the kitchen spun.

One of his fingers was gone. The little finger had been chopped off at the knuckle. There was surprisingly little pain, but he was bleeding, and bleeding badly. Shock tried to seize him, but he shook it off and jammed the stub against his side to staunch the flow.

The servant was coming at him again, weaving figure eights in the air with the meat cleaver. He was grinning at his feat. "That was only the beginning," he said.

"Wrong," Lin said. "You will whittle on me no more." He drew his Colt and put a slug between the man's eyes.

Those eyes widened for a heartbeat, and then the man in white folded, the cleaver clattering as it struck the wood floor.

Lin was worried the punchers over at the bunkhouse had heard the shot and would investigate. He had to ride the wind, but first he must stop the bleeding. He glanced about the kitchen for something he could use as a bandage, squandering time he could not spare.

A loud crackle gave Lin an idea. He turned to the flames. Gritting his teeth, he lowered his left hand and pressed the stub of his little finger to a burning towel. Intense pain coursed up his arm, but he held the stub there for a mental count of three, then jerked his hand out of the fire and backpedaled. Smoke was curling from his sleeve, and his hand felt as if it were on fire, but it was not burned. The stub, though, was black at the end, sealed as effectively as if he had used hot wax. The bleeding had stopped.

Lin wheeled to go and nearly stepped on the end of his finger. He tore his gaze away, and ran.

The cool night was invigorating. Lin climbed into the saddle and flicked the reins.

Shouts rose from the direction of the bunkhouse.

Bending low so he was not an easy target, Lin brought the buttermilk to a trot. No shots boomed, but he did not slow until a couple of minutes had gone by without sign of pursuit.

Lin held his left hand up to his face. Conflicting emotions tore at him. Part of him wanted to be sick. He told himself that it was only the end of the finger, and he could get by without it. That did not help much, but at least the contents of his stomach stayed where they should.

Sudden fatigue washed over him. He was sweating and sore and could use some rest, but he had Etta June and the children to think of.

The thought gave Lin food for more pondering. Here he was, regarding them as if they were his own family when they were not. He had to keep reminding himself that he was just a hired hand. Although Etta June had shown an interest, he must not, as the old saw had it, count his chickens before they hatched.

Lin liked her, though. God, how he liked her. She was forthright and practical and had a good head on her shoulders. For some men that might not matter. All they would be interested in was her body. But Lin wanted a smart woman. He was not all that smart himself, and by marrying a woman with more brains than he had, he would make it through life making fewer mistakes.

Suddenly Lin stiffened.

Hooves drummed behind him — a lot of riders coming on fast. Bar M punchers were after him.

Lin was only partway across the grassy valley. He had no place to hide. But he did have a trick up his singed sleeve.

Quickly drawing rein, Lin swung down. "Easy, fella," he said as he gripped the bridle. The pounding of the hooves was louder, but he still might have time. "Down," he said, pressing on the buttermilk's shoulder. He hoped the horse would remember. They had done it only a dozen times or so, a lark on Lin's part after he heard about an outlaw who had trained his horse to do the feat.

With a low nicker, the palomino sank to the ground and rolled onto its side.

Lin eased down beside it and stroked its neck to keep it calm and quiet. "Keep still," he said soothingly.

A knot of silhouettes acquired form and substance. Six or seven men and their mounts were a score of yards to the east of him.

Lin tensed. If one of them should glance his way and spot a dark bulk where there should not be one — Lin caught himself and held his breath, his right hand on the Colt.

Like a storm cloud pealing with thunder, the riders swept on by and rumbled to the north.

Lin waited until the pounding faded before he rose and tugged on the bridle to get the buttermilk to rise. Once again he stepped into the stirrups. To keep from blundering onto his pursuers, he rode west for about half a mile and then reined north again.

Lin shifted in the saddle. A small sun blazed where Seth Montfort's house stood. It was fully engulfed and would burn to cinders.

Good, Lin thought; it was what Montfort deserved. But now he could add arson to his list of crimes. If the law ever caught up with him, he would wind up behind bars for twenty years. If he wasn't sentenced to a strangulation jig for murder, that is.

Lin sighed. All he had ever wanted was to live a peaceful, law-abiding life, running his own ranch. He never intended to become a badman. Circumstances had turned him into one. He shook his head. Sometimes he was as dumb as a tree stump. How could he think of marrying Etta June with the shadow of the gallows hanging over him?

As if that were not enough, the range war was far from over. Seth Montfort and the rest of his paid assassins had to be dealt with. More blood would flow. More lives would be forfeit.

"Why me?" Lin asked the stars. "What did I ever do to deserve this?"

The stars did not answer.

CHAPTER 30

Chancy spun and crouched. At the end of the alley reared a tall figure wreathed in gun smoke. Chancy triggered an answering shot, and the figure leaped from sight.

Bass would expect him to run, but Chancy took the bit in his mouth and did the last thing Bass would guess: He charged toward the street. He was puzzled when Bass did not reappear. His puzzlement grew when he came to the end of the alley and the street was empty.

Lute Bass was nowhere to be seen.

Chancy wondered if he had hit him. He looked for blood, but there was not enough light. Much of the settlement was plunged in murk and shadow. Careful to keep his back to the front of the building, he sidled toward the saloon, replacing the spent cartridge as he went.

Mason might as well be a morgue. Not so much as a cat or dog stirred. A gust of wind raised small swirls of dust, and down the street a shutter swung and creaked.

Where are you? Chancy almost yelled. But it would be a mistake to let Bass know exactly where he was.

Something moved across the street. Instinct compelled him to dive flat, and it was well he did.

Three shots cracked; three slugs smacked into the wood above Chancy's head. He replied and the night went quiet.

Chancy mopped at his brow. He did not like being hunted; he did not like it at all. He crawled to an old water barrel and rose on his knees. It was empty and the top was gone, but it was cover. He remembered Lin telling him to always reload as soon as he could, and he groped his belt for a cartridge.

Chancy supposed he should be grateful that the good citizens of Mason were not taking a hand. The way his luck was going, they would probably side with Bass, and then where would he be?

From the other side of the street came a scraping noise.

Chancy held the Colt with both hands to steady his aim, but no one appeared. Maybe Lute Bass was trying to draw him into the open.

"Can you hear me, boy?"

The shout came from off to the left, from the vicinity of a pair of ramshackle cabins.

"Can you hear me?" the killer asked a second time.

"What do you want?" Chancy responded. He suspected Bass was in a cluster of trees between the cabins.

"To offer you a chance to give up."

"Don't hold your breath!" Chancy yelled.

"I do not want to be at this all night, boy. Throw out your pistol, and come out with your hands over your head, and I will let you live."

"You must think I have no brains at all," Chancy said.

"I am doing you a favor. We both know it is only a matter of time before I give you what you gave Rufus."

"You will try."

A string of oaths amused Chancy. A man in Bass' trade had no business being so temperamental.

"Listen to me, youngster. I am an old hand at this. I could carve seventeen notches on my revolvers if I wanted, but I have always thought that is too showy."

"You are a saint," Chancy responded.

"I am practical. I do not want anyone to try and make their reputation at my expense. I go up against enough lunkheads like you without inviting more."

" 'Those who live by the gun die by the gun,' " Chancy quoted what someone had once told him.

"I would rather do what I am doing, living as I damn well please, than live to old age under the heel of someone else. I have my principles."

It had never occurred to Chancy that hired assassins might have scruples. "Next you will tell me you go to church," he scoffed.

"I did when I was little," Lute Bass said. "Ma made me. She made all of us. We did not have shoes or socks, but she would line us up, single file, and march us to church as if we were soldiers going off to war. During the sermon she would say 'Amen!' with the rest of the congregation and smack those of us who did not do the same."

Chancy could not understand why Bass was telling him all this. He did not give a good damn about Bass' childhood.

"I was more black and blue after a church service than I was after most of the fights I have been in," Lute Bass went on. "My ma never was bashful about hitting us. On the street, in the general store, in church, whenever she felt we deserved it, she hauled off and walloped us."

"Too bad she did not use an ax," Chancy hollered.

Lute Bass laughed. "She would have done you a favor, huh? But for all her faults, our ma cared for us. How about your ma? Did she look out for you?"

Chancy almost smacked his ears to be sure he was hearing right. What on earth did Bass care about him and his mother? "Are you drunk?"

"It takes more than half a bottle to put me under the table," Lute Bass bragged.

Chancy was trying to spot Bass in the trees but couldn't. He decided to keep him talking. Cupping a hand to his mouth, he said, "How about if *I* do *you* a favor?"

"This should be interesting. I am listening."

"Holster your pistol and ride out, and there will be no hard feelings," Chancy said. "I will let you live."

"*You* will let *me* live?" Lute Bass roared with mirth. "Damn, boy. You are the funniest pup I have ever had to rub out. I thank you for the offer, but this is to the death."

"Are you as agreeable when you smother kittens?" Chancy taunted. But he did not feel as lighthearted as he let on. Something was bothering him. A vague worry gnawed at the back of his mind, a sense that all was not well. He scanned the street but did not see anyone.

"Still there, boy?"

Chancy did not answer.

"Bryce?" Bass shouted urgently. "Answer me!"

Chancy's vague worry grew stronger. He rose from behind the barrel and backed toward the corner. He was so intent on the trees that he did not pay any attention to the darkness close at hand. Suddenly it disgorged a shambling apparition that tittered like a lunatic.

A revolver spat flame and lead, and a searing pain speared through Chancy. He fired back.

It was Mort! But Mort was dead, Chancy thought. He had seen him fall with his own eyes.

As if the killer could read Chancy's thoughts, he said, "Always be sure, boy, or you will regret it." He squeezed off another shot.

Chancy was hit again. He responded in kind and had the satisfaction of seeing Mort crumble for the second time that night. He moved toward him to be sure, but rapid footfalls bore down on him from the rear. Chancy whirled, or tried to, but his legs would not cooperate.

Lute Bass had a Remington in each hand. Both became slug-spewing thunderbolts.

Hot pokers seared Chancy's body. He squeezed off a shot. Squeezed off another. The Remingtons echoed his Colt. Lute Bass seemed to be falling in slow motion. Chancy extended his arm to take aim, but the world was fading. He felt himself strike the ground.

Then there was nothing — nothing at all.

The children were asleep. The house stood quiet under the stars. Except for the occasional yip of a coyote and the low of a cow, the ranch was as peaceful as could be.

Etta June did not feel at peace. She sat in the rocking chair on the porch, a rifle across her legs, and slowly rocked. This was one of her favorite times of the day, after the kids were tucked in, when she had precious time to herself — when she could relax and think and plan. Although tonight, as with every night since Lin had left, she could not relax no matter how she tried.

She rocked and stared and hoped, and marveled that she hoped. Her wonder was natural, given that she was not the sort given to romantic whimsy.

Etta June prided herself on having a clear, level head. When she fell in love with Tom

Sr., she fell in love in a levelheaded way. He appealed to her practical side because he was practical himself. Even his courting was practical. He never brought her flowers, and only once took her to a church social. After they were married, he indulged in intimacy once a month and only once a month. Again, that was his practical side showing itself in his wish to have a family.

But this was different. Lin stirred Etta June in ways she had never been stirred. She thought of him when she was not with him. She daydreamed of doing things with him she never daydreamed of doing with Tom.

It was all the more surprising because Etta June had known him such a short while. She had known Tom for years before he proposed. Yet already she was thinking of how it would be to have Lin in the empty rocking chair next to hers, rocking at her side.

A sound stiffened her.

Etta June half rose, then sat back down. Hooves slowly clomped toward her — a single horse and rider. She put her hand on her rifle. A round was already in the chamber and the hammer was pulled back, so all she had to do was snap it to her shoulder and fire.

The man and the animal came out of the night, so plainly exhausted that when the man drew rein, both looked fit to collapse.

"Mrs. Cather."

"Have you forgotten already? It is Etta June and only Etta June."

Lin stiffly dismounted and came up on the porch. "I have been in fear for you. I am glad you are all right. If that is too bold, I apologize."

"You know how I feel. How can it be bold?"

"I have some notion," Lin said. "But we have never said the words, so I cannot be sure."

Etta June leaned the rifle against the rail. She got out of the chair, walked up to him, placed her hands around his neck and kissed him full on the lips. She kissed him long and she kissed him hard, and when she was done, they were both breathing heavier. "Does that settle it in your head for once and for all?"

"It does, and I thank you." Lin enfolded her in his big arms and asked into her hair, "Are the children all right?"

That was when Etta June let herself think the word her heart had already formed. Her tongue felt thick as she said, "You are a fine man, Lin Gray."

Lin trembled slightly. "Bryce."

"How is that again?"

"My real handle is Lin Bryce. I am wanted by the law for killing two men down Cheyenne way."

Etta June barely hesitated. "I do not care."

"A banker came to repossess our ranch, and my brother started shoving, and one thing led to another."

"Again, I do not care. What is past is past. We are now."

"I thought you should know," Lin said softly. "It is the first and only lie I will ever tell you."

"I am grateful," Etta June said, choking up.

"That is not all. I have had to kill again. Seth Montfort did not take kindly to your message."

Etta June listened to his recital of events. Her eyes moistened and she said in heartfelt sorrow, "Pat and Sue?" When he was done, she clasped his hand and brought him over to the parlor window so the light from within spilled over his face. She saw what they had done, and her love swelled until it was boundless. "I will kill him myself if he comes here."

"No, you will not. I will spare you that burden." Lin paused and gazed toward the stable. "Where is my brother? He is supposed to be looking out for you."

Etta June squeezed his hand tighter. "You are not the only one who makes mistakes. I was afraid he would go to Montfort's and get himself killed, so I sent him into Mason to take his mind off his worry." She paused. Something did not feel right about his hand. She raised it into the light. "Lord, no," she breathed. "They did this, too?"

"The butler mistook me for a chicken."

"Oh, Lin," Etta June said, and kissed him again. Afraid she would burst into tears, she remarked, "Your brother should have been back by now."

"He is a grown man," Lin said. "Or almost."

"We can go into Mason ourselves if you want."

"Not with Montfort about to move on the Dixons. I gave them my word I would be there to help. I head out at dawn."

"We head out," Etta June said. "And you will sleep in an extra hour and have breakfast before we go."

Lin grinned. "A man steps into your loop and all of a sudden you are bossing him around."

"I am female," Etta June said. "And I thank you for the step."

They shared their third kiss, the longest yet. When the ardor passed, Etta June rested her cheek on his broad chest. "Are you sure about this? I demand a lot from my men."

"You are worth the demands." Lin kissed her forehead. "I am a simple man. You are getting the worst of the bargain."

"No more talk like that, ever," Etta June said. "And you must make me a promise."

"Anything."

"Do not die on me. It is new for us, but it is strong, and it would crush me if you died."

"If I can help it, I will go on breathing for you." Lin coughed. "I suppose I should bed down my horse."

"Bed yourself down," Etta June said. "I will see to him."

Lin grinned down at her. "Will you always take this good care of me?"

"Until the day I die."

Lin went in.

Etta June took her rifle and led the buttermilk toward the stable. Midway there she looked up at the heavens. "Thank you," she said.

CHAPTER 31

Lin was awake, but he did not open his eyes. He felt too good, too wonderfully comfortable and warm, and he did not want to spoil the feeling. He was happy, truly happy for the first time in years. He could not remember the last time he had felt this good. Grinning, he nuzzled the pillow, his stubble rasping on the cover.

Then someone coughed and a small voice said, "Are you awake yet? Ma sent us to fetch you."

Lin's eyes snapped open.

They were over by the door, brother and sister, smiling a trifle nervously.

"Ma says you should wash up and come down to breakfast," Beth told him.

"She says you can take your time," Tom Jr. added. "And that you can put on some of Pa's clothes if you want."

"Thank you," Lin said.

They turned to go, but Beth looked back

and hesitated. "Are you going to be our new pa?"

"Yes," Lin said. There was no doubt, not after last night.

"Will you treat us like our pa treated us?" Tom asked.

"He was awful nice," Beth added.

"I can never be him," Lin said. "But I promise you I will be the best pa I can be."

They smiled and departed.

Lin smiled too. He was on the threshold of a new life, of having a wife and kids and a ranch, everything he had ever truly wanted. All he had to do was live long enough to step over that threshold. Casting off the blanket, he sat up and scratched his chin. Yes, he definitely needed a shave.

The aromas of eggs and bacon and coffee greeted him when he made his way downstairs. He had washed and used his razor, but he wore his own clothes. He did not feel entirely right wearing Tom Sr.'s. Not yet, anyway.

They were at the table, waiting. The chair at the head had been pushed back for him. Lin sat and saw Beth reach for a fork. "Grace first, don't you think?"

Etta June was radiant. She did the honors, then passed him a bowl heaped with scrambled eggs, a plate piled high with bacon and another heaped with toast.

"Land sakes," Lin said. "Do you always eat this much?"

"We have healthy appetites."

"A year of this, and I will be a hog," Lin joked. "You can take me to market and sell me for top dollar."

The kids laughed, and Etta June's eyes mirrored the depths of her affection. For a while all was well with Lin's world. He ate until he was fit to burst and washed the food down with hot black coffee. When he was done, he smacked his lips and sat back. "A man could get used to this."

"A woman hopes so," Etta June said.

"Do you want me to get the buckboard ready, Pa?" Tom Jr. asked. "Ma told us we are going to visit the Dixons."

"I am not your pa yet," Lin said. "So Lin will do for now."

"Mr. Bryce," Etta June corrected him. "I will have manners and common courtesy."

"Yes, Ma," Tom said.

"And I would rather ride than take a wagon," Lin mentioned. For Etta June's benefit, he noted, "The faster we get there, the better."

Etta June smiled at her offspring. "Why don't you two scoot to the stable, and I will be there in a minute? I have something to say to Mr. Bryce."

Dutifully, they scampered out.

Lin refilled his coffee cup to hide his unease. "Did I say something wrong? I am new at this."

"You told them you will be their new pa."

"I am sorry. That was yours to do, wasn't it?"

"When?" Etta June said.

"When what?"

"When do you intend to become their new pa? We should set a date."

Lin was flabbergasted. "You do not let any grass grow under you, do you? How about a year from now? I will court you and we will get engaged and have a church wedding with all the trimmings."

"I was thinking next week."

"What?"

"All right. Two weeks, if you want, but no more than that. And a justice of the peace will do."

"What?"

"Why do you keep saying that?"

"Two weeks!" Lin exclaimed. "That is hardly any time at all. Won't folks talk? We should do it proper."

"Do you want me or not?" Etta June asked.

"More than anything in the world," Lin

confessed.

"I would do it tomorrow, but we have this Montfort business to settle. As for folks talking, which folks are you talking about? Abe Tucker and those in Mason? Abe is nice enough, but the rest I do not know, and what any of them think counts for less than a cow patty. As for proper, when you are in love, love is all the proper you need."

"You sure have a way of putting things," Lin marveled.

"If I am wrong in any respect, dispute me."

Lin reached across the table, she did the same and their fingers entwined in the middle. "I will do what you want, when you want. Forgive me if I am rattled. I have not done this before."

"I have had one husband, but I am as bewildered as you," Etta June said. "I never thought the miracle would happen twice. It is the same and yet it is different, if that makes any sense."

"Two weeks," Lin said again, quietly.

"We can make it two weeks and a day if you are scared," Etta June teased.

"What about after?"

Etta June blushed. "Now, *that* was bold. Don't expect me to be any less nervous than I was on my first wedding night."

"No, no, no," Lin said, and grew warm with embarrassment. "That is not what I meant. Newlyweds do something special, don't they? I could take you to visit the geysers and whatnot." He had heard that was a popular pastime.

"We have a roundup to finish and cattle to ready for market," Etta June said. "Geysers are not as important as keeping our ranch afloat."

A longing filled Lin, a longing such as he had never known. She had said "our." "You will not regret this."

Etta June grinned. "I better not. I own a rolling pin."

"You will be a handful," Lin predicted, grinning. He did not want to let go of her hand, but he did.

"I better get to the stable," Etta June said, rising. She set down her napkin and looked into his eyes. "About after the vows." She blushed again. "I am not prissy."

"Oh, my," Lin said. He watched her walk out, gladness filling his heart, and his eyes started to moisten. Coughing, he shook himself and gulped a mouthful of coffee. "If this is what love is," he said to the cup, "it is glorious."

He had not worn his Colt to breakfast; he did not think Etta June would think it fitting. Now he went back to the bedroom and strapped it on. As he turned to go, he caught his reflection in the mirror. "I should pinch myself to see if I am dreaming," he told his image. But he didn't. If it was a dream, he preferred the dream to the reality.

The morning air was cool. Lin stood on the porch, stretched his arms wide and breathed deep, delighted to be alive.

The stable doors were open, but no one had come out yet. Saddling four horses took a while when two of those doing the saddling were kids. Lin went down the steps.

To the east the sun was an orange ball. To the east too lay Mason. Lin wondered what had happened to his brother. He hoped Chancy had not taken to cards and drink and forgotten about the Cathers — and him.

Someone came out of the stable.

Lin stopped in shock, his sense of well-being shattered. His hand flicked to his Colt, but he did not draw for the simple reason that the other was not wearing a revolver or carrying a rifle. "You!" he blurted.

"Me." Seth Montfort grinned.

"Where are Etta June and the kids?" Lin glanced past him, but the inside of the stable was in shadow.

"Permit me to offer you a compliment,"

Montfort said. "You are harder to kill than a cockroach."

"I asked you a question." Lin doubted the rancher was alone. Stone and the other gun sharks must there, as well.

"Your concern is touching," Montfort said. He raised his right hand and snapped his fingers, and out of the stable walked Stone and half a dozen assassins. One was behind Etta June, holding her by the arms. Two others had the children.

"Let them go," Lin said.

Seth Montfort laughed. "I would be more worried about myself, were I you. You and I have unfinished business." He snapped his fingers again, and two more of his hired killers came around the left side of the stable, three more came around from the right.

Lin grew cold inside, but not from fear. He had expected odds like this. "Are you sure there are enough?"

"Oh, quite sure," Montfort said. "These are your last minutes on earth, so treasure them."

Etta June tried to pull free, but the man holding her would not let go. "Seth, you have gone too far."

"Stay out of this, my dear. It is between your new admirer and me," Montfort said glibly. "I warned him. I told him I had staked a claim, but he refused to listen."

"I am not one of your cows," Etta June said. "I do not have your brand on me."

"Not a brand that anyone can see," Montfort said, "but it is there."

"I don't have a say?"

"You are a woman."

"So?"

"So no."

Lin was strangely calm, given his plight. He was worried more about his new family than about his own hide. "I will say this once more. Let them go and ride out, and no more blood need be spilled."

"Does that include your brother's?" Montfort asked.

"What about Chancy?"

"The last I saw him, he was lying in Abe Tucker's store with a hole in him," Montfort related. "And no, before you ask, I did not put it there. Three men have come all the way from Cheyenne hunting him and you."

Lin's calm evaporated and was replaced by a knot of anxiety. "How bad was he hurt?"

"They were keeping him alive until you showed," Montfort said. "I should not be telling you, but what the hell. You will never step foot in Mason again."

"You might be surprised."

Seth Montfort snorted. "Oh, please. What can you do against this many? I admit you surprised me when you found out I sent Griggs to spy on Etta June, and later when you showed up alone at my ranch. But the surprises end here."

"I have a few more," Lin told him. "The first is that Lassiter is dead."

"What?" From Stone, who took a step toward him.

"The second is that before I killed him, he murdered Patricia and Sue Dixon. Since he was working for you, that makes you partly to blame. Under the law, you can have your neck stretched."

"Only if the law finds out," Seth Montfort said, "and I am not about to tell them."

"I will," Etta June declared.

Montfort glanced at her, his irritation plain. "Why must you be like this when I have only your best interests at heart?"

"Liar. You only want to keep your neck out of a noose," Etta June said. "But Pat and Sue were friends of mine, and I will see that justice is done."

Montfort sighed and faced Lin. "Any other surprises before the lead starts to fly?"

"Just one more," Lin said. "I burned down your house."

"Sure you did," Montfort said, and laughed.

"You had gone off to Mason, your punchers said. I shot the three leather slappers you left to watch your place, and one of your hands, and I had to kill your butler or whatever he was, besides. Then I set your house on fire."

"Damn," Stone said, and chuckled. "You are a hellion."

Seth Montfort did not share the man killer's admiration. "Do you realize how much that house cost me? How long it took to build? The furniture, the furnishings, were the best money can buy. Now you tell me it all went up in smoke?"

"Consider it an omen. Your dream of claiming the Big Horns for your own is about to go up in smoke too."

Montfort drew himself up to his full height and tried to square his rounded shoulders. "I have had enough of you. Mr. Stone, he is all yours."

"At last," Stone said.

Lin was eager to end it too, but not quite yet. "Etta June and the children. Get them out of here."

"They stay," Seth Montfort said.

"But they might be hit."

"I am beginning not to care," Montfort

378

said. "Mr. Stone, what are you waiting for?"

"Nothing," Stone said, and his hand swooped low.

CHAPTER 32

Lin drew and fired so fast, the deed was done before his brain realized his hand had moved. He fired too fast, though. The slug he meant to core Stone's heart instead caught Stone in the shoulder and spun him half around.

Other pistoleros were grabbing for their revolvers.

The smart thing to do was retreat to the house. But in his fear for Etta June and the children, Lin threw all caution to the breeze. Roaring like a riled grizzly, he hurtled forward, snapping a swarthy killer taking deliberate aim. The man dropped in his tracks. A second killer was raising a rifle. Lin cored his left eye.

Seth Montfort bolted, shrieking over his shoulder, "Shoot him! Shoot him! Shoot him!"

With two of their own down and Stone on his knees, the rest were scattering. The as-

380

sassin holding Etta June let go and darted toward a corner of the stable. She, in turn, bounded toward the two men who had her son and daughter. The pair took one look at Lin and decided their companions had the right notion; they forgot about Tom Jr. and Beth, and hunted cover.

"Into the stable!" Lin shouted to Etta June.

Revolvers cracked. Bees whizzed over Lin's head and on either side of him. He responded in kind. Etta June had reached her kids and was flying toward the stable with an arm around each one. Covering them, Lin backed after her. He was shot at, and returned the lead.

Suddenly a shadow fell over him. They were in the stable. A figure to one side flamed and thundered. Lin's answering shot brought a cry and a thud.

In the quiet that fell, Lin heard ringing in his ears.

Etta June and the children were hunkered next to the wall. She was hugging Beth and stroking her hair.

"Are you all right?" Lin needed to know.

Nodding, Etta June said, "She is scared, is all. How about you?"

"I am fine," Lin said. If by that he meant trapped in a stable ringed by paid killers out to earn their pay and with a woman and her two children to protect, then yes, he was fine.

"What do we do?"

Lin wished he knew. He warily peered out. The men he had shot lay where they had fallen. Of the rest, there was no sign. Suddenly a shot pealed and the wood near his face spit slivers. Ducking back, he squatted.

Seth Montfort's laugh had the same effect as fingernails on a blackboard. "Did that get your attention?"

Lin did not answer.

"I have the stable surrounded. You are not going anywhere. Make it easy on yourselves and give up."

Like hell we will, Lin almost yelled.

"How long can you hold out without food and water?" Montfort shouted. "Because that is how long I will wait if I have to."

Beth began crying. Etta June hugged her and assured her everything would be all right, but over Beth's shoulder Etta June's eyes met Lin's and reflected her worry.

Montfort had more to say. "You are on your own. Your brother is in Mason, and Cody Dixon does not know of your plight. There is no one to help you."

Lin could not keep quiet any longer. "Tell me something I don't know!"

"How about this?" Montfort said. "I am not patient by nature. I *could* wait until you stagger out weak from hunger and thirst. Or I can have my men burn you out."

"There are children in here!"

"Accidents happen, Bryce. A brat bumps a lantern and a stable burns to the ground with the brat's family and a friend inside."

Etta June stood. "You would do that, Seth? After all your talk of taking me to be your wife?"

"I want your land, woman, more than I want you," Montfort answered. "And fate has given me the means to my desire."

"You wouldn't!"

"What else did you expect? You have chosen your hired man over me. Since you care for him so much, it is fitting the two of you die together."

"But Tom and Beth!" Etta June cried.

Lin took a gamble. He ran toward Etta June and the children. A revolver spoke and his sleeve gave a tug. He weaved and ducked as more slugs sought him and he felt a pang high on his left arm. But he made it.

Etta June flung her arms around him. "Why did you do that? Were you trying to get yourself killed?"

"We are in this together." Lin could protect them better if they were close to him. He checked his arm. The slug had broken the skin, but that was all.

Seth Montfort was laughing. "When I first set eyes on you, Mr. Bryce, I took you for a big, dumb ox. You have done nothing to improve my impression."

A small hand fell on Lin's leg.

"I am so afraid," Beth said, her cheeks wet with tears. "Don't let him hurt us!"

Lin's throat did not want to work as it should. He had to try twice to say, "I won't, little one."

"You have ten minutes!" Seth Montfort hollered. "By then I will be ready to set the stable ablaze." He paused. "Banner! Richards! Run to the house and fetch as many lamps as you can carry. I don't know where she keeps her kerosene, so we will use what is in the lamps."

"I use lard oil," Etta June whispered to Lin. "I can't afford kerosene."

Not that it mattered, Lin thought. The lard oil would burn just as nicely. He scanned the stalls. "How many horses did you saddle?"

"None. They grabbed me as I came in. I tried to shout, but the man who grabbed me had a hand over my mouth."

"Can you ride bareback?"

"Of course."

"All of you?" Lin gestured at little Beth.

"She will ride with me," Etta June said. "What do you have in mind? They will shoot us the moment we are out the door."

"Not if I keep them busy," Lin said. "Follow me." Staying close to the wall, he hustled them to the stalls. Tom Jr. needed a boost onto a bay. Then Lin held Beth while Etta June climbed on a sorrel. "Wait until I give the word." He handed Beth up and went from stall to stall, bringing each horse out and forming them in a bunch around Etta June and the children.

"Nothing to say in there?" Seth Montfort taunted.

"Not to you," Etta June said quietly. She added something under her breath that Lin did not catch but which caused Beth to bleat in surprise.

"Ma! You told us never to use those words."

"I am sorry, Daughter," Etta June said. "Folks say I have the forbearance of a saint, but even saints have their limits."

"What is a saint?" Beth asked.

Lin was watching the front. "Stay in the middle of these horses," he instructed. "Keep low until you are out of rifle range."

"Wait a second," Etta June said. "Where will you be? How do you intend to keep them busy?"

"They cannot shoot at you if they are shooting at me."

"No! I won't let you." Etta June shifted to climb down, saying, "Get down, Tom. We can't have him fight them alone."

But by then Lin was behind the horses. He raised his left arm. "Think of them and not me," he said, and brought his arm down, smacking the last animal on the rump. At the same time he let out with his imitation of a Sioux war whoop.

The effect was everything he hoped it would be.

All the horses broke into motion. Etta June shouted for Tom and Beth to hold on as they were swept up in the panicked flight.

Yipping and screeching, Lin was hard on the hooves of the last animal. When they broke into the open, he was only a few steps behind. He spotted a man wedging a rifle to his shoulder and shot him dead. Another assassin darted out from the left side of the stable, raising his revolver to shoot either Etta June or Tom Jr. Lin shot him dead too.

"Forget them!" Seth Montfort bawled from somewhere off to the right. "Kill Bryce! A hundred dollars to whoever drops him!"

Lin ran toward the sound of Montfort's

voice. He was almost to the corner when an assassin came flying around the other side. They fired simultaneously. The man, rattled, missed. Lin did not. As the man fell, Lin tore a Colt from his grasp.

A revolver in each hand, Lin plunged around the corner.

Most of them were there. Revolvers crashed and boomed. A pain seared Lin's side, and he lost part of an earlobe. Firing first one revolver and then the other in swift cadence, Lin gave a good accounting. Enemies fell, thrashing. He stared into a rising muzzle, but a muzzle of his spoke first.

Seth Montfort was near strident with panic. *"Kill him! Kill him! Kill him!"* he shrieked as he raced toward the rear of the stable.

Lin started after him. A hand grabbed his ankle, and he nearly pitched onto his face. It was one of those he had shot, still very much alive. Lin pointed a Colt, but a shoulder slammed into his back. He tripped over the man on the ground, and was down.

A knife thudded into the earth an inch from Lin's face. Twisting, he sent a slug into the forehead of the knife's wielder.

A rifle was thrust at Lin's face. He swatted it aside just as it went off. For a moment his hearing went, and he was blinded by the gun smoke. He jammed his Colt against the ribs of the culprit and triggered a shot of his own.

Lin's vision cleared.

Montfort had disappeared.

Lin heaved to his feet and gave chase. So long as Seth Montfort lived, Etta June would never know a moment's peace. He was almost to the back of the stable when he was reminded by the thunder of a rifle behind him that Montfort was not the only one left. In midstride Lin whirled and snapped off the last shot from the Colt in his left hand. The man fell, and Lin dropped the revolver.

Then Lin was past the stable. Only three horses were in the corral, milling in a panic. On the far side, their reins looped around the top rail, were the mounts of Montfort and his men.

Seth Montfort was swinging onto one.

Lin climbed the rails. Holding the Colt with both hands, he aimed more carefully than he had ever aimed in his life. As Montfort wheeled the horse, Lin stroked the trigger.

A squawk and a tumble ensued. But Montfort was up on his hands and knees in an instant. He glared about him, spied Lin and lurched to his feet.

Lin took quick aim, but Montfort doubled

over and ran toward the stable. Thanks to the corral rails, Lin could not get a clear shot. He had no recourse but to go after him.

Lin vaulted into the corral. The three horses shied away. Running full out, he crossed to the other side and was about to lever his body up and over when a rifle spanged.

Lin went prone. The shooter was at the rear of the stable. Aiming under the bottom rail, Lin shot the man in the leg. The man cursed and toppled, and his head became a target Lin could not resist.

Reloading as he went, Lin climbed over the rail and sped along the side of the stable. He had lost sight of Montfort, but only temporarily. When he reached the front, Montfort was bounding toward the house like an oversized jackrabbit.

Lin went after him. He did not like being in the open, but it could not be helped. Montfort made it inside before Lin could shoot. He almost failed to spot a gun shark who appeared to rise up out of the ground. They fired at the same split second, and it was the gun shark who pitched over.

Lin's boots thudded on the steps. Montfort had left the front door open, and he barreled inside. Someone was in shadow at the far end of the hall. A revolver spat, and Lin replied. There was a loud grunt. The man's revolver spoke a second time, and again Lin answered.

The man fell against a wall. Gasping and gurgling, he melted to the floor, leaving a scarlet smear.

Cautiously moving forward, Lin kicked the revolver from fingers gone limp. "You have got your due," he said.

"It can't end like this," Seth Montfort said. Two holes in his chest were oozing more scarlet.

"All the money you paid your pack of killers, and what did it get you?"

"I hate you," Montfort said.

"I have heard that a lot lately."

"How can this be?" Montfort said, asking himself, not Lin.

"You brought it on yourself. You had more land than you needed, but it was not enough."

"Bend down and I will rip out your throat with my teeth," Seth Montfort growled.

"Try to die with dignity."

Montfort coughed, and now blood was coming out of his mouth. "To think a no-account like you has done me in."

A racket outside caused Lin to turn. But the person who flew toward him wore a dress. She came to a stop, her chest heaving with emotion.

"You were supposed to keep going," Lin said.

"And leave you?"

Then Etta June was in his arms, and for as long as he lived, Lin would never forget that moment. They looked down at the man who had tried his utmost to destroy them.

"You picked him over me," Seth Montfort said in disbelief. "You pretend to be a lady, but you are a whore."

"Just die, will you?" Etta June said.

Montfort opened his mouth to reply, but all that came out was a strangled whine and a last exhale. His portly body sagged.

"Good riddance."

Lin guided Etta June out onto the porch. "Where are the children?"

"Safe out back."

They stood arm in arm and surveyed the slaughter.

"You are safe too," Lin said. He added with a tired smile, "Even your stable is still standing."

Etta June gave a start. "Yes, it is, isn't it? We will have to do something about that."

EPILOGUE

The rider was caked with dust. He had gray at the temples, and a smattering of gray marked the stubble on his chin. Pinned to his shirt was a battered badge. In his holster nestled a Colt with well-worn grips. He reined up near the house and shifted in the saddle to regard the charred beams and blackened pile that had once been the stable.

Etta June came out, her arms folded. She was wearing her apron. "How do you do," she greeted him.

The lawman doffed his dusty hat and smiled a weary smile. "You are Mrs. Cather, I take it?"

"That I am. And you are the marshal who showed up in Mason a few days ago."

"Word gets around fast. Yes, I am Marshal Conklin. Did you also happen to hear why I am here?"

"You are after a couple of killers," Etta

June said.

"Lin and Chancy Bryce. I have seen Chancy's grave, and know he died swapping lead with man killers sent by a certain gent in Cheyenne."

"Then you must be here about Lin."

Marshal Conklin nodded. "I have been told that you hired them, and that he was involved in this Montfort business." The lawman motioned at what was left of the stable. "Is that where it happened?"

"Yes, that is where Lin died," Etta June said sadly. "I don't know what he did that you are after him, but Lin Bryce gave his life saving mine and the lives of my children. I will always think fondly of him."

"I knew his father," Marshal Conklin revealed. "A good man."

"There was not much left of Lin," Etta June said. "I can show you where I buried the little there was, if you want."

"That won't be necessary." Marshal Conklin, staring at the blackened ruin, gave a slight shudder. "Burned alive. I would not mind any way but that."

"Can I interest you in coffee or food?"

"No, thank you, ma'am." Conklin raised his reins. "I just had to see it with my own eyes for my report. I will leave you to your chores." He smiled and touched his hat brim.

Etta June watched until the lawman was a speck in the distance. Then she went inside and down the hall to the kitchen table. Lin was filling three cups with coffee, and looked up.

"Did it work?"

"He believes you are dead."

"I am grateful. But I still don't think we should have burned down the stable."

"Our story had to be convincing," Etta June said, and grinned. "It is a small price to pay for a new husband."

Crutches clomped, and Chancy came over from the stove balancing a plate of eggs in the same hand as his right crutch. He was pale and thin and his hair was down to his shoulders. "A husband and a brother-in-law. Or don't I count?"

"Of course you do," Etta June said.

Lin set down the coffeepot. "You are lucky it was Abe Tucker who found you and that he kept quiet about you being alive."

"We have been lucky all around," Etta June said.

Chancy's features clouded. "Except for Pat and Sue."

Lin did not like being reminded. "Enough

gloom." He raised his cup. "How about a toast?"

Etta June and Chancy imitated him.

"To the future!"

"To the future!"

Lin Bryce smiled.

ABOUT THE AUTHOR

Ralph Compton stood six foot eight with his boots. He worked as a musician, a radio announcer, a songwriter, and a newspaper columnist. His first novel, *The Goodnight Trail,* was a finalist for the Western Writers of America Medicine Pipe Bearer Award for Best Debut Novel. He was also the author of the *Sundown Riders* series and the *Border Empire* series.

The employees of Thorndike Press hope you have enjoyed this Large Print book. All our Thorndike and Wheeler Large Print titles are designed for easy reading, and all our books are made to last. Other Thorndike Press Large Print books are available at your library, through selected bookstores, or directly from us.

For information about titles, please call:
  (800) 223-1244

or visit our Web site at:
  http://gale.cengage.com/thorndike

To share your comments, please write:
  Publisher
  Thorndike Press
  295 Kennedy Memorial Drive
  Waterville, ME 04901